I0761454

# The Widow Hamilton

ALSO AVAILABLE BY MOLLIE ANN COX

The Eliza Hamilton Mysteries

*The Lace Widow*

# The Widow Hamilton

## An Eliza Hamilton Mystery

Mollie Ann Cox

NEW YORK

Books should be disposed of and recycled according to local requirements. All paper materials used are FSC compliant.



Published in the United States by Crooked Lane Books, an imprint of The Quick Brown Fox & Company LLC.

Crooked Lane Books and its logo are trademarks of The Quick Brown Fox & Company LLC.

Library of Congress Catalog-in-Publication data available upon request.

ISBN (hardcover): 979-8-89242-391-5
ISBN (ebook): 979-8-89242-392-2

Cover design by Lynn Andreozzi

Printed in the United States.

www.crookedlanebooks.com

Crooked Lane Books
34 West 27th St., 10th Floor
New York, NY 10001

First Edition: February 2026

The authorized representative in the EU for product safety and compliance is eucomply OÜPärnu mnt 139b-14, 11317 Tallinn, Estonia, hello@eucompliancepartner.com, +33757690241

10 9 8 7 6 5 4 3 2 1

*This book is dedicated to my sister, Becky, so brave in her cancer battle. When I write about Eliza and Angelica, I often see reflections of us. Keeping fighting—we need you!*

*A cup of tea. That was all she could remember. The pink flowers on the cup—they swirled and danced, taunting the edges of her mind. Then, darkness. Everything engulfed in black. Where was she now? She tried to move, to sit up. Nothing. Her limbs, her back—nothing responded.*

*Who gave her the tea? The memory slipped away, a shadow, a dream. A menacing laugh, low and womanly, broke the silence in her mind's ear, echoing, faceless. And a hand—was it soft? Plump? Just another trick of her unraveling senses?*

*She rolled onto her side, the damp floor pressing cold against her skin. The musty stench was her sole connection to life. If not for its anchor, would she still be here?*

*Her thoughts tumbled, colliding in the darkness, each one slipping away before she could hold on to it. The tea. The plump hand. Why couldn't she remember? Where had everything gone? She clawed at the void, desperate for a hint—just a sliver. But nothing came. Not even her name.*

# Chapter 1

Eliza Hamilton knocked again.

She hadn't sent her card ahead, but that was not her practice with Alice and her friends. The women who lived at Pearl Street House had always been accommodating. Eliza shivered, pulling her cloak and scarf closer to her. She dropped the basket of ginger cake, oranges, and cider on the doorstep.

Eliza, surprised the Pearl Street House residents would all be out, rubbed her gloved hands together for warmth. It was the first Sunday of Advent, after all. Not one of them was inside working on a lace tablecloth or weaving a rug?

Not one person was home?

The house usually brimmed with the activity of the women who lived there. Widows and grown orphans. They sold their handmade linens, weaving, and lace throughout the city and rarely had a day of leisure. The quiet unnerved Eliza as she still stood in front of the door.

Had they moved their household?

Surely not. Someone would've told her. It had been a few months since she'd seen them, but she was certain that they'd have informed her if they had found another home. Peering through the crack in the curtains, Eliza sensed something was amiss. The house, usually so full of life, seemed cloaked in an unnatural stillness. A shiver, not from the cold, ran down her spine.

She tucked her card inside the basket. Maybe she'd call on them after the service. The wind whipped against her back. Eliza repositioned her scarf and pulled her arms closer to her body before she stepped away. She'd be late for the service if she didn't go soon.

She turned from the house and walked toward the street, as an odd prickling sense traveled the back of her neck. People scurried around. It was bitterly frigid, and they were heading for warmth, Eliza guessed.

Three women huddled together at the end of the street, gradually making their way toward her. As they drew closer, Eliza recognized them. She approached them but stopped in her tracks. Something was off. Why were they huddled so? Their movements were sluggish and unsteady, as if each step required a great effort. She slowly moved toward them. Something was not right.

Alice, René, and Paulette advanced toward the house, at first not noticing Eliza as she stood on the walkway.

"Alice?"

Alice turned and the others followed.

"Eliza? I'm sorry I didn't recognize you beneath your cloak." Alice's speech was slower than usual. "What are you doing out today in this frigid weather?"

"No bother," Eliza said. "I'm on my way to church and dropped off a basket for your household."

As Alice drew closer, her dark-circled, puffy eyes became pronounced.

Worry twisted in Eliza's chest. She shivered from the prickling at her neck. "Alice, has something happened?"

Alice's chin quivered. "Our Rebecca. It's our Rebecca. And Jo. Jo!"

"What is it?" Eliza's mind swirled with possibilities.

Paulette approached Alice and wrapped her arm around her stooped shoulders. She lifted her face to Eliza. "Rebecca is dead." Her voice trembled.

Stone cold dread swept through Eliza as she fought to breathe. Rebecca. She was one of the newer women in the house, but she and Eliza had had many conversations over the past year. She was a dressmaker whose delicate skill belied her broad stature.

The wind whipped against Eliza's back, each gust feeling like a physical blow. But it was Alice's words—"Rebecca is dead"—that nearly brought her to her knees. The basket of ginger cake and oranges sitting on their stoop felt mockingly inappropriate. Around them church bells called the faithful to worship, their familiar peals now seeming more like mourning bells.

"I couldn't protect her." Alice's voice cracked. Even though she still stood, she crumpled into herself. "Where's our Jo?"

"We need to get her inside," said René. She'd lived with Alice from the start. They'd met at the Widow Society. Her large, gray eyes locked with Eliza's, her wrinkles more evident with worry.

Eliza's chest burned with concern and shock. She followed them to the door. Paulette took the basket inside. *What did she mention about Jo?* Eliza's mind attempted to make sense of what she was hearing.

"Come in." Paulette gestured to Eliza.

Eliza entered the row house, and warmth embraced her, remembering the kindness of these women after she'd lost her husband. They welcomed her and offered help when her son was in trouble. Now something terrible had happened to them.

*Rebecca is dead. Where's our Jo?*

The familiar warmth of Pearl Street House felt wrong today, its usual comfort turned numb. The rhythmic click of knitting needles, normally so soothing, was silent. Everywhere Eliza looked, she observed traces of the dead woman: an unfinished piece of lace draped over a chair, a book of patterns marked with

Rebecca's careful notes. Even the air seemed thick with loss, the usual scents of beeswax and lavender now mingling with the sharp tang of grief. Through the thin walls, she could hear someone crying—the sound bringing back memories of her own first days of widowhood, when even breathing had seemed an impossible task.

How would they survive with one person gone from the group? Rebecca, who was nimble with her fingers, mostly worked as a dressmaker but also made lace and embroidered linen. Among the group, she was a front person who often dressed as a man in male-dominated places. Jo had done that as well. Eliza wondered where she was.

*Rebecca is dead. Where's our Jo?*

Alice appeared to be in shock as the other two women helped her off with her thin cloak and accompanied her to the sofa.

Eliza slipped off her gloves and went to Alice, crouching down in front of her. She reached for Alice's hands, roughened by years of needlework, and cupped them in her own. Eliza and Alice had held each other through the darkest days of their respective widowhoods, had shared tea and tears and midnight confidences. Now those same hands clutched Eliza's as they faced another loss together. The candlelight caught the silver in Alice's hair.

"Alice?"

Alice blankly stared at her.

"Let's get her a cup of tea," Eliza said.

"Kettle's on." Paulette entered the space, her words breaking the silence.

Eliza rubbed Alice's thigh for a few moments, then stood and regarded Paulette. "What happened to Rebecca? I don't understand. She was young and healthy."

Eliza imagined Rebecca in her mind's eye. Tall and broad, with kind brown eyes and a dimpled chin. Unlike the others, she was not a widow. She was an orphan they'd encountered at the

Widow Society. They took her in and taught her how to make lace and embroider. She had also learned to sell and move about the city unnoticed, disguising herself as a man.

"Someone killed her," Paulette said.

"An accident of some sort?" Eliza had read of young women being plowed down by careless carriage drivers and of others falling into the river.

"Murder," Alice said in a deep, guttural voice.

The taste of uncertainty lingered on Eliza's tongue, as her breath stilled in her throat. She sank onto the couch beside Alice, wrapping her arm around her.

"Murder?" The word felt foreign, impossible. Eliza had had enough murder to last a lifetime. "But why? Who would do this to Rebecca?" She glanced at René and Paulette, mother and daughter. "Who would want to harm her? She was such a dear."

The room became silent once more, until the tea kettle rumbled in the next room.

Alice stared off into space while Paulette fetched the tea. The room remained quiet except for the spoons against cups and saucers, stirring sugar and cream into the steaming brew.

Paulette cleared her throat. "We've just been to identify her body." She stirred sugar into her tea. "It was her."

"She'd been missing for a few days," René said. "We were beside ourselves with worry."

Eliza had so many questions. But the moment did not warrant them. At least not yet. Instead, she sat with the rest of the women, drinking tea in silence. Her heart thundered in her chest, each beat echoing the terror that threatened to overwhelm her. Memories of Hamilton's death, the suffocating helplessness, clawed their way to the surface. She pushed them down, focusing on the present.

The warm tea did little to chase away the chill that had settled deep within her bones. *Murder.* The word hung heavy in the air, casting a shadow of dread over the room.

As Alice's words sank in, Eliza's mind drifted, unbidden, to her own loss. Hamilton, gone now for over a year. She had vowed to preserve his legacy, to see his biography published. After all, Alexander Hamilton was a founding father of this country, the first Secretary of the Treasury, a brave general, and George Washington's loyal assistant throughout the Revolutionary War. But now, sitting in this house of fresh grief, she reminded herself her work was far from over—both for her husband's memory and for the living who needed her.

"Where are the others?" Eliza asked.

Alice's haunted gaze drifted, lost in a sea of grief and disbelief.

"Making deliveries," Paulette answered. She often helped Eliza with sewing projects.

"Who'd want to harm Rebecca?" Eliza's voice trembled as she voiced the question that echoed in the recesses of her mind. That was the one question she considered fine to ask. Rebecca had been a beacon of kindness and resilience. The notion of someone snuffing out her light filled Eliza with righteous indignation.

But as she observed the faces of the other women, fear lurked behind their facade of stoicism. Fear of the unknown, fear of what lay beyond their doorstep.

Eliza's mind continued to race with questions, each more unsettling than the last. Who had committed such a heinous act? And why? She would not get any answers here today. They had just visited the body of their dear friend who had been murdered.

Her mind went back to her husband, cared for by the city's top doctor, but his life force had faded. She'd stayed by his side until he was gone. She had no memory of the hours just after that.

René's voice cut through the silence, measured but trembling. "We mustn't jump to conclusions, but . . ." She hesitated, the weight of her next words hanging between them like a storm cloud. "We haven't seen Jo since Friday. She went out to search for Rebecca."

The air evaporated. "Jo is missing?" Eliza's heart pulsed against the collar of her widow's weeds.

Alice wouldn't meet her gaze. René barely nodded, then turned her eyes downward.

"We've been searching for her all night," Paulette sobbed.

The matter became clearer to Eliza. *Rebecca was dead and Jo was missing.*

"We mustn't jump to conclusions," René said again. Eliza understood the words this time.

As her tea grew tepid, she vowed to help find justice for Rebecca. But first, they needed to find Jo. She set her trembling cup and saucer on the table. "We'll find her. Jo is a survivor." They all were. Jo was possibly the scrappiest among them.

Alice glanced at Eliza with something like hope in her eyes, which hadn't been there until now. "Aye, that she is."

A thread of optimism hung in the air. Eliza clung to it. If anybody understood how to live with threads of hope, it was her.

# Chapter 2

After Eliza left, she made her way to the constable's office. She needed to be quick about it. The temperature was dropping, and soon McNally, her driver, would be scouring the streets for her, as he was expecting her at Trinity Church. She did not want that to happen. It would set tongues wagging.

Walking a few blocks, she located the constable's office after turning the corner. It was the same constabulary she'd escaped to after being held on a farm at the edge of town. The memory of her cracked, swollen feet often woke her up in the middle of the night. She opened the door.

As she entered the constabulary, the chill in the air seeped into her bones, a grim reminder that justice, like warmth, was something hard won in the city.

The place reeked of stale tobacco and sweat. She took a moment to steady herself. She'd never find a handkerchief beneath all her clothes. And the constables would not appreciate such a gesture.

"Mrs. General Hamilton?" Constable Schultz stood up from behind his desk.

"It is you. How lucky I am." She pushed away memories of her struggle last year. He had helped her. But it wasn't good to dwell on the past.

"How can I help you?" He moved toward her and the two others in the office were straining to view her from their desks.

She placed her hand in his and they shook hands. A simple, congenial gesture, but it warmed her. "I'm here about Rebecca Dickens and Josephine Ambrose."

His eyebrows rose, creasing his forehead. "Ah. I see. Please sit down."

She glanced at the chair he offered. "I'm sorry I don't have much time."

"It is a gruesome business. Are you certain you can't have a seat for a moment?" He gestured at the chair.

Eliza had been at the bloody bedside of her husband and countless soldiers during the Revolution, had lost her son, husband, and almost lost her own life last year. She did not feel the need to sit, yet she did.

The constable sat down behind the desk. "What can I tell you?"

"The most urgent matter is the whereabouts of Josephine." Eliza took off her gloves and clasped her hands on her lap.

"There is a search for her as we speak," Schultz replied. She hadn't seen him in a year, and he'd aged considerably. There was gray throughout his hair and pronounced creases around his eyes. His Prussian accent had diminished.

Eliza leaned in, her voice low and urgent. "Any leads on where she might be?"

"I'm sorry, madam, there are not. I can make enquiries for you, of course, and am happy to do so," he replied. "Maybe by tomorrow we'll have found her. But in any case, I'm happy to get a message to you."

She unclasped her hands and discreetly wiped them on her cloak. "About Rebecca. I've just been to visit the women who lived with her. They are quite distraught, of course, and they tell me she was murdered. I did not ask for details. What exactly happened?" She leaned forward.

He glanced down and placed his arms over his protruding stomach. "What I know is that she was reported missing a few days ago." He lifted his eyes to meet her gaze. "We found her dead in the early hours of the morning."

"How was she killed?"

"We don't know yet. No wounds, no marks that would suggest a struggle."

"Could she simply have died? I mean, how do we know it was murder?"

He cupped his hands together on the desk. "We don't. We know nothing yet about how she died."

"Yet her friends—"

"Yes, they are sure she was murdered, but we pressed them to tell us why and they couldn't. They just kept saying she was very healthy and would not succumb to the cold or just up and die. They are certain, but we are not." The harsh "t" on the end of "not" jabbed at Eliza.

Sometimes people just died. Their bodies gave out. Sometimes they'd harbored a disease for years without realizing it. But the women had a close bond with Rebecca, were familiar with her habits and preferences. "Surely the investigation will tell us."

He frowned and leaned in. "There won't be much of one, I'm afraid."

"Why not?"

"We don't have the resources to investigate every suspicious death in New York City now, do we?" One of his wiry eyebrows lifted.

Resources. His meaning was money, and she fully understood the absence of it.

Eliza swallowed. "She was a dear friend of mine." Her voice cracked, even though she didn't want it to. She didn't want to cry in front of him. "I'd like justice. It would help her friends as well. Besides, if there's a killer on these streets after women, wouldn't it be best for you to find him, so he doesn't kill again?"

He sighed, a flicker of discomfort in his eyes. "She was found near . . . a disreputable place, Mrs. General Hamilton. You know how these cases often go."

"What? Her presence there doesn't imply anything. She made a living selling lace, linen, and dresses." Eliza's face heated.

Schultz's face reddened in turn. "I am sorry, Mrs. General Hamilton. I personally will take this matter on. I promise you. I'll do my best."

Eliza questioned the quality of his best, with him hinting that Rebecca was a prostitute. "Thank you, Constable Schultz. One more thing, if I could ask you. May I see her?"

His jaw dropped. "Why?"

"I just have this need to see her." Eliza tried to avoid using her status for personal gain, but in certain cases there was nothing else to do. She was the widow of the great General Alexander Hamilton, whose untimely death by duel roused the whole city to line the streets during his funeral. His words would go on forever in documents like *The Federalist Papers,* and the U.S. Constitution, yet his death left his family with no money. Their house would be sold back to the bank any day now. But most people were unaware of their precarious financial situation and so she maintained her social status.

"Very well. Follow me," he said.

Following him, she navigated through meandering offices, hallways, and a narrow alleyway. He opened the door.

"Can I help you, Constable?" a man dressed in a guard uniform said.

"I'm accompanying Mrs. General Hamilton to view the body of Rebecca Dickens."

The guard glanced at her. "Highly unusual, Mrs. Hamilton. Are you certain about doing this?"

"Of course, I am." She lifted her chin.

Constable Schultz nodded. "A friend of hers, sir."

"Carry on," he said.

Eliza followed Schultz. It wasn't as if she *wanted* to see another dead body. She believed she had a responsibility to Rebecca and to the women she'd resided with. The pulse in Eliza's neck throbbed against her wool collar. She drew in a breath, trying to will her heartbeat to slow, and her stomach to settle. *This was for Rebecca.*

As they entered the dimly lit, windowless morgue, a faint scent of decay lingered in the air, mingling with the sharp tang of disinfectants. Cold enveloped Eliza, even dressed for winter.

The morgue's stone walls held the deep chill of death itself. Sparsely furnished, the room had bare stone walls, and a few crude wooden tables scattered about. Only one body lay in the room, covered by a thin muslin sheet. Eliza had encountered too many rooms like this during the war. Too many lives slipped away while she held bloody hands and whispered prayers. But this was different. Rebecca's body lay alone, unclaimed but for their small group of friends—no family to mourn her, no clergy to pray over her soul.

Eliza regarded the constable, who stood near the doorway. "May I?" She held the sheet in her hands.

He nodded.

She pulled the cloth down to reveal Rebecca's face. As she did so, a strong, sweet scent came from the body. It was Rebecca all right, complete with the dimple in her chin and long black eyelashes. Small wrinkles at her eyes and mouth. Unnatural dark circles rimmed her eyes.

*Poor Rebecca.*

Eliza's chest tightened with an all-too-familiar ache. How many times had she stood over the dead? Hamilton, Philip, her father—each loss carved deeper into her heart. But this was different. Rebecca hadn't died surrounded by loved ones; she'd been discarded like refuse. The injustice of it burned in Eliza's throat as she studied the unnatural darkness around the young woman's eyes, the bluish tinge to her skin. Even in death, Rebecca's hands showed the careful grace of a craftswoman. What secrets had those skilled fingers taken to death?

A few flickering candles cast dancing shadows across the room, created an eerie glow over the scene. The light played tricks, lending an otherworldly quality to the somber tableau.

Eliza reached out, the candle's flame flickering in the dim light as it drew near Rebecca's face. "Is that dried blood in the corner of her mouth?"

The constable leaned closer. "I believe so. Yes."

"She must have been sick. Vomiting blood." A tear welled up, hot and unbidden, as the unyielding reality of Rebecca's death settled into Eliza's bones.

Schultz pointed out the absence of that in the coroner's report. "I'm sorry. It's not written on the report."

"How can that be?" Eliza asked.

Schultz shrugged. "I'm sure I don't know."

Eliza turned her attention back to Rebecca.

"She also smells oddly. It's not the scent of death. I know it well." *Too well.* "There's something off about her eyes." She walked to Rebecca's feet and pulled the sheet up there. The skin on her feet was also almost black. "And her skin. The coloring is off." It was plain to see this was no natural death.

Why did the examiner overlook these things? Did he pay her no mind because they assumed she was a woman of low moral character?

Schultz walked over to Eliza. "You're right. Madam—"

"I believe the women at Pearl Street House are correct. Rebecca was murdered. Poisoned, I should think. Arsenic." Eliza had witnessed it once before during the war. A woman had used it to follow her soldier husband to the grave.

"But they've already examined her. No mention was made of this. She's going to be released for burial in the morning."

"Please request another examination based on what we see here." Eliza's jaw was so tight that she could barely get the words out. She was aware that they could analyze the blood to check for the presence of poison. They obviously had not bothered.

"I will do my best and bring the results to your home."

"No need, Constable Schultz. I'll be back tomorrow."

She took one last glimpse at Rebecca, then slipped the sheet over her, shuddering. What had Rebecca faced in her final moments? And why?

And most importantly, who had done this to her?

# Chapter 3

Eliza tossed and turned that night, Rebecca's discolored face taunting her. The other thing that taunted her was the medical examination of Rebecca's body. Why did nobody observe what she had? Had they even tried? Hamilton used to say that if you were poor and dead, a lonely grave awaited you. Now she grasped what he meant.

But it wasn't as if Rebecca had been poor. She just wasn't wealthy. Rebecca and the women she'd lived with had built a thriving concern selling their handiwork to the fine homes in New York City. The fact that Rebecca was found outside a gentlemen's club tugged at Eliza's heart. What had she been doing there? She'd been missing for a day. Had someone taken her? Had she been conducting affairs for their handmade textile concern?

And where was Jo? Somehow it seemed wrong for Eliza to be resting in her bed while Jo might be in danger. Even though Schultz said they were searching for her.

Eliza remembered the women at the Widow Society, where she had met Alice. Most of them would never overcome their plights. Few remarried; those who weren't wealthy often relied on the church or organizations like the Widow Society. Some, inevitably, had to sell their bodies.

But the women who lived together on Pearl Street had found another way, by gathering and strengthening their forces, selling their goods, such as lace, embroidered linens, and the like.

Eliza gave up trying to sleep and rose from her tangle of quilts. She welcomed the brisk cool air, which further awakened her. She warmed herself by the fireplace, then heaved another log on it. As she watched the flames dance, she closed her eyes and prayed she'd find answers to Rebecca's death and Jo's whereabouts. She assumed that there was a connection between them. But was there?

She dressed and made her way downstairs to the breakfast table. The children were already there, except for her two older boys—who were now young men, she reminded herself. Alexander Jr. was renting accommodations near the law practice he was clerking at, and James would be home for the holiday, a school break. His studies were almost complete.

Looking at her large table, with only four children and no Hamilton, she always needed a moment. Alexander's and James's chairs were empty. Fanny, the Hamilton's adopted daughter, had recently married. She was with child and could not be there. But Hamilton and Philip were gone. Loss was her constant companion. Gratitude swept through her as she watched the children. They were free from harm, had food, and a place to lay their heads. How long would they stay in this big, cold house? For everything that her Hamilton had been, he'd left her with no funds to pay for it. In fact, he'd left her grappling with debt.

"Mama!" Little Philip, named for his late older brother, raised his three-year-old arms. Sitting on his sister Angel's lap, he reached for Eliza, who lifted him to her and buried her face in his hair.

Eliza had much to be grateful for, even without her husband at her side.

★ ★ ★

The journey to Manhattan was two hours from the Grange, the house Eliza and Hamilton had built in Harlem, where she and their children still lived. For now. Eliza disliked the long distance on Bloomingdale Road, and the bitter weather, and she almost canceled her meeting with Isabella Graham, her partner in creating an orphanage. But nothing would stop her from seeing Alice and the other women. Nor from checking in on Constable Schultz to see how the search for Jo has progressed, as well as the further examination of Rebecca's body.

When Eliza arrived at the door of Alice's home, she was surprised to see Constable Schultz standing there holding a slip of paper on the stoop. He glanced at her and put the slip of paper in his pocket. A flicker of something—discomfort? guilt?—crossed his face. Eliza made a mental note to ask him about it later, though she suspected the answer would not be straightforward.

"Good morning, Mrs. General Hamilton." He tipped his hat. "I was just about to knock and tell Rebecca's friends about the examination."

"Very well. We'll go together." Eliza was pleased she did not have to go to the constabulary. She was also curious about what he had stuck in his pocket.

The constable knocked on the door. A weary-looking Alice opened it. "Please come in." She brightened when she glimpsed Eliza.

"We arrived at the same time," Eliza said. She embraced Alice. "How are you?"

Alice shrugged. "I'm certain I don't know." Alice appeared well turned out in a black wool mourning dress, like Eliza. She turned to the constable. "Please, both of you, sit down."

René and Paulette entered the room, clutched together, Paulette sniffling.

After they sat, the room was silent, with all eyes on Schultz.

He cleared his throat. "I regret to tell you that we've not yet found Josephine. We had a lead and followed it to a dead end. Did she run away with someone? A man? Did she owe anybody money?"

Alice moaned. "We went over this yesterday. The answer is no to both questions. She loved her life here with us. She would not run away with a man. She had plenty of money and was not in debt. And before you ask again, she did not have a taste for drink."

"You said you had a lead?" Eliza leaned forward.

"It led us nowhere. We'd learned about a man, perhaps hurting women, keeping them in his home. But he's no longer in the city. He left several weeks ago. We will continue to search for her." He paused, then turned to Alice. "Mrs. Rhodes, I agree with Mrs. General Hamilton. She was right to assert that your friend Rebecca was murdered. Most likely poisoned."

Alice raised her eyebrows. "I told the other man that. He wouldn't listen."

His face reddened. "There were mitigating circumstances."

Alice and René exchanged looks.

Eliza leaned forward. "Go on," she said.

"I may regret telling you . . ." Schultz gazed downward, and his fleshy face grew pink.

"Please. It would mean so much to us," Eliza said.

His eyes cast downward and he shuffled his feet. "I don't like to speak of such matters with ladies. But they found Miss Dickens dressed in male clothing. In fact, when we found her, we registered her as a male."

Alice coughed, which turned into a laugh. René turned her face to keep from laughing.

"That's not odd, Constable," Alice explained. "She often dressed as a man to tend to our handmade goods concern."

Schultz's jaw dropped.

"It's regrettable but true that people treated her differently because she was dressed as a man," Eliza said. Eliza had initially found it uncomfortable and surprising, but it wasn't all that unusual.

Hamilton had told her stories of women disguised as men who fought in the war.

Schultz cleared his throat. "It's against the law."

"For a woman to dress as a man?" Eliza was incredulous. She had done it herself. She wasn't aware it was illegal. Dressing as a man provided women access to establishments and circles otherwise unavailable to them. She tugged at her collar, which scratched against her neck.

His jaw tightened. "For her to pretend to be someone she was not."

"Aye. There was no pretending. She was always Rebecca," Alice said.

"But, but . . ." Constable Schultz struggled with finding the right words, his lips moving but nothing coming out.

"Constable Schultz," Eliza interrupted. "Can we move past the fact that she was a woman dressed as a man and ask what you and your colleagues are doing to find her killer?"

His eyes traveled from woman to woman, as if he were confused, then focused on Eliza. "We've had a second examination of the body. We determined she was poisoned, but . . . finding where she got it from is another matter. I'm under orders to leave this alone—it's above my rank. Believe me, Mrs. Hamilton, I wish I could do more."

"What if I disappeared for a day and then turned up dead? Poisoned. Would you be so cavalier about it?" Eliza placed her cup on the table.

"Of course not, Mrs. General Hamilton."

"Then why are you not pursuing justice in this matter?"

"My superiors have put a stop to me investigating this matter—and several others. I can't say if they are investigating, because I don't know." He shrugged.

Eliza had had dealings with Schultz before and had surmised he was an honest man trying to make a living for his family. His discomfort was reflected in his stance. Sometimes following orders went against the grain for soldiers, as well as constables.

"Others?" René said. "Have other women been murdered?"

Hamilton used to say that women, especially poor ones, were vulnerable in the world and if they met a bad ending, justice often shrugged its shoulders and focused elsewhere. Authorities disposed of their bodies in mass graves.

"There are always murders of women. You don't hear of them because there's nobody to tell the newspapers. They are alone in the world." Eliza paused. "That's what makes this house and the women in it special."

"Aye." Alice eyed the constable. "We need to find Jo before they kill her like Rebecca. And we need justice for our Rebecca."

"I cannot go against a direct order, madam." Schultz's face grew red once more.

Silence filled the room. Paulette sniffled in the corner.

"Who's your superior?" Alice questioned.

"William Trist."

Alice grunted. "I know of him. He'll do nothing for Rebecca, let alone Jo."

Eliza swallowed the surge of anger creeping up her throat and leaned forward. "Then tell me, Constable, if we uncover the truth—if we bring you her killer—will you have the courage to arrest him? Or will he slip through your fingers?" Her voice did not quiver with anger or fear; it was merely edged in annoyance.

He shifted in his chair. "I recommend you avoid that. It could be very dangerous, given where we found her body. Besides, maybe one of my superiors is investigating. I have no way of knowing. I'm sorry, I must go now. I am so sorry for your loss. We'll be releasing the body tomorrow."

As he left, Eliza ruminated about whether justice would ever be served for Rebecca and the many women whose stories were lost with them. But one thing was certain—she wouldn't stop until she had an answer.

There had been no justice in the loss of her dear Hamilton. Burr had slipped away, hiding like the rat he was. Even as she had campaigned against him after Hamilton's death, he was a free man. The last she had heard of his whereabouts was that he was staying with a relative in the South—gone from the city, at least. She hoped he would stay away forever. She used to lie awake at night praying for his death, but now she saw even death as being too good for the likes of Aaron Burr.

# Chapter 4

After the constable left, quiet filled the room, except for Paulette's sniffles. She sat in the corner in the rocking chair and cried. Paulette, René's daughter, had done seamstress work for Eliza. Eliza gathered that Paulette's father was African, as René was fair-skinned, while Paulette was not.

Eliza had questions but figured she had to tread carefully. The women were still reeling from Rebecca's death. Even Alice, usually so lively, sat in stunned silence. How could Eliza broach the subject amidst the thick fog of grief that enveloped them—even as she wrestled with her own shock? But time was slipping away if they were to find Rebecca's killer.

Two new women entered the house, their presence casting a brief shadow over the room. Eliza recognized them from earlier visits, but they had never been introduced to her.

"How is she?" one of them asked with an Irish accent.

René shook her head and shrugged.

Alice blinked, realizing they were talking about her. She glanced at them. "Did you make your deliveries?"

The house was in mourning, had crepe in the windows, and all wore black. Yet they were still conducting business. Didn't these women ever stop? But of course, they couldn't, Eliza realized.

"Yes," the younger of the two said.

Alice nodded absently, her mind elsewhere. "Good." She then turned to Eliza, her expression hardening. 'You spoke of justice for Rebecca. The constables won't lift a finger—we both know that."

"It seems so." Eliza folded her hands in her lap. "Though I wonder. He mentioned the matter was out of his hands. So I wonder if someone else has taken on the case."

Alice's jaw tightened.

"But perhaps we should give it a little time," René said. "None of us are in any condition—"

"Time?" Alice sprang to life, with gleaming eyes and straighter posture. "No! We should find out who killed her as soon as we can. We don't want anybody else to get hurt, do we?"

"Alice, we are talking about a killer." René's voice cracked. "What can we do against a killer?"

Alice smacked her lips. "Turn him over to the constable!"

"Such folly!" The Irish woman moved closer to the group. "You are not thinking right, Alice. If the police don't have the means, we certainly don't."

All eyes were on Eliza now.

Many assumed she was wealthy. After all, she was the widow of Alexander Hamilton. But the truth was far different. Instead of inheriting a fortune, she had inherited her late husband's debts. And now, the home she had fought so hard to keep might slip through her fingers.

"I'll do what I can," Eliza assured them.

"I'm sorry. I didn't see you sitting there." The older of the two redheads stepped forward and offered Eliza her hand. "I am Brigid, and this is my sister, Mary."

"I am—" Eliza began.

"Mrs. General Hamilton," Brigid finished. She shook Eliza's hand, and so did Mary.

"Mary and Brigid are our weavers," René said with a weary voice.

"Very nice to meet you, but I'm sorry for the circumstances," Eliza said. When Eliza had stayed in this house with these women, the thwack and thumps of the weavers working provided background noise to the day. But Eliza had never introduced herself, as the weavers kept odd hours.

"We have a funeral to plan. There's no time to figure out who killed Rebecca," Mary said.

Alice's jaw twitched. "There's no reason we can't do both." Her words cut through the room, silencing the murmurs.

"Rebecca attended St. Paul's. I'll stop by there tomorrow on my way to deliver a quilt to the Van Horns," René said.

Alice fixed Eliza with a sharp gaze. 'So, what's our next move?' The question hung in the air, loaded with expectation.

"Don't you think you should take time and mourn before you—" Mary started.

"I do not," Alice interrupted. "Rebecca was dear to me, to us. Someone murdered her. The best thing we can do to honor her memory is to help bring justice to this matter. I'm not one to dwell on my losses."

Eliza related to that. Neither was she. "We need to trace her steps. Where was she heading the day she left? Who did she speak with?"

"Maybe each person we speak to can lead us to the next," Alice agreed.

"And to her killer," René said.

A shiver ran through Eliza, despite the warmth of the room. The weight of responsibility pressed on her. She had to honor Rebecca's memory by seeking justice, but dread coiled in her gut. This would be no simple task.

What had Schultz said? He'd reported that Rebecca's body had been discovered outside a brothel in a shady part of town, and that she'd been dressed in male clothing. "We need to speak with William Trist." Eliza's voice was firm with determination.

Alice's expression darkened as she twisted the gold locket at her neck. "Trist is an unpleasant man, and speaking with him will get you nowhere. He will only waste our time."

Eliza was not acquainted with him. But she was sure he'd know her. Everyone did—or at least recognized her. And maybe this time that would be a good thing. "I shall meet with him."

A sharp knock at the door shattered the somber silence. René rose, her knees creaking like old floorboards in the stillness.

It was Eliza's driver, McNally. "Good afternoon, ladies. Please allow me to express my condolences. Mrs. General Hamilton, we need to go. The snow is blowing fiercely and shows no sign of stopping." Bits of snow were caught in his red beard and on his shoulders.

"Thank you. I'll be there soon. I need to gather my things." Eliza turned to Alice. "I will be back as soon as possible and will talk with Trist. In the meantime, please try to get rest. You will need your energy."

Eliza stole one last glance at the group of women, all of them weary and bereft. But Alice most of all. It went against Eliza's impulse to leave Alice, yet McNally waited.

"We must hurry to Trinity," Eliza said to McNally. "I'm meeting Mrs. Graham. I believe she just has a few papers for me to review. Perhaps I can take them with me."

"Madam, I—"

She held up her hand. "I know what you're going to say. I must take care of this matter, and I will be quick about it."

The church where Isabella Graham waited was only a few blocks away. It was such a short distance that Eliza would walk, if it were not for the snow piles and icy patches. When McNally pulled the horses into the lot, a man approached their carriage. Eliza recognized Martin, one of Isabella's butlers, even though he was wrapped up in many layers of clothing. She opened the door. "Martin! Whatever are you doing here in the snow?"

"Mrs. General Hamilton! I'm waiting for you. Mrs. Graham sends her regrets that she could not be here. She wanted me to deliver this satchel to you." He handed the snow-covered, wet leather bag to her. "She will be in touch."

"Thank you. Please go and get warm!" Eliza said and shut the door.

"No worries, madam, I will."

Eliza peered inside the bag as they pulled away. It was full of papers neatly bundled together for her to review. She looked out the back window of the carriage. Martin was gone.

The journey home was swift and safe as the roads were not quite covered with snow. Eliza looked over the papers and spotted a few misspelled words—she'd be sure to mark those when she returned home. There were spaces for signatures, as well, on documents of intent. Her breath caught in her throat. Was this orphanage really going to happen?

# CHAPTER 5

Disjointed and chaotic, Alice's thoughts were mere leaves scattered by a gust of wind. Nothing made sense. *Rebecca. Gone.* She'd only been with them for less than a year, but she had bonded with the group.

And Jo. She'd been with Alice from the start. Finding the house to rent. Setting up the concern. She was her partner. Younger. Smarter. Wily. *Where was she?*

Could Eliza help them? Could she find Rebecca's killer, when all Alice could do was sit here, drowning in her own helplessness? Eliza Hamilton was stronger than most women . . . but this? Finding a killer to clear your son of a murder charge was one thing. But finding the killer of a woman dressed as a man was a different story.

Alice recognized that brothel—after all, they needed linens same as everyone else. And she knew Lucille, the owner of the establishment. Alice had dealt with such customers herself, as nobody noticed an old woman creaking about. She'd never send the young women into any kind of a dangerous situation. But Lucille's place itself was not dangerous. Usually. It was the area where it was located that was questionable.

What in God's name had Rebecca been doing there? Alice had warned her enough times. She didn't belong in that part of town.

*Rebecca. It was so hard to believe she was gone.*

Rebecca Dickens was the youngest of them, in her twenties. Alice had found her through the Widow Society—another lost soul, the daughter of a widow who'd passed away too soon. The Society had taken her in, given her a purpose. But now Alice wondered—had it all been for nothing? Rebecca had cleaned and cooked and did any chore they asked of her. With her free time, she made lace in her room. A skill her mother had taught her. A connection to her that never passed.

Rebecca also crafted dresses for the widows and the workers, often making them from bits of fabric, old clothing, and linens. Dressmaking was a line of their concern that had not grown. Alice and Jo seized the opportunity, and they kept her busy.

Alice fiddled with her locket, the cool metal of it pressed against her fingertips, grounding her in the present. A tear escaped, tracing a furious line down her cheek. Lost in the storm of grief. Rebecca murdered. A fresh cut, deep and raw, that left her breathless. How could she keep moving forward when every step threatened to shatter?

*Accident.* Maybe it had been an accident, just as they first reasoned. Maybe Rebecca had eaten something tainted with poison, too trusting of the street vendors Alice had warned her about.

The memory of Rebecca's laugh, carefree and defiant, echoed in Alice's mind. When Alice first met Rebecca, she was alone—surrounded by widows and orphans, yet isolated. Rebecca had been pretty, her black hair gleaming like polished onyx. Those soft brown eyes, distant, gleaned something others couldn't.

Whatever haunted her, it ran deep. And she'd never let them in, never shared the shadows that lingered. Despite her beauty, Rebecca never sought friendship or male companionship. Aye, she'd been hurt deeply. But she rarely spoke of it. Like most of the women. The past was best left alone.

Even Eliza Hamilton would agree to that.

# Chapter 6

Nighttime was the hardest. In the quiet darkness, Eliza withstood the sharpest stab of his absence. Hamilton had belonged to the world during the day, a figure of strength and intellect. But at night, he had been hers alone, the one who held her close and chased away her fears. Rebecca's murder brought up the intensity of his death again. Grief was like that. She felt fine for a few days or a week, until some reminder dredged it all up again.

Eliza also dwelled on her father, who had died a few months after Hamilton. She was at peace, aware she and her children had provided comfort to him, even as he grew feebler and feebler. Even Fanny, the Hamilton's adopted daughter, was able to stay with them and helped take care of him and the house. They'd stayed until the end of his life. Her father had died last November, and the holidays were a blur of mourning. She was determined that her children have a better Christmas than last year, having just lost their father and grandfather.

She rose from her bed and walked toward the window. The room was bathed in blue light and snow blanketed the ground. The weather would delay her. McNally would not risk travel on the snowy roads, unless necessary. Last winter, several carriages had met their tragic end, sliding off icy roads or plunging into the frigid river waters. The thought sent a shiver along Eliza's spine.

But she needed to get to town. Time was of the utmost importance. She'd learned that from her experience dealing with the authorities after her son Alexander Jr. had been accused of murder. Thank goodness it had turned out all right and his name was cleared.

Her older sons were expected to arrive any day now, so she hoped the snow would melt soon. A thread of worry moved through her. "It's pointless to worry, Betsy. What will be, will be," Hamilton had often said to her.

Eliza pulled her robe tighter around her, trying to ward off the chill that had crept into the room as the fire died. The snow-covered landscape glowed with the early morning, casting an eerie light. "Please, let it melt," she whispered, her breath fogging the cold windowpane.

The Grange wasn't built for winter. Hamilton had envisioned it as a summer house. And it had been that for a while. But she and the children loved it so much that they spent most of their time there, in the house Hamilton had dreamed up for them.

Eliza closed her eyes and shivered as the image of Rebecca's body lying on the table refused to leave her mind. She feared she'd always remember her that way, rather than her laughter or silliness. She'd seen Rebecca dressed as a man countless times. It was the only way to succeed as a woman who ran her own concern. Most women had a male relative working alongside them. But Rebecca was clever. And the women who lived at the Pearl Street house were better for it. Eliza cracked a smile.

The constable said it was illegal for someone to pretend to be someone else. Did someone figure out Rebecca was a woman and attack her for it ? Is that what happened to her?

Eliza's fists balled as she watched for the sunrise, hopeful that the sun's heat would melt the snow. She needed to get out of the house to see William Trist.

The Grange seemed to hold its breath in the predawn darkness, waiting for the household to stir. Eliza moved through the familiar rooms by memory and touch, discerning exactly which floorboards would betray her early rising. The house still creaked and settled in ways Hamilton had never lived to learn—each sound a reminder of how briefly they'd shared this dream. From the kitchen below came the first sounds of Mrs. Cole beginning her day, the scrape of the hearth rake against iron promising warmth and sustenance for the children who would soon wake. The family would take their morning meal in the warm kitchen, while the rest of the house took its time heating.

By noon, the sun's warmth had melted the snow, and Eliza wasted no time preparing for her trip into town. She hoped the authorities would soon tell her they had found Jo and that they had found Rebecca's killer. The urgency of her mission pressed against her, driving her forward as she set off to see William Trist.

All eyes followed Eliza as she entered the constabulary. She hated it but was also prepared for it. "I'm here to see William Trist."

The young man who approached her lifted a finger. "Yes, Mrs. General Hamilton. Please follow me."

When she entered the office, a short, balding, stout man greeted her with a handshake. "William Trist. Very pleased to meet you. I knew your husband. Please accept my late condolences."

His handshake was limp. Eliza followed his gesture to sit. "Thank you. Have you found Josephine yet?"

"I'm afraid not. We have a team of men and volunteers searching for her. Do you have any idea where she could be?" he asked.

But it was Eliza who had come to him for answers. Was Alice right? Would this be a waste of time? "None, unfortunately. She could be anywhere."

He frowned. "Now, I understand you are interested in Rebecca Dickens's case."

"I was acquainted with her, and I know the house where she was living. They are fine, upstanding women, providing a service to many households in this city. They make fine lace, linens, quilts, blankets, and so on." Eliza cupped her hands and placed them in her lap.

Trist shifted back in his chair, and it squeaked under the weight of him. "I see."

"I was shocked to learn there would be no investigation," Eliza pressed, her voice firm. "Doesn't Rebecca deserve the same justice you would afford for someone like me?"

A few moments of silence passed as he seemed to consider her words.

"Mrs. General Hamilton," Trist said and cleared his throat. "As Constable Schultz explained, we presumed she was a man. And we found her in the Water Street district. "

"I cannot see the significance of that," Eliza said.

"Of course you don't. You're a comfortable widow. You've had a better than average upbringing. A good family life. You're innocent of a certain way of life."

Eliza had been near to battlefields, tended bloody soldiers, and worked with widows in horrible circumstances. She understood just about everything that could happen to women. But she attempted to maintain composure.

"That may well be true. But as a Christian woman, I believe every life has value."

Flummoxed, his beady eyes shifted back and forth, then finally rested on her. "In an ideal world, that would be the case. But we have limited men, limited money, and I must make tough decisions. We typically find people in that area because they are criminals themselves, the very people we aim to get rid of. So why waste our resources?"

Eliza grimaced.

"But I can see this young woman was not a criminal. So, I ask you, what was she doing there?" he asked. "And why was she dressed in disguise?"

"I don't know why she was there. None of her friends do either. But I can tell you why she was dressed as a man. She was representing their handiwork concern. Men do not take women seriously in such matters. So sometimes they dress as men to avoid that."

"That is against the law."

"It's also clever."

One of Trist's eyebrows rose. "You are a law-abiding citizen. I am shocked to hear you say that."

Being law-abiding had done little to protect her family. After all, Aaron Burr walked free, despite all he had done. But Eliza held her tongue, knowing better than to challenge Trist. Her Hamilton had been a lawyer, and they'd had many discussions about the law in this new country. So she had a basic understanding. Eliza kept her own counsel, not wanting to make the chief cross. "Did you test her blood for poison?"

"Yes. Yes, someone poisoned her."

"Good—on that we agree."

"Since she seemed to be a friend of yours and there may be a matter of mistaken identity, I will put my best men on this case. I can see she means something to you, and I had the greatest respect for your husband."

"Very well. I will call on you later. I'm interviewing all those familiar with Hamilton for his biography. We've engaged a writer to help me." She hoped that stroked his ego a bit. But she had no intention of interviewing him. He was not of the same ilk as the soldiers she'd been talking with. Not at all.

She stood. "Please keep me informed."

# Chapter 7

A frigid wind burned Eliza's face as she stepped out of the constabulary. Had the temperature dropped while she was inside?

Eliza's feet, clad in sturdy leather half boots, were growing numb despite her wool stockings and the carriage's foot warmers McNally had filled with hot coals before her journey. Around her, merchants' wives hurried past in their fur-trimmed pelisses, while working women wrapped themselves in thick shawls. Eliza moved quickly toward Pearl Street.

A grim-looking René let her into the house. As Eliza stepped inside, a wave of warmth embraced her, offering brief relief from the biting cold.

"I'm sorry, Eliza, but I'm the only person who is here. The others are out. May I get you some tea?" René asked.

Tea would warm her bones, but she didn't want to stay—and she didn't have the stomach for it. "No, thank you. I've just been to speak with William Trist, and he tells me that the police will investigate Rebecca's death."

René sank onto the settee, her energy drained. "Thank you. I'll tell everyone. They've postponed the burial—the ground's too frozen solid in places."

"How are you, René?" Eliza sat down next to her.

"I still can't believe this happened. And Paulette is very distraught." Her eyes were wet and hollow.

"The constables will find her killer," Eliza said. "And Jo will come walking into this house any minute."

"I doubt that," René said. "I know you've just come from there, and I don't wish to dash your hopes, but the law has not been helpful. It's hard for me to believe they will help now."

She might be right, but Eliza wouldn't give up. "Do you have any idea what Rebecca was doing there?"

"None. That's what is so frustrating. I don't believe she was killed there. She must've been killed elsewhere," René said.

"And moved? That would be a great deal of trouble."

"It'd take a lot of muscle. Rebecca was no waif."

Eliza contemplated. "Who was the last customer she helped?"

"That'd be Thursday. She was delivering an embroidered tablecloth to the Van Horns."

Eliza was acquainted with the family. Not well, but enough that she could question them about what had happened. "I'll talk with them. Maybe they can tell us something about Rebecca's state of mind or where she was heading next."

"Thank you," René said. "But please be careful."

Eliza stood. "I will." She spotted a trunk in the corner. "What is this?"

"We've cleaned out her room. Alice planned to deliver it to the Widow Society today, but it was too heavy."

"I can get McNally to fetch it and we will drop it off."

"That would be wonderful. Thank you."

McNally loaded the trunk into the carriage.

"Let's stop by the Van Horn residence. It's on Fifth Avenue."

McNally nodded, but one eyebrow lifted. "The weather. There's more snow coming, mum."

Eliza had had enough of winter, and the solstice was still weeks away. "Let's make it quick, then."

As they drove toward the Van Horns', Eliza formulated a plan, a line of questions, but she recognized that she had to be careful. The Van Horn family were notorious gossips. Eliza couldn't abide it. She'd refused several of their invitations because of it.

Once they'd arrived, she knocked on the door. A butler answered. "Mrs. General Hamilton to see Mrs. Van Horn."

Eliza reflected on having just come from the simple but comforting house on Pearl Street to this one. The respective furnishings told a story of class. Mrs. Van Horn's imported silk wallpaper versus the Pearl Street house's whitewashed walls; gilt framed mirrors versus simple polished brass; Turkish carpets versus scrubbed wood floors. But it was the subtle things that spoke the loudest—the ways Mrs. Van Horn's servants moved with careful deference, while the Pearl Street women shared their work with easy camaraderie. How one house smelled of expensive perfumes and beeswax polish, while the other carried the honest scent of laundry soap and newly baked bread.

The butler led her into a large marble hallway. Luxurious red velvet chairs were situated against walls on which paintings covered every inch. A floral painting caught her eye—hyacinths in painstaking detail. Her Hamilton had loved them and had them planted in their garden. Eliza was so intent on the painting that Mrs. Van Horn's sudden appearance startled her.

"Mrs. General Hamilton! How wonderful to see you." Mrs. Van Horn's shrill voice echoed through the cavernous hallway.

Eliza turned and embraced her, kissing both cheeks. "I'm dreadfully sorry that I didn't send in a card. This visit is truly last minute."

"You are welcome here anytime, my dear. Let's go into the parlor. Tea?" Statuesque, graceful, Mrs. Van Horn gestured toward the parlor.

"No, thank you. My visit has a mission, and I need to be quick about it as my driver is concerned it may snow again." Eliza followed Mrs. Van Horn into the parlor, where they both sat on elegant pink couches.

"What can I help you with?" Mrs. Van Horn smiled, her blonde curls framing her cheekbones.

Eliza remembered that Mrs. Van Horn didn't know Rebecca's true name. Maybe she didn't need to know it. "I am inquiring about your recent purchase of embroidered linens."

"Yes. We get them from the House of Pearl."

This was the first time Eliza heard someone refer to the craftswomen's concern by name. "The person who delivered them, um . . . I'm sorry the name escapes me . . ."

"Oh yes, Rob. A delightful young fellow."

"Did he, by any chance, mention where he was going after his visit here?" Eliza asked.

"I don't believe so." Mrs. Van Horn's eyebrows knitted.

"Where could he have gone?" Eliza said, almost to herself, absentmindedly. "I just don't understand."

Mrs. Van Horn's hand flew to her chest, her eyes wide with alarm. "Are you looking for him?" she whispered.

There was no point in hiding anything from her, except the truth of his gender, which might not sit well with her.

"No. He's dead."

Mrs. Van Horn gasped, her hand covering her mouth. "Oh, my word."

Eliza remained silent, giving her time to gather her composure.

"How? He was so young. I just can't imagine."

"He was murdered," Eliza said. "A constable may be around to speak with you about this matter."

"Oh dear, oh dear, dear, dear," Mrs. Van Horn said, standing and pacing back and forth. "I'm trying to remember our conversation." She continued pacing the floor between the window and the couch. Her chest rose and fell with quick breaths.

Eliza noted what she thought was an overreaction to the news of a worker's death. Was she quite well?

Eliza stood and moved closer, resting a hand gently on her shoulder. "I'm so sorry," she murmured, pulling Mrs. Van Horn into a tentative embrace. The woman's body remained stiff and unyielding, so Eliza released her.

"Do you have any idea where Rob went after he delivered here?" Eliza asked again.

She shook her head. "He may have mentioned something about the apothecary. I'm not sure if it was this visit or an earlier one. Said his mother was having trouble." Her cheeks were mottled with the shock of the news.

Eliza wondered if her memory was correct. "Which apothecary?"

This might be the chance they need. Arsenic was available at apothecaries. But would Rebecca have purchased it herself? That didn't make any sense. But maybe someone there had seen her. Maybe with another person. That could shed light on things.

"I'm uncertain. There are two close by. Johnston's Apothecary is the closest, but Manhattan is just around the corner from there."

Eliza would visit both, since they were in the same vicinity. "You've been very helpful."

Mrs. Van Horn's eyes met Eliza's, but something was off. Was it just the shock of Rob's death, or was there something more? Something deeper that Mrs. Van Horn was reluctant to reveal? "Are you quite all right?"

Mrs. Van Horn opened her mouth, then shut it, wringing her handkerchief as if she was twisting the life out of it. "It's just a shock. He was just here." She crumpled into herself and landed on the settee, resting her head in her arms on the side of it. Her shoulders shook as sobs escaped. "He was just here."

Eliza went to her and rubbed her shoulders. "I'm sorry to bring you such shocking news. I had no idea you were so fond of him."

She lifted her head, revealing a wet and red face. "We all were. He was . . . endearing."

Eliza had never seen a lady display such emotion about a hired person. Questions burned the tip of her tongue.

"Has anybody else been around asking about him?" she asked.

"A young man came here to make sure we'd gotten our delivery and asked about Rob."

Eliza had figured as much. Jo had come here looking for Rebecca.

A house servant entered the room. "Mrs. General Hamilton, your driver is at the door. He wishes you to know it's snowing."

*Of course it was.*

# Chapter 8

The sound of Mrs. Van Horn's sobs echoed in Eliza's mind, where they sat, hovering. Was Mrs. Van Horn an overly emotional person, or had she genuinely cared for Rebecca? What was the relationship there? Would René or Alice know? Or would she have to visit with the Van Horn matron again?

Eliza and McNally flew home as fast as they could while wisps of snow fell. But by the time they'd gotten to the Grange, the snow was coming down in thick chunks and forming mounds on the ground. They weren't the only ones who made it before the snow had gotten so bad that you could hardly see. Eliza stepped into the warmth of the Grange, and her heart lifted at the sight of her older sons gathered in the parlor with the younger children.

After embracing them, she took in the happy tableau in front of her. Her children circled the fireplace in the parlor, a game of backgammon on the floor. Angel, her oldest daughter, was embroidering on the settee. "Mama," she said, "You didn't bring Philip with you?"

James cast a glance at Eliza. "We tried to tell her that Philip is gone."

Philip had died in a duel, years before Hamilton. Angel had never recovered.

"Angel," Eliza said in a soft tone. "Remember, we lost Philip in a duel. Philip is dead."

Angel's face crumpled, her eyes widening with a fresh wave of disbelief, as if she were hearing the news for the first time all over again.

"I don't believe it." She dropped her embroidery onto her lap. She stood and ran into Eliza's arms, sobbing.

"There, there," Eliza said. "Let's get you some warm milk and then you can go to bed for a nice, long nap."

Angel nodded, childlike, even at twenty-two years of age. She walked with her mother downstairs into the warm kitchen, where Mrs. Cole was kneading dough for bread.

"It smells lovely here, doesn't it, Angel?" Eliza asked as she poured milk into a pan and placed it on the stove.

"I'll take care of that, Mrs. Hamilton," said Mrs. Cole.

"Nonsense. I'll handle this. You make bread. We're going to need it. We have a full house. The only people missing are my siblings and their children." She doubted she'd see her brothers, none of whom were speaking with her, since she let her feelings erupt about their father's will. It was a conflict that sometimes awakened her in the middle of the night. She didn't enjoy disruptions in her relationships, let alone with her brothers and sisters.

Her brothers accused her father of giving her thousands in cash to help support her family when Hamilton died. She had gone to her father's home after the funeral for a respite. But they thought he'd given her money. Little did they know, their father had no money to give. Their father did, however, deed over eighty acres of land to her, also disputed by her brothers. She left her father's home without the deed in hand. It was finally found amongst his papers and her brothers were not happy about it. As men, they felt they were entitled to more because they had families to support.

But so did she.

Eliza would not sign the deed over to them—her father had wanted her to have it. And she needed all the money she could get from the sale of the land. She closed her eyes and prayed that all would resolve.

This time of year was so busy with family and church obligations. Angelica was ensconced back in London with her brood. And all Eliza wanted was a miracle—for them all to be together again.

Just before the milk boiled, Eliza removed it from the stove and poured the thick white drink into a cup. Angel was sitting at the table, staring blankly.

"Let's go, Angel." Eliza gestured to her daughter to follow her upstairs to her room. The quiet room stood watch as the women entered it. Angel sat at the edge of the bed.

"Drink your milk, my love, then lie down and have a rest." Eliza placed the milk on the table next to the bed. It warmed her chilled hand.

"Why did he do that?" Angel said.

"Who do what?" Eliza asked as she walked to the other side of the bed, turning down the cover.

"Why did Philip die?" Angel's voice cracked.

"Oh, my dear," Eliza came back around the bed and sat next to Angelica. "Ours is not to question the ways of God. And all ways are his. There are no answers."

Even as the words left her lips, doubt stung at her. Did she truly believe them anymore? Faith had once been her anchor, but now it often felt as hollow as the prayers she recited.

Angel nodded. She reached for her drink and gulped it. Eliza tucked the covers in around her. She sat back down until Angel drifted off to sleep. Would her daughter ever experience peace? Would Eliza?

Eliza reentered the parlor, where her children were gathered around a large object. Her gaze fell on the open trunk, and a chill ran through her. Rebecca's trunk—how could she have forgotten?

James turned to his mother. "What's this?" He held a book in his hands.

"That trunk belonged to Rebecca, a friend of mine who passed away. Her friends packed up her belongings for the Widow Society, and McNally and I intended to deliver them today. But with the snow, I completely forgot."

"I would not want to see some of these things at the Widow Society," James said. "I don't think anybody there would need these journals and books."

"And commonplace books," Alexander Jr. said.

Dread washed over her. "Perhaps we shouldn't be looking through her things. She just died a few days ago."

"Well, Mother, she is dead. What care does she have that we're looking through her things?" Alexander said.

"I'm sorry to hear that, Mother. Were you close?" James asked.

"I knew her, but friends of mine were quite close to her."

"How did she die?" With a solemn expression, Alexander closed the lid of the trunk with gentleness, as if sealing away the remnants of Rebecca's life.

Eliza lowered her voice, as her other children were playing backgammon and paper dolls close by. "She was murdered."

"Mother!" James exclaimed and embraced her.

"Have they found who did it?" Alexander asked, brows knitted.

Eliza's stomach turned. "Not yet."

She didn't want her sons to know the details. She wanted to shove every bad thing in the world away, like the books they had shoved into the trunk. Eliza wanted the Grange to be filled with as many happy memories as possible, even as sadness lingered in the walls and floorboards, just as it surely did in that trunk.

# CHAPTER 9

Dinner with her children finished, Eliza went to her room, newspapers in hand. Paper delivery would be impossible for the next few days due to weather. She missed reading the news daily, which added to her sense of isolation, especially now, with the snow falling steadily. There would be no way to get into town tomorrow, or perhaps even the next day. Rebecca's funeral and burial would be further postponed if the snow was deep on the ground.

Eliza brought the candle closer and carefully arranged the newspapers in chronological order. She needed to catch up on each day's news, one by one.

Thomas Jefferson was getting ready to run for the president's office again. *No surprise there.*

Frederic Tudor, a Boston businessman, had shipped a cargo of 130 tons of ice out of New York City, bound for the island of Martinique. *Very clever—and how did he manage such a thing?*

A body had been found in an alley behind the notorious Lucille's Gentlemen's Club.

Eliza held her breath and read further:

> *The body was in curious condition since there were no marks indicating how "he" died. But even more curious indeed was that this*

*person was not a man as supposed, but a woman in disguise. And since the lewd creature was found near Lucille's, one can only imagine the depravity that got it in such a condition.*

Lewd creature? Eliza swallowed a scream forming in the center of her chest. She cast the paper aside, its words echoing in her mind. *Lewd. Depravity.*

Poor Rebecca, remembered this way in the newspaper. Did anybody but the women she lived with know her? Yes, she had been an orphan, but what of her life before? Eliza examined the paper again. There had been no mention of Rebecca's name, thank goodness.

Eliza had only known her briefly, but her association with the women of Pearl Street House had rendered her trustworthy.

A sharp pang formed between Eliza's shoulder blades. Something was off about the whole story. She stood and walked toward her window, watching as the snow fell. Could she get to the city tomorrow? She didn't expect so. McNally didn't like taking the horses out in snow. And Eliza recognized it wasn't safe. She felt so helpless.

Eliza ached to reach the apothecaries, to uncover Rebecca's next steps—if they knew anything at all. It was strange that Mrs. Van Horn had known where Rebecca had gone, and even stranger was her overly emotional display. Something didn't sit right.

She pulled her robes closer over her. The fire was dimming. Red veiny patches glowed on the logs. She added another log to the fire. She had no more house staff to help her with such matters. They were only able to afford Mrs. Cole and McNally, and she wasn't sure how much longer she could manage to pay them. She turned and made her way to bed, glancing at the papers, unable to read any more.

The memory of disguising herself as a man to retrieve information gnawed at her, a secret she'd kept buried deep. What would the papers say if that ever got out? Imagining her children reading such words . . . she couldn't bear it. It rolled around in her mind, escaping as a nervous giggle. What did it matter? What did any of it matter now? The widow of the great Alexander Hamilton had lost almost everything. And would most likely lose her house. What else could people do to her?

Then she considered her children. She could never let what she had done come out, even if it had ultimately been to save her son. They deserved a brighter future than what their father had left them with.

Here it was the beginning of Advent, when they should be focused on family and faith, and her heart was still mired in grief and loss. And now, she was distracted by Rebecca's murder. As much as she tried to will the sight of Rebecca's face away when she closed her eyes that night, she could not.

⋆ ⋆ ⋆

Eliza awakened before the sun to a dark room with a biting chill. She untangled herself from the covers and lit her bedside candle. A theory had occurred to her sometime during her fitful sleep. The trunk downstairs might hold clues to Rebecca's last days.

Rifling through a deceased person's belongings felt unseemly, especially so soon after their death. But sometimes necessity overruled propriety. She herself had packed Hamilton's clothes and given them to the almshouse. His sons were either too large or too small to fit their late father's clothes. But his books and writings still sat in his study. She and her sons had organized everything for Hamilton's biographer. But they remained untouched.

It was difficult to even handle the papers and books Hamilton had loved so much. He who was gone, physically, but still seemed a part of their lives. An energy vibrated on each page of his writing and in each book that had once rested in his hands.

Candle in hand, Eliza left her room, her resolve hardening with each step. She must search Rebecca's trunk—clues might be hidden within, clues that could lead her to Jo.

Eliza still sometimes woke at night, in a haze between this world and the dream world, transported back to the barn where she had once been held captive. She prayed that Jo was in a safe, dry, and warm place. Maybe she was just stranded somewhere because of this dreadful weather. Maybe she had not been stolen away.

Eliza opened the door to Hamilton's study, where Rebecca's trunk had been placed. The children were warned to stay away from this room. As it did each time she entered, the bright green room summoned her grief, still fresh and jabbing at her chest. She blinked back her burning tears, as she'd done countless times. Would it ever get any easier?

★ ★ ★

The trunk lid creaked when Eliza opened it. The trunk smelled of something—lavender, perhaps, or was it lilac? The same scent conjured her last conversation with Rebecca, when she had laughed about some customer's impossible demands. How quickly laughter could turn into silence.

Eliza set her candle on the floor next to her, its light flickering against the shadows on the wall. She peered inside, spotting several small books, a few larger ones, and clothes. The clothes could easily go to the Widow Society, but the books? Perhaps the women in the house couldn't read. Could Alice? Eliza had never thought to ask. But Rebecca could read, and she had read for pleasure, evidently, Though Eliza noted the absence of a Holy Bible, which she believed everyone should possess. Rebecca must have been educated—or at least taught how to read. Reading was important. It allowed people to be familiar with the Bible personally. Eliza had taught several of the children who'd stayed with them over the years to read just for that reason.

The clothes were neatly folded, some worn and patched, others almost new. A delicate lace handkerchief, tinged yellow with age, lay on top—a token, perhaps, from a lost loved one? A small, intricately carved wooden box nestled at the bottom of the trunk caught her eye. Inside, she found a rose-shaped brooch, its petals chipped in places, suggesting it had been well-used, well-loved. Eliza wondered who had given it to Rebecca—was it a gift from a suitor, or perhaps a memento from her mother? The only things left, ordinary objects, remnants of a life that ended abruptly.

Most belongings in the Grange had been Hamilton's. Eliza had only a few dresses—two mourning day dresses, one mourning dress for the evening. She'd given most of her clothing away, save for her blue dress that she'd saved for one of her daughters. She always wore a locket, inside of which was an old paper on which Hamilton had written her a love poem. She clasped it now as she reflected, wishing he were here, instead of just his words.

She also wore a ring her father had made for her and in it was a lock of her Hamilton's hair. She wondered if either of those possessions would have meaning to anybody in the future. How could they understand her attachment to these items? The countless stories and emotions behind each item.

Eliza cracked open a volume of William Wordsworth, the scent of paper mingling with the lingering traces of lavender. The collection of poems spoke of nature, of a longing for simplicity, and of the profound emotions that stirred beneath the surface of ordinary life. What had these words meant to Rebecca? Had they been an escape from the harsh realities of her life, or a source of inspiration for her own desires?

Eliza wondered if Rebecca had seen herself in *Charlotte Temple* or *Evelina*, both tragic heroines who navigated the treacherous waters of society, only to be undone by them. Was Rebecca's life a reflection of these tales, where the pursuit of independence was met with society's cruelest judgment? She set the book aside, just as the sun began to rise. She wanted to sort everything before the children woke.

She spread the books on the floor. *Charlotte Temple* by Susanna Rowson, *Evelina* by Fanny Burney, *Belinda* by Maria Edgeworth.

Eliza lifted *Charlotte Temple* and warmed. She and Angelica had read the book together. It was a tragic tale of a British schoolgirl seduced and abandoned in the United States. They'd found it gripping.

What an odd collection of books. The oddest one being the Wordsworth. Rebecca had diverse taste in reading. Eliza's heart ached, not only for Rebecca but for the many women who lived on the fringes of society, vulnerable to its harshest cruelties. How many young women such as Rebecca had met their end in dark alleys, their lives deemed unworthy of investigation because they were poor, or because they dared to step outside the boundaries society had set for them? The injustice of it kindled a slow-burning anger within her. Rebecca had been more than a victim—she had been a person, a woman with dreams and desires, who had tried to carve out a place for herself in a world that gave her little room to breathe.

She reached into the trunk and found a large leather-bound book. Eliza had no leather-bound books, but Hamilton had a few. They were expensive. The book's pages were soft from frequent handling. Eliza's candle cast a warm glow over the careful sketches—dresses, hats, dreams put to paper, now stilled. A pressed flower fell from between the pages, so delicate. She flipped through the pages of drawings of dresses and writing. Beyond those pages were scraps of fabric pasted to pages, some cut into the shapes of dresses, some shaped into hats. More writing.

Eliza carefully placed the books back into the trunk, except for the commonplace book. That might hold the key to understanding Rebecca's past—and perhaps lead the constables to her killer. She needed to examine the book more closely, but she would do that alone in her own room. She rummaged through the clothing, and at the bottom of the trunk she found something. She lifted out a group of letters tied with a ribbon.

Eliza hesitated, the weight of the letters in her hands suddenly a burden. What right did she have to pry into Rebecca's most personal correspondences? Yet her intuition gleaned that these letters might contain answers—answers that Rebecca herself could no longer give. Would she be dishonoring Rebecca's memory by reading them, or would she be doing what she would have wanted—finding justice? The line between propriety and necessity blurred in her mind as she held the delicate bundle, the ribbon frayed from handling, as though it had been opened and closed many times before.

The sounds of her children rustling around upstairs snapped her out of her thoughts.

Eliza closed the trunk and tiptoed back to her room with the commonplace book and the letters. She hoped to find people acquainted with Rebecca by reading the letters and studying the book. Her eyes skimmed her bedroom, landing on the newspapers. She'd need more fortitude to read further. She simply could not read one more word of anything, not with Rebecca's body waiting to be buried and Jo missing. How to go on with everyday life, while so much hung in the balance?

# CHAPTER 10

Alice peered out of the small, frost-edged window, the fresh mounds of snow piling up like silent tombstones. Snow usually brought her a sense of peace, the kind that settled like a warm blanket over her thoughts. But today the snow suffocated her, a white shroud trapping her within the house, within her own mind. She didn't understand why she cared that Rebecca couldn't be buried yet. What did it matter? She was dead.

Dead, cold, beyond the reach of the living. Still . . . the idea gnawed at Alice, refusing to let her be. Burying was the way of things—an end, a closure. Not just for the dead, but for the ones left behind.

Where was Jo? They'd scoured the streets searching for her.

Alice's mind turned to the worst. What if Jo's fate was tied with Rebecca's in some uncanny manner?

The Van Horn staff confirmed that Rebecca had been there, made a delivery, and then gone to an apothecary. She and René and Paulette had followed what they assumed may have been the path taken to both nearby apothecaries. Nothing had been out of the ordinary—there were no poor beggars about on those streets, nor were there any clues to a crime, let alone a murder committed in the vicinity. The area was tidy, with plenty of establishments and houses, along with one public house.

The woman behind the counter at Johnston's had said yes, she was familiar with Joe, but that she had not seen him for a few months. Something about the woman made Alice uneasy. It wasn't just the patch over her left eye, though that alone would have been enough to unsettle anyone. It was something deeper, something she couldn't name—a sense of wrongness that clung to her like a second skin. Each time Alice crossed paths with her, she tamped down an inexplicable urge to flee, as though the woman carried a darkness within her, one that might seep into anyone who lingered too long in her presence. But what was it? What was it that made Alice's skin crawl every time they met?

Where was Jo? The question persisted and unsettled her. It was as if Jo had vanished, leaving only questions in her wake. And what if . . . No, she couldn't allow herself to consider the worst. But the idea crept in, dark and unwelcome. What if Jo had found something she wasn't meant to? What if that discovery had sealed her fate, just as it had for Rebecca?

Something else gnawed at Alice. Perhaps Jo had followed Rebecca to the alley where they'd found Rebecca's body.

Jo was clever. Would she do that?

But Rebecca had been clever too. Too clever to go in the alley behind Lucille's Gentlemen's Club on her own.

It made little sense. Which was the problem.

But then again, nothing in life rarely made sense anymore.

Life had once flowed with rhythm, steady and predictable, like the ticking of a well-made clock. As a girl in Belgium, Alice's rhythm of family, friends, and school provided a neatly ordered day, each moment carrying the comforting weight of routine. Then the rhythm had shifted, a sweet melody of domesticity and her husband's embrace in the quiet hours. But when he died, the music stopped. Silence. Emptiness. It was as if the world had lost its tempo, leaving her adrift, searching for a tune that might never come.

How had she clawed her way back to an orderly life years ago?

Alice's bones creaked as she descended the stairs, each step a reminder of the years that had worn her down. The warm scent of fresh biscuits wafted up to meet her, a fragrance that usually brought a smile to her lips. But today, the sweetness turned sour in her stomach, a wave of nausea rising unexpectedly. Even the comforts of home could not banish the unease that had settled deep within her.

# CHAPTER 11

Eliza's children sat around the breakfast table in the dining room. Her sons had gotten up early and the fire was blazing. Eliza took them in: Angelica, whom they called Angel, named after her sister, William, James, Alexander Jr., John Church, little Philip, and little Eliza—all except her poor Philip, who died in a duel a few years before his father did. She contemplated their faces as little Philip raised his arms to her. He had just turned three. She lifted him to her.

As she sat at the breakfast table, little Philip in her arms, surrounded by her children, Eliza couldn't help but consider the world outside their walls. The country that Hamilton had helped to build was now under the sway of men such as Thomas Jefferson, men who had little use for his vision. And what place did a widow such as her have in this new world, where the memory of her husband was fading like ink on a well-worn letter?

"Good morning, Mama," Angel said.

"Good morning," Eliza said. "What do we have here?" Eliza studied Angel's face, searching for any sign of the shadows that sometimes darkened her daughter's eyes. Eliza had tried everything—distractions, outings, even consulting the doctor—but nothing lifted the cloud that hung over her. It broke Eliza's heart to see her once vibrant daughter reduced to this fragile state. She wished she could do more, but what could a mother do against such sorrow? All she could do was pray and hope that time would heal the wounds.

"Mrs. Cole made a lovely morning meal," James said.

Eliza wished she had an appetite, for Mrs. Cole had indeed laid a splendid table. She glanced over at the food. A stack of smoked meat, boiled eggs, and fresh biscuits mocked her nauseated stomach. The thought of maybe letting Mrs. Cole go made her sickness worse. She was unsure of how much longer they could afford her.

"Are you quite well, Mother?" James asked.

She nodded. "I'm just not hungry at the moment."

He poured her tea. "Perhaps tea will set you right."

"The strawberry jam is delicious. Nothing like the taste of fresh strawberries in the middle of winter," Alexander mused.

Eliza sipped her tea. Those strawberries were the pride of Hamilton. How he had loved their garden. He had found respite during his few years there.

But every time Eliza bit into bread slathered with the strawberry jam, all she tasted was regret, worry, and fear.

"Snow!" Little Philip pointed out the window.

Eliza smiled. Sitting in the dining room, with its large floor-to-ceiling windows, gave the illusion of being outdoors. Which is what Hamilton had wanted. The light from the snow and blue sky reflected through the open room.

With a sudden swift stab, despair engulfed Eliza as she contemplated Jo, wanting her safe and comfortable. Dreading she had been caught in the storm. The past few days had been frigid with snowstorms. She closed her eyes and said a silent prayer for Jo.

When she first met Jo, Eliza was struggling because Alexander Jr. had been accused of murder, just two weeks after Hamilton had been killed. At one point, she had to stay with Alice and her friends. One morning, Eliza spied a stranger at the table. And she had been shocked when Josephine revealed that she had disguised herself as a man. Despite herself, Eliza cracked a smile. What a moment that was! The disguise both startled her and shifted something within her. All things were more possible for men. At least on the face of things.

The rest of the meal was dotted with family talk and good food. Eliza ate a buttered slice of bread while her sons planned to clear away the long, hilly driveway that led to their home. The children were eager to go outdoors, and Eliza wondered if more play than work would be happening.

"Are you going to join us?" James asked.

"Not today." She forced a smile. She couldn't bear the idea of playing in the snow, not with the weight of their future pressing on her. There were letters to read, debts to tally, and she had to sift through Rebecca's papers. Distractions were a luxury she couldn't afford. Her smile hid her worry from her children, a smile she'd perfected over the years.

"Very well, but if you change your mind, we'd love it," James said.

"Thank you." Eliza smiled.

Soon, Eliza sat on the settee with a stack of mail to open. Much of it was debts that Hamilton had owed. There were one or two pleasant notes from local women, wishing her a wonderful holiday, which Eliza mostly had forgotten about. It wasn't top of her mind. Again. Last year, her father had died and there was no time or mood to celebrate. This year, she had been bound and determined to give her children a nice memory. She was uncertain she could lift her mood enough to do so. Maybe by Christmas, they would have at least buried Rebecca and found Jo. She prayed for both conclusions.

The last envelope she opened carried the weight of a death sentence. The bank was foreclosing on the Grange. Each word on the white paper stung. Her eyes traced the edges of the room, the place Hamilton had dreamed of and fought for, the place where they had hoped to grow old together. But now the highest bidder would take all those dreams. The notion of leaving this house, of losing the last tangible link to him, was another death to grieve. But she couldn't afford to wallow, not now. Her children needed her to be strong, to plan their next move. There was no time for tears, only for action.

She wasn't even angry anymore. Hamilton did not fathom that he was going to die at the hand of Aaron Burr that morning. There was not enough time for him to put their affairs in order.

Eliza would not dwell on the loss of him, the loss of their home. She needed to plan her next move. Where would she and her children reside? Was there a place for her and her family in this ever-changing city?

# Chapter 12

With the children outside and little Philip napping, Eliza slipped off into her room to more intently read the rest of the newspapers and to search through Rebecca's things for any hint of what might have become of her. Maybe something in her belongings held a clue. One could only hope.

First, the newspapers. She scoured the newspaper for any other mentions of Rebecca's death. Nothing. There was an odd advert from a group called the Women's Morality Alliance on the last page of the last paper. There was that word, "lewd" again. She read further:

> *It has come to attention that some women of this city have gone against nature and are dressing as men and living together, without a man in the home. If you think this should be stopped, please attend our meeting on December 1.*

Eliza wondered who would attend such a meeting. Before meeting Alice and the women she lived with, Eliza had to admit that she'd never imagined such a life. She might have thought it curious. But unnatural?

It was an odd choice of words.

Eliza frowned as she reread the ad for the Women's Morality Alliance. It wasn't the first time she'd encountered such sentiments—the fear of anything that challenged the strict social order seemed to be growing with each passing year. But the vehemence of this group, their readiness to condemn women who dared to step outside the prescribed roles, sent a chill through her. Was this what Rebecca had faced? An entire society ready to judge and punish her for merely existing outside their narrow definition of womanhood? Eliza had never taken notice of the group before, and she kept well-informed. How had she missed them?

With a sigh, Eliza set the newspaper aside. There were no more clues in its pages—only ominous warnings and hateful rhetoric. Her gaze drifted to the stack of letters. Perhaps, hidden among these folded papers, she would find the answers she sought, or at least a glimpse into the life Rebecca had led before it was so brutally cut short.

She reached for the letters, unfolded the first one and read:

*I warn you that your soul is in eternal danger.*

Eliza's heart sped in her chest. What was this? She read on:

*You are an unnatural creature and will be struck down. Take a husband soon.*

*Will be struck down.* The words echoed in Eliza's head. Rolled around and formed a stone-cold fear. Fear for Jo, fear for the other women who lived in the house on Pearl Street. Even for herself. Such depravity existed in the world. This she recognized. But her marriage to the great Alexander Hamilton had protected her. Even though she'd been on the battlefield, lived near the battles, she never once feared for her life. Not until after Alexander died and her son was accused of murder.

The letter trembled in her hands as the words leapt off the page. A shiver traced her spine, the fear seeping into her bones. Who could write such venomous words? And what had poor Rebecca done to deserve them? Eliza's breath came faster as she tried to make sense of it all.

Her heart banged a wild drumbeat in her chest as she read over the words. A glacial fear crept into her bones. Who could harbor such hate?

There was no signature, of course. Coward. The words led Eliza to believe that this person had been watching Rebecca. Had they been watching all the women who lived in the house? Or just Rebecca?

Poor Rebecca. She must've been harassed for quite some time. Why didn't she tell anyone? Maybe she had. Maybe the other women were aware but hadn't told Eliza. But perhaps Rebecca had told no one. Perhaps she had kept this burden to herself, either out of fear or a misguided sense of duty. Eliza shook her head, trying to push away the dread that gnawed at her. Time was of the essence. Imperative!

She folded the note and set it aside. Reading more was the only measure she could take, being stuck inside.

*My dearest Rebecca,*

*I hope this letter finds you well. I'm writing to express my dearest condolences on the loss of your mother. I hope you are faring well, dear cousin.*
*Mother is not doing well. I wish you might travel to Williamsburg to be with your family. I know you do not have the funds. I also know that your brother Jacob certainly has the money to send you here. Why doesn't he help you?*
*I find it shameful that he set you and your mother out after he inherited the establishment. Perhaps you could persuade him to send you here.*
*Williamsburg is lovely. It's without the crowds you must be used to by now.*

*My heart aches when I think of you alone in that big city. Please speak with Jacob.*

*Your dear cousin,*
*Lily*

What was this? A more detailed picture of Rebecca was forming. She had family in Williamsburg, Virginia. Why had she not gone to them? Perhaps she would have. Rebecca had a brother, Jacob. Eliza needed to find him. He should be told about Rebecca's death. Eliza assumed he was in the city. She needed to find Jacob Dickens.

She'd only read two letters and had already learned so much about Rebecca. She glanced at the remaining stack of letters. She needed paper and a pencil to take notes, as she sensed there was much more to Rebecca's story there in that stack of mismatched notes and letters.

# CHAPTER 13

Was it night or day? The room never grew light. Constant darkness. Constant dank and must. Someone had given her a ratty, pilled blanket that stopped her from shivering. Still, she was not warm. It must be winter. But what day was it? Did it matter?

Time stretched into something unrecognizable—a looping, endless dark. Was it minutes, hours, or days? The frigid air seeped into her bones, gnawing at the edges of her mind. She tried to remember . . . anything. But every thought was like a wisp of smoke, curling away before she could grasp it. Who am I? Where am I? The questions echoed in the hollow spaces of her mind, unanswered and growing louder with each passing second.

The room's darkness had weight, pressing against her skin like a living thing. Only the occasional drip of water marked time's passage—how many drops since her last meal? Since the bitter tea that had started this nightmare?

Beyond hunger now, the pangs had disappeared. She'd soiled herself and stank of urine. She was wet everywhere, which made her even more cold. Her thirst had grown beyond thirst. The metallic taste in her mouth grew, and her teeth and tongue were dry imposters in her own mouth.

Still, she could only remember that teacup with the dancing pink flowers.

Dancing pink flowers.

Bitter tea in her mouth.

Dropping to the floor.

White, soft, fleshy hands.

The teacup, delicate and fragile, spun in her mind, the pink flowers blurring as they danced. The jeweled fingers sparkled in the dim light. The ice-cold, hard floor meeting her with a final, brutal clarity.

No memories remained: her arrival here, the location, even herself. She pushed against a wall in her head. *Who am I? Where am I?*

But this, this was not right. This wasn't her life. For this could be nobody's life, lying in filth, legs and arms tied. She turned on her side, staring at the only thing visible in the darkness: the wall. She closed her eyes, trying to force herself to remember.

Dancing pink flowers.

Bitter tea in her mouth.

Dropping to the floor. The floor was cold and hard.

White, soft, fleshy hands. The fingers sparkled with jewels.

Then the wall in her brain slammed shut.

The frigid air curled around her limbs, digging into her joints. It chewed on her, sharp and relentless, until she was sure her bones would shatter from the pressure. The ropes—rough and unyielding—bit into her skin with each movement, sending spikes of pain through her wrists and ankles. The scabs were a cruel reminder of her futile attempts to free herself, each one a tiny scream etched into her flesh.

A cramp traveled from her hip to her knee. She groaned and lurched, making her back seize. She rolled over on her back and tried to relax against the searing pain.

She had moments of almost clarity. Lucidity. Dream or reality? She wasn't sure.

The sound of the door creaking open sliced through the suffocating silence, sending a jolt of terror through her. Was it real?

Or just another trick of her fevered mind? She strained to listen, every nerve on edge, as the floorboards groaned under the weight of unseen footsteps. Her breath hitched, fear curling tight in her throat. Someone was there, in the room with her. The darkness pressed closer, and she fought the urge to cry out, to beg for mercy from murky shadow.

# Chapter 14

The tiny needle felt at home in Alice's hand. A strand of red silk lace had formed. Ordered from a dressmaker for a special client, it was one of the most delicate patterns Alice had ever worked. But the material was exquisite. Other craftswomen's orders validated their work. Other women who made their living making dresses, hats, and collars recognized good handwork, and they paid on time and well.

As she dipped and pulled the needle and fine silk yarn, she pondered Rebecca's poor body still waiting to be buried. She whispered a prayer—not a prayer but an incantation to whatever god or creature would hear her that Jo's fate would not be the same as Rebecca's.

*Please bring Jo back to us.*

Long ago, Alice believed in a god, but she given that belief up years ago when her husband had been cruelly taken from her. No god would have allowed that, after everything they'd been through. After being shunned by their families because they wanted to be together. After making the trip on the ship that left them at the New York Harbor. After all the lean times, life became easier, then her husband got sick. No god would allow that.

Still, on the off chance: *Please bring Jo back to us.*

Pulling the thread through, looping it, twisting it. The motions comforted her, for she had been doing them since she was a child, before she'd come to the new world.

They'd done everything they could—ran a missing person advertisement in the newspaper, placed an order for pamphlets to be hung around town. But in the meantime, the sky dumped snow so deep that many establishments had halted service, as it was difficult to get out of one's home, let alone tend to business matters.

It eased her mind that Eliza had taken Rebecca's things to the Widow Society, for other women could use them. No need to keep any of it in the house. Rebecca had shared a small room with Jo. The two of them had become close. Alice clicked her tongue. 'Twas a good thing they liked one another as it was tight quarters.

When they'd pieced together that Rebecca was missing, Jo's face had contorted into rage and worry. "I'll find her. If it's the last thing I do."

"Please, Jo," René had said. "Think about this. If someone has her, they might take you too."

Jo puffed her chest. "I dare them to take me!"

She'd stormed out of the house. It happened so fast that Alice was not even sure if Jo had worn a winter cloak.

René, embroidering a collar, sat in the corner. Alice watched her. "Was she wearing a cloak? Our Jo?"

René frowned. "Her cloak is still here, Alice. We talked about that yesterday, remember?"

She did not remember. But she would take René's word for it.

# CHAPTER 15

After tucking the children in, Eliza read one more of Rebecca's letters, even though she herself was ready for sleep. This one was from Jacob:

*Dear Rebecca,*

*We send you wishes for good health. I am sorry to inform you I cannot send you to Williamsburg. I simply don't have the funds. Julia is expecting another baby, and we already have children whom we need to feed.*

*I'm sorry. I hope to sell the inn. If that should happen, I will send you money. I know this will upset you. But times are hard for innkeepers. People want to stay now in the new, larger hotels. We often get people who cannot pay what we ask.*

*Still, I know it has meaning to you—as it does to me—but father's time was different.*

*With love,*
*Jacob*

Thank goodness Alice had found Rebecca, or God knows what would have befallen her. The streets surely would have taken her. How could a man turn his back on his sister? When had this happened? The letter had no date on it.

Eliza's heart tightened as she read over Jacob's words again. Memories of her own struggles—of nights spent worrying about her children's future—flooded her mind. Yet, how many times had she penned similar letters, full of apologies and unfulfilled promises? The helplessness of it all stirred her fears, fears that lived just beneath the skin, traveling through her every day, unescapable. She tried hard to pretend they weren't there. She was Mrs. General Hamilton and still had a measure of pride left in her.

She dropped the letter onto her writing table. Weariness moved through her, and she lifted herself from the chair to the bed. Eliza glanced around the room as she sat down on the edge of the bed, the flickering light of the candle casting long shadows on the walls. The heavy curtains, drawn tight against the cold, did little to keep the winter chill at bay. The fire still had embers, giving off heat. She pursed her lips and blew out the candle.

* * *

The sound of running water awakened Eliza the next morning. The thaw was upon them. She gazed out the window from her bed and watched the water stream down her windows. Thank God—now perhaps she could visit Alice and her friends and tell them what she'd learned. They needed to find Jacob and his family.

A sliver of hope sliced into Eliza's heart. Perhaps Jo would be back at the house by the time Eliza arrived. Warm and safe in the bosom of her friends. The idea warmed Eliza as she lifted herself from her bed to the cold floor and made her way downstairs.

"I cannot believe you want to go into town today," James said to her. "Why don't you stay home with us? It is Advent, after all."

James's tone was so like his father's—steady, calm, but with an underlying current of concern. It wasn't just about the roads or the weather; Eliza sensed in him a need to protect her. This realization both comforted and saddened her. How quickly he had grown, this son of hers, now more man than boy. His eyes had the same Hamilton determination that had drawn her to his father all those years ago.

"I'd love nothing more. But my friends are in great difficulty right now. One of them has died and another one is missing. I want to help if I can."

"Missing?" James said.

"It was the same with Rebecca, the woman who died." She explained it to James as he sat at the table with her, finishing breakfast while the others were already playing.

"Sounds like a dangerous business, Mother. I'd tell you to stay out of it, but I know better." He grinned. "By the way, I've inspected the work you've been doing on Father's papers. You've made significant progress."

Eliza's heart warmed. "I have so much more to do. More interviews. I can only travel so much. But when I hear that someone is in town, I go to them."

For the past eighteen months, Eliza had poured herself into her work, each document a piece of her husband's legacy, each interview a chance to keep his memory alive. The task was monumental, overwhelming, but it was all that kept her from drowning in her grief. She had spent countless hours sorting through letters, speeches, and legal papers, her fingers stained with ink, her eyes strained from late nights spent by candlelight. The work had helped her endure. Gathering interviews and documents about Hamilton and organizing them for William Coleman, the biographer she'd engaged. It kept her mind engaged, which eased the burden on her heart.

"Father had a wide circle." James said.

"He touched many lives. We lost him too soon. It's vital that we make sure his life story is written," she said. "Not just because I'm his widow, but because he was a great man." History would not forget him. She would make sure of it.

"Is Coleman making any progress?" James asked.

"He claims to be. Though I've yet to see any evidence of that." He'd come to their home and read through Hamilton's papers, taking notes. How long would it take? She was wondering if it would ever get written.

"Writing a biography is no straightforward task," James said, as if he were reading her mind. "It is Advent, Mother. One of your favorite times of the year. Do you know these women well enough to take you from your family? And to risk the plague?"

"The plague? It's winter. Everybody knows it's worse in the summer," Eliza said.

Her face heated. How to tell her grown son that the bonds she shared with these women were as important as what she shared with her family? Her children were paramount, but she and the women had forged a bond during a difficult time. "Some things in life can't wait. Death is one of them. We've lost a dear woman, and she's yet to be buried. I need to find out when that will happen. And if I can help find Josephine . . ."

She couldn't abandon them now. The thought of Josephine out there, alone and afraid, was unbearable. These women were her family, in many ways, just as much as the children playing in the next room.

James cleared his throat. "Very well, I'll go with you."

"But—"

He held up his hand. "The roads may be treacherous. McNally may appreciate another hand. I won't hear of you going alone. Alexander and Mrs. Cole can see to the children."

Eliza's intuition tugged at her—there was more to her son wanting to accompany her. What sort of devilment was he up to?

# Chapter 16

Eliza slipped her feet into her boots, pulled on her cloak and hat and wrapped two wool scarves around her neck. She didn't care to be cold.

James shook his head at her outfit and grinned. "Mother, we are only going to Manhattan, not Iceland."

She ignored him as they walked out the front door, where McNally awaited with the carriage. "G'day, Mrs. General Hamilton, Mr. Hamilton." He opened the door for them. "It might be a rough ride."

"Yes, we know," Eliza said. McNally had a keen sense of the obvious and sometimes Eliza couldn't contain herself. "First stop, the Manhattan Apothecary."

As they made it down the long driveway, with little slipping and sliding, Eliza gazed out over the snowy hills of Harlem, spots of grass poking out as the snow melted.

"Do you need something from the apothecary? Are you quite all right?" James asked.

"No, I need nothing from there. But Mrs. Van Horn told me that Rebecca was going there after she delivered linen to her. She mentioned two of them. Johnston's and the Manhattan. We know that Josephine went looking for her. Most likely following her footsteps. I want to visit both, ask questions, then tell Alice what I learn. Then we might need to go to the constabulary, as I've found out that Rebecca had a brother," she said.

"What is his name? Might I know him?"

"Jacob Dickens. He owns an inn, has a wife and several children."

McNally made a sharp turn, and Eliza and James grabbed on to the seat.

"Sorry!" McNally yelled.

James's brows knitted as if in consternation. "I don't know the name. If she had a brother, why was she in the Widow Society? Could he not care for her?"

"Evidently not. She also had a cousin in Williamsburg that wanted her to come and live with them but could not send money for the means to travel."

He frowned. "We are very fortunate."

"We are. Even though the bank wants the house, and I have no means to do anything about it. We have our good names, which count for something."

"Mother, I want to help, but as a clerk, I—"

"I know. No worries. I've been through worse, Son, and will manage." She'd figure out something. God was with her, guiding her. All she needed was to watch for the signs. Losing the house would be heartbreaking. It was the only house she and Alexander had ever owned. He'd put his heart and soul into working with the architect, especially planning the gardens. There was so much of Hamilton in that house—in each floorboard, window, and wall.

⋆ ⋆ ⋆

Eliza walked into the Manhattan Apothecary. Medicinals and herbs assaulted her with their pungent scents, a reason she disliked the apothecary.

The woman behind the counter wore her hair swept off her face, but a strand of it fell sloppily out of her cap. Moles dotted her face. She was stout and quick about her motions, flitting from jar to jar.

She lifted her chin and regarded James. "Can I help you, sir?"

James smiled. "It's my mother whom you can help." He pointed to Eliza.

Eliza took off her hat, her white widow's cap beneath it.

"Mrs. General Hamilton! I am so sorry to not recognize you. How can I help you?" Her face blotched in embarrassed red.

"I'm inquiring about a man who may have been in about five days ago."

"Man?" James said. "I thought—"

Eliza elbowed him. Had she forgotten to tell him that Jo had been dressed as a man?

"Yes, a small man named Joe. He seems to have disappeared. After delivering items to the Van Horns, he said he was going to the apothecary. Yours is the closest."

"I see. I know the name Joe, but so many men have it. What did he look like?" She leaned in.

"As I say, he was small, not much taller than me, dark hair and eyes." Eliza gestured, showing Jo's height.

The woman squinted her eyes. "I believe I know who you mean. He has been here from time to time. Not recently, though." She paused, as if forcing herself to think. "You say he's missing?"

Eliza nodded. "He's been gone since before this snow came."

"I'm sorry. Can't help. I've not seen him." She crossed her arms.

"Well, thank you," James said, offering his arm to his mother. "Shall we?

When they exited the store, they walked toward the next apothecary, but James stopped. "You didn't tell me Jo is a man. In fact, I'm certain you said Jo is a woman."

Eliza's face heated. "We shouldn't talk about that on the street."

"When should we talk about it?" He tilted his head, much the same way Hamilton did when amused or agitated.

"Once we are in the carriage."

"What are you involved with? Should I be worried?" His voice was low and tense.

"Right now, I'm just trying to help my friend. You should be worried about her, not me." She matched his tone.

"Very well," he said after a moment of studying his mother. He slipped out his pocket watch and glanced at it. "Let's be off then."

They hurried to the next apothecary, Johnston's, which was large and cleaner, though scent still always lingered in these places. Eliza and James waited for the man behind the counter, who was helping someone. Behind him there was a shelf with scales, a mortar and pestle, and a long row of glass bottles with herbal concoctions in them. A young woman swept the floor around the edges of the place.

Another woman soon popped out of nowhere to help them.

"A good day to you," she said. "How can I help you?" James, not Eliza, held her gaze. One eye, patched, made it hard to read her expression. Her face had deep planes and angles and was withered and shadowed.

"We're searching for a missing man. We presume he came here the day he went missing," James said.

"What day was that?" the woman asked.

Eliza spoke up. "Friday."

"There were a lot of men in here Friday. It was a busy day." She scratched her head.

"He's quite small, dark, big eyes," Eliza said. "Might have been looking for someone. His name is Jo."

The woman's face lit. "Aye, he was in here searching for another man."

"Good," Eliza said. "Did he say where he was off to next?"

The woman frowned. "No. Not to me. Samuel?"

The man behind the counter approached them.

"You remember Joe," the woman said. "He was here on Friday, looking for his friend Rob."

"Yes, yes, I do," he said. "I told him that Rob was here the day before, and then Joe mentioned going to Water Street to meet a friend for a drink."

Eliza's heart raced. "Did he say which establishment they were going to?"

The man appeared to be trying to remember. "I don't think so, but most young men go to Murphy's. Seems to be a popular place for them, but that's not a place for ladies." He crossed his arms.

"Of course not," James said. "But I can ask a few questions there."

Eliza thanked James, then turned to the man and woman behind the counter. "Thank you both very much."

The way became apparent to Eliza then. James would go to Murphy's and she to Alice's, both delivering and seeking information.

# CHAPTER 17

The weather had done more than just impede travel; it had pushed the city's usual corruption into sharper relief. In wealthy neighborhoods, teams of boys were paid to clear paths and spread ash for traction. But here, near Pearl Street House, the snow lay in pristine drifts, forcing people to risk life and limb just to go out.

The snow around Alice's home was clinging in large clumps. And the walk was not clear. Eliza's feet were frigid, and she longed to be inside out of the wet and cold. She knocked on the door. Paulette opened it and fell into Eliza's arms, sobbing. Eliza held her for a few moments.

"Who is there? It's cold. Come in and shut the door!" René came up behind them, prompting the break of their embrace and rushing them inside.

"Eliza, how wonderful to see you!" René said.

"I wanted to see you all. Where is Alice?" The letters burned in her mind. Eliza wanted to know if the others were aware of them.

"She went out first thing this morning. She is keen to bury Rebecca. But the ground . . ."

"I understand." Eliza supposed there was nothing to do about that but wait. But she might be wrong. "Have we learned anything about Jo? Has she turned up yet?"

"Nothing." René's voice was rough. Her hair had not been pinned and her clothes were not quite clean.

Eliza reached out and squeezed her hand. "I hope she returns soon." Eliza paused. "I had errands to run this morning, myself and I've yet to tell you my news." But she didn't want to blurt out that she found those awful letters. She'd ease her way to the subject.

"What's that?" René leaned in.

"When I left here last time, I visited the Van Horns and found out where Rebecca was heading the day she disappeared."

"Johnston's Apothecary?"

Eliza nodded.

"We've done the same and gotten nowhere." There was a flat note of discouragement in René's voice.

"I'll put a kettle on," Paulette said and left the room.

"We know Rebecca went to the apothecary—that's something to go on. We can assume Jo followed, once she found out where she was," Eliza tried to maintain a lightness, hope, in her voice.

"Yes, but where to next?" René shrugged, staring away, barely noticing Eliza's hand on hers.

"The man behind the counter at Johnston's said Jo was meeting a friend for a drink. He did not know where for certain, but said a lot of the young men go to a place called Murphy's on Water Street. Do you know it?"

"Murphy's? No." René said. "I try not to go to that area, if possible."

"Murphy's?" Paulette said as she came back into the room with a tray of tea and cookies. "I've heard of it."

"What do you know of it?" René said. "It's not a place for a young mother like yourself."

"I've not been there." Paulette served the tea. "I've just heard they pour a good drink there and host card games."

"Thank you, Paulette." Eliza took her tea and held the hot cup in her hand, relishing the heat from the brew.

René squinted. "Card games, you say?"

"What do you know, Mother?"

"I know our Rebecca loved to play cards." René sipped her tea.

Eliza's heart sank. Did Rebecca get involved with some card players and owe someone money? Did she lose her life because of a debt? She shuddered. Hamilton often spoke of those men. "My son James is there now. He accompanied me today. He's worse than a mother hen, but it turned out to be helpful because he's going to ask questions at Murphy's." She paused. "Would Jo go there?"

"She would if she believed Rebecca might have been there." René sounded resolute.

A baby cried in the next room.

Paulette stood. "That would be my Alexander." She left the room.

Eliza and René sat in the room, listening to Paulette's gentle voice in the next room.

"The constables are paid to avoid such places," René said, quietly.

"What do you mean?" Eliza asked.

"The corruption in our constable force is rife. They often make more money from establishments, paid to ignore their activities, than their own paychecks." René folded her hands in her lap.

"Surely that's not true," Eliza said.

Paulette came back into the room with baby Alexander on her hip.

"Oh, my goodness! How he has grown!" Eliza set her tea on the table.

Alexander smiled and raised his arms to Eliza. Paulette handed him over. Eliza could lose herself in his big, brown innocent eyes and the sweet scent of him. "Aren't you beautiful?"

"Aye, but a handful!" Paulette beamed.

Eliza wondered, once more, about Paulette's husband's whereabouts. What did he do for a living, and why did Paulette spend so much time here, rather than in her own home? But she kept her own counsel. It was none of Eliza's concern. She'd have stayed with her own mother longer if she could, but as a young married woman, she longed to be with her husband and in their own home. Such as their homes had been. They'd always lived in cramped rental quarters until they'd had the Grange built.

The front door opened, and Alice hobbled in. "'Tis a frightful day." She took her cloak off and hung it on the rack next to Eliza's. "Good day to you all," she said. "The news I have is that we may bury our Rebecca on Saturday, if the weather continues to warm."

"I am happy to know it," Eliza said.

"Tea?" René gestured to the table.

"No. I'm sorry. I'm going to have a lie-down. I'm not up to talking."

The room quieted as Alice climbed the stairs. Even as the weight and warmth of the baby calmed her, Eliza held her breath, for this was not like Alice at all.

Eliza struggled to find words. She studied Paulette and René, both not wanting to meet her gaze. "Is Alice ill?"

Paulette took the baby from Eliza. "She isn't herself, but I don't think she's ill."

"She mourns for Rebecca," René said. "Is worried for Jo. She has been keeping busy, making lace. But . . ."

"But what?" Eliza's heart raced. She and Alice had a long history. They'd first met at the Widow Society. Alice, one widow who'd made herself so useful, even as she tried to scrape her way back. They'd lost touch, but Alice showed up last year when Hamilton died.

René frowned. "She is not thinking right. Not remembering things."

How old was Alice? It was hard to judge. She'd looked the same since Eliza had first met her. Was she in her sixth decade? Seventh? "My mother had similar leanings as she aged."

"It's hard to imagine Alice that way," René said. "I tried to stop her this morning as she left the house. But she'd not have it."

"Of course not," Eliza said.

Paulette, feeding her baby in the corner, spoke up. "Losing Rebecca has been hard on her. Then the possibility of losing Jo? It's too much." Her words hung in the air for several minutes.

"Oh! I'd quite forgotten," Eliza finally said. "I took Rebecca's trunk to my house. We left here in a hurry. It began to snow. My children opened the trunk and found more than clothes inside. There were letters and a journal. I've read a few of the letters and from what I gather, Rebecca had a brother. He lives here in town somewhere. Has a family and runs an establishment."

"Rebecca never said!" Paulette exclaimed.

René's demeanor changed, as if she wanted to speak. Her eyes shifted.

"What is it, René?" Eliza asked

"I knew of him," René said. "But he was unkind to Rebecca."

"Still, should we not tell him that his sister is dead?" Paulette asked.

"No," René's voice trembled. "I should think not."

Eliza searched for the right words but could not find them. She had believed she was giving good news. Now she suspected she'd stirred unpleasantness in René.

"Very well," Eliza said. "We shan't inform him of her death." Eliza had wanted to be helpful, but the only news she'd brought to them was that both women might have been to Murphy's. They had already learned the rest of it. What unkindness had Rebecca's brother shown her? It must've been horrible for René to say that they should not contact him concerning his sister's death.

A knock at the door interrupted her contemplation. Paulette rose and answered the door.

"James Hamilton to fetch my mother," a voice said.

Eliza had been so deep in her contemplations that she'd forgotten about her own son.

"Please come in, sir," Paulette said.

James entered the room. "Good day. Mother, are you ready to go home?"

"Yes, of course. What did you find at Murphy's?"

"It is a seedy establishment." He placed his arms behind his back. "I warrant you ladies would not grace its doorstep."

"But?" Eliza asked.

"Your friend Rebecca owed a man named Ramsay money over a card game."

Eliza caught her breath.

"Would someone kill a person because they owed them money?" René said. "He'll never get it now."

"It's more complicated than that, I suppose. And he may not have killed her. We can't make any assumptions. Just consider it a fact." James shifted his weight.

"And Jo?" Eliza asked.

"No news of Jo," he said. "I'm not sure if that's good or not." He eyed the women in the room. "But I hope you will not venture there. I hope to never return." He focused his attention on his mother. "Shall we?"

Eliza paused. She wanted to stay with the women. But as she took in her son, she recognized hurry and expectation in his gestures and in his eyes. He appeared uncomfortable.

James reached for Eliza's cloak and helped her on with it. Eliza couldn't speak. The day hadn't gone as she wanted. Jo was still nowhere to be found, Alice was unwell, and Rebecca had dark secrets that may have played a part in her death. Eliza shuddered despite the warmth of the house.

# Chapter 18

"We need to stop here at the constabulary," Eliza told McNally. "We shall be there only for a few minutes."

"Constabulary? What?" James pulled out his watch and examined it. "This won't do."

"Why do you keep looking at your watch? I need to see what progress the police investigation has made on both Rebecca's death and Jo's disappearance. You can wait here if you like." She exited the carriage and began to walk toward the constabulary.

"Wait! Wait! I can't let you go to such a place unaccompanied." James's voice was tinged with worry.

He was so sweet. And clueless. She'd been here countless times before, unescorted. She held back a grin. Better to let him think he was needed. It would be good to have him by her side. He held out his arm, and she rested her hand there as they walked.

Eliza girded her loins before they stepped inside. As usual, the place smelled of stale tobacco along with body odor and maybe a hint of something sour—urine? She glanced at James, who'd once been in prison for a night, and hoped this did not bring up any unpleasant memories.

They walked through to Constable Schultz's desk. Looking up from his desk, the constable spotted James and stood quickly. "Mrs. General Hamilton."

"Greetings, Constable Schultz. This is my son, James."

"Very pleased to make your acquaintance."

"Likewise," James said.

"How can I help you?" Constable Schultz asked.

"We're here to see if there's been further investigation into the Rebecca Dickens case or the missing person case," Eliza said.

"The sergeant isn't in," Schultz said. "But I know they've been working on it. I'm just not privy to it."

"Oh dear, I am sorry to hear it. When will he return?" Eliza shoved her balled-up hands into her cloak.

Schultz shrugged. He glanced nervously at James.

"Can you get a message to him?" Eliza asked.

"Certainly."

"Might you have a piece of paper and a pencil?'

After rummaging on his desk, a pencil emerged, as well as a piece of paper.

Eliza wrote for the sergeant to contact her soon with any news. Then she wrote down that they'd found out that Rebecca owed someone money—a man called Ramsay, who frequented Murphy's. She also wrote that she had threatening letters that had belonged to Rebecca.

"Do you know Murphy's?" Eliza asked Schultz as she handed him the paper, her words scrawled on it.

He paled. "Yes. I know it. It's no place for a lady."

"Indeed."

"It's no place for most of us," James muttered.

Schultz's head cocked. "Have you been there?"

He nodded. "Just today. And even in broad daylight, there were many activities I will never be able to forget."

"He's the one who brought me the information about Ramsay," Eliza said.

"Ramsay, you say?" Schultz's bottom lip quivered slightly. Eliza was sure of it. "Best to steer clear of him."

"Rebecca owed him money from a card game," Eliza said quietly. "Could he have something to do with her murder?"

"Card game at Murphy's? Dressed as a man, I assume?" Schultz asked.

Eliza nodded.

"Mother. You are making wide leaps in logic. It's not like you. There is no evidence to support that accusation," James chided.

"Your son is right, madam. Best to leave this to us. I'm sure we'll be in touch."

Eliza wasn't so sure they'd be in touch. She was certain they'd love to ignore Rebecca's murder and Jo's disappearance. And they'd like to ignore her. James tugged on her. "We best take our leave, Mother."

What was his hurry? Why did nobody see the urgency? A killer was roaming the streets of Manhattan. And Jo was missing, maybe taken by the same person who'd killed Rebecca. Where was Jo? Was she still alive? Eliza teetered on the edge of optimism but was also prepared for the worst. And she was helpless—as they all seemed to be.

"If you're sure there's no other news?" she asked Schultz.

"I wouldn't know, Mrs. General Hamilton, but I'll get the note to the sergeant, and we will call on you as soon as we can."

* * *

Eliza used to love this time of the year. Even loved the snow. But that was back when she was a married woman and had nothing to do but tend to Hamilton and her children. Now the winter and the snow just served to keep her from doing what she deemed she must. Maybe it would not snow anymore. Maybe they could bury Rebecca on Saturday, and Alice would at least have that one matter lifted from her mind.

She stepped up into the carriage, James helping her, even though it was unnecessary.

"Now, Mother," he said as he sat down next to her. "I need to know what you've gotten yourself into. Why has a woman named Jo turned into a man? And why are you so attached to her?" One of his eyebrows lifted.

She explained that several of the women in the house often dressed as men to conduct the affairs of their concern, making and selling lace, linens, embroidery, weavings, and the like.

James groaned.

"Do you not see the genius in this?" Eliza protested as the carriage moved slowly.

He took a breath. "It is not unheard of." He paused. "I'm not certain I'd call it genius. Perhaps these widows would be better off married?"

Eliza gazed out the carriage window. She understood his inclination. But knowing Alice and her group, she doubted they could ever be married now. Not after their taste of freedom, going about the city unfettered by the expectations of society and husbands, and making enough money to live well. But what did she know about it? Here she was, from all outward appearances, Mrs. General Hamilton, the widow of the great man, living in a beautiful home, surrounded by her children. Nobody was aware she'd soon have to find another place to live. Her sister Angelica used to say that appearances were everything. But Eliza begged to differ. Appearances could be deceiving. In fact, Eliza surmised that most were.

"You've always been a charitable person. We've often had other children who lost their parents living with us. I always loved it." James paused again. "But I'm not so sure you should concern yourself much with these women."

"Why?"

"I mean, they associate with people you should not. Murphy's, for example, which is not a good place for any New Yorker, let alone you." He rubbed his hands on his trousers.

"What did you see there?" Eliza asked.

His face reddened. "I don't wish to discuss that with you. But it's more than drink and card games, I can assure you."

Eliza couldn't imagine Rebecca in such an establishment. Yet, that was most likely where she had been, albeit as a man. You never knew about people. She'd learned more about Rebecca from her death than she ever had while she was alive.

Eliza laid her head back against the carriage seat and glanced at her son, who was gazing at the snowy fields they passed. She pondered everything they learned today—and everything they did not. Maybe she hadn't helped at all. Her one small sliver of hope was that Schultz would get her message to Sergeant Trist, who could then use it to find Rebecca's killer and maybe also find Jo.

# Chapter 19

Rebecca's body was in the dead house, waiting for burial, and it gnawed at Alice. She imagined the cold stone floor of the dead house filled with the dead waiting to be buried. Wrapped in a warm quilt on her bed, she still shivered.

Alice didn't like it. Not one bit. She'd never care for the idea of the dead waiting to be buried. It felt wrong. Unnatural. Where was Rebecca's soul? Was she free? Or in a dark purgatory?

She closed her eyes, weary, but sleep evaded her. She should arise and get work done. It did no one any good to wallow in grief and sorrow. This she recognized. But every bone ached in her old body, and she was full of cracks and creaks every time she moved. Her body was a map of old aches, each joint stiff with the years of toil.

Best to lie still.

Tomorrow, others could take over her duties.

Yes, they would.

Alice willed herself to dream, imagining Jo walking in the room, cracking a joke, making an interesting observation about something she had seen that day or a person she had talked to. Alice envisioned it in her mind's eye.

*Jo, shivering, alone in some dark corner of the world, waiting for a release that might never come.* Wasn't that purgatory too? The living had their own limbo with grief hanging over them in an unseen cloud. Maybe Jo was already free. Perhaps death held the only escape from this miserable wait.

Should she hope for Jo to be alive or dead? The longer Alice lived, the more death seemed to be a kind of freedom. She hated to imagine Jo cold and alone. Frightened. Or worse. Tortured by someone. *Better to be dead.*

Alice sat up in her bed, leaned against the icy wall and grabbed the center of her chest, clutching her nightdress in her fist. Alice's life had been full of loss. Whose life was not?

Streams of hope had existed. This house. These women. The good women at the Widow Society. The many people she sold goods to. All good people.

What else could you do but savor the moments or a friendly handshake, a smile on the face of someone you worked for as you handed them fine lace, a drink of ale with other hard-working women?

But those streams of hope evaded her now. This loss was too much. The weight of it pressed on her chest, stealing her breath, filling her heart with a darkness. Escape, impossible.

What remained when even hope had turned to dust?

# Chapter 20

Eliza could not believe her eyes—there, standing in front of her, was Angelica, a vision in sky blue. For a moment, Eliza stilled, then a cry of delight escaped her lips as she ran into her sister's arms. The rustle of Angelica's dress filled the room, mingling with the crackling of the fire.

"What are you doing here? What a wonderful surprise!" Eliza squealed.

"'I ran into James and Alexander in Boston." Angelica slipped her arm through Eliza's. "They almost ruined the surprise! You didn't let it slip, did you?' She turned a pointed glance at James.

"Of course not," James said. "I had to hurry her on her errands, though."

*That's why he was looking at his watch.* It made sense to Eliza now.

"I've just been enjoying your children," Angelica said.

Eliza took in the scene before her. The fire in the hearth cast a golden glow across the room. Angel played the pianoforte, her fingers gliding over the keys as little Eliza hummed along beside her.

Angel played her brother's favorite piece with technical perfection but none of the joy she'd once brought to it. The sunlight caught the silver threads appearing in her dark hair—too early, much too early for a girl her age. Eliza watched her daughter's face, searching for any hint of the vibrant girl who'd existed before Philip's death.

The boys, William and John, sat on the floor near the fireplace, absorbed in their backgammon game.

"You're nearly frozen," Angelica said. "Come, let's sit by the fire."

"Where is your family?" Eliza settled into a chair before the hearth.

"I left them in London." Angelica paused. "I became nostalgic for the Christmases of our youth. My husband and children had no interest whatsoever and if I forced it, there'd be no rest."

"You traveled alone?" Eliza spread her hands toward the flames.

Angelica nodded. "It's not the first time." She paused. "And you still wear widow's weeds! It's high time you were out of mourning."

Eliza laughed. "I told you I've no need for fashion. I'll be Hamilton's widow forever. I don't want people to forget. I want them to be reminded of him every time they see me."

Eliza's joy shifted as she perceived something in Angelica's eyes—an exhaustion that ran deeper than travel. Her smile held tension, a fatigue that even the cheerful fire couldn't chase away. What wasn't her sister telling her?

"You must be exhausted. Why don't you take a rest?" Eliza asked.

"I can rest when I die." Angelica sat in the chair next to her. "I understand you've been involved in dark happenings in the city."

Of course, Alexander had told her what Eliza was doing in town. Angelica was acquainted with the women who lived in the Pearl Street House. She recognized how much they meant to Eliza.

Eliza bit her lip. She didn't enjoy giving bad news to someone who had just come from traveling a great distance.

"What's happened?" Angelica persisted. "Alexander only told me bits and pieces." She gestured with her hand in a rolling motion. "Get on with it."

Eliza took a deep breath and told her the news. All of it.

It silenced her. And that rarely happened with Angelica. *She is not herself*, Eliza thought, then shivered, even as the warmth of the fire circled her.

Angelica squinted. "Who is this group you mentioned from the newspaper? I've heard whispers about them." She trailed off, leaving Eliza with a creeping sense of unease.

"The Women's Morality Alliance?" Eliza asked.

"I think we should pay them a visit."

"Whatever for?"

Angelica paused and leaned toward her sister. "Because, in some ways, women like that are more dangerous than places like Murphy's."

"You don't think a group of well-meaning women could be more dangerous than Murphy's," Eliza said, frowning.

"I know they can be," Angelica said, her voice low. "They mask their intentions behind good works. But sometimes, sister, it's the righteous who are most dangerous."

Eliza understood what she meant. But James had been in Murphy's and had warned her about it. It must be a terrible place. She doubted a group of well-intentioned but off-putting women could be more dangerous.

"We need to find the WMA and pay a visit," Angelica said again.

"We can always ask someone at the paper." Eliza had sway there, since her dear Hamilton had started the paper and had written for it often. "I can send them a note."

"Balderdash! Let's visit them."

Eliza nodded slowly, her mind made up. "You're right. We can't wait. I'll speak to McNally. Let's find out exactly what these women are hiding."

Angelica grinned. "We should to Murphy's while we're at it."

"You know they won't allow us in," Eliza said. "Besides, James said it was horrible!"

"I say we walk in and get a gander at the surroundings, before they kick us out. We can always feign ignorance. After all, we are nothing but silly women." Angelica laughed.

Eliza's curiosity had been sparked by James's report. She never would visit on her own, let alone with her son. But with Angelica? She could do anything with Angelica by her side.

# Chapter 21

Eliza awakened the next morning to the crinkling of paper. Angelica was not next to her, as she had been when they slept last night. Her sister was on the floor surrounded by newspapers.

"What are you doing?" Eliza sat up in a haze.

"I didn't mean to wake you, but I read this article in your paper and searched for more." She smoothed over a page.

"And what did you find?' Eliza reached for her robe at the bottom of the bed. Even though the fire was still lit, the room bore a chill.

"Last Sunday, this piece was in the paper. The article about them finding the body of whom they supposed was a man, but discovered was a woman." Angelica's eyes were lit with passion.

Eliza's brain was still half asleep but connected the dates. "Yes, that's right. I visited Alice on Sunday, and they had just come from identifying Rebecca. That's who they are talking about."

"The next day is this advertisement from the women's group." Angelica paused and scrutinized the paper. "It looks like they ran an ad every day that week."

Eliza had stopped reading the paper because the article had angered her so much. "They must have a sum to spend."

"Precisely. These are not poor women." Angelica folded a newspaper and set it aside. "Now, this letter to the editor talks about unnatural women and it's signed by the same group."

"I read that." Eliza disengaged herself from the covers and placed her feet on the floor.

"Do you know if they were . . . unnatural?" Angelica pressed, her voice low but insistent.

Eliza blinked, her cheeks warming. "Unnatural? What are you saying?"

"Do they lie together, as man and wife?' Angelica didn't soften her gaze, and Eliza shifted uncomfortably, surprised by her sister's bluntness.

Eliza's face heated. "I don't know." The room silenced. "And what's more, what care have I? What care has anybody? That is nobody's concern, except for those involved, I suppose."

Eliza had to admit that it never occurred to her that Alice and the women at Pearl Street House might sleep together as husband and wives do.

"You stayed there yourself," Angelica pointed out.

"I had a private room and didn't ask who was staying in which room, let alone if anyone slept together." Eliza walked toward the fire and stoked the logs. "They are women who are widows. They were married, had children, and were destitute until Alice found them, and they gathered their talents and made something for themselves. To suggest otherwise is vile."

Angelica tilted her head. "I see. But do they not long for touch? Why are there no men in their lives?"

"Angelica! Many women live with no men in their lives. They are widows. They do without men." She paused, trying to calm her racing heart. "They are very busy making lace and other things and selling them. I warrant they have no time for men."

The room quieted, except for the pop and hiss of the fire.

Eliza normally loved the quiet spaces when she and Angelica were in the same room. She loved their conversations as well. The comfortable quiet usually soothed her when Angelica was there.

Angelica's voice softened. "Eliza, I worry about you. You're still young, still beautiful. You could marry again, find security—someone who can help you keep the Grange. You shouldn't be alone forever."

Eliza's stomach heaved. The idea of marrying again sickened her. "I miss my husband, certainly. But I do not want another." Her voice was a whisper, as the pressure on her chest was almost too much to get air to speak. "I loved him. And will not love again."

She wouldn't marry for money. She didn't marry Hamilton for it and wouldn't do so now. If she lost the Grange, then so be it.

Angelica gathered up the newspapers. "It's far too early in the morning for such conversations. I need tea and food. Are you ready to break your fast?

Eliza's stomach waved more. She crouched by the fire and stared into it. Angelica, of all people, grasped how much she loved Hamilton. To even suggest that she take another husband stirred displeasure throughout her body.

The fire hissed and crackled as Eliza poked at the logs, sending up a swirl of embers that briefly brightened the dim room. The air smelled faintly of smoke and old wood, the chill of the morning pressing.

"Eliza? Are you ready to go downstairs? Let us forget this strange conversation and eat good food."

Eliza glanced at Angelica, her closest sister. She was here, had traveled a long distance to be here. She took her hand, stood, and they went downstairs together. As they walked downstairs, Eliza squeezed Angelica's hand, grateful for her sister's company but unable to shake the unease of their conversation. Marry again? The notion weighed heavily on her, an unwanted burden in a heart still full of love and loss.

# Chapter 22

She had decided not to eat anymore. She'd starve. Death would not be far off, and she welcomed it. Why live through this endless torment? Her spirit suffered as much as her bruised body. Any dreams of better days slipped away. What care had she? She'd be dead soon, anyway, and made her peace with it. She didn't discern who she was, where she was, or what was happening to her, but this was no kind of life: lying in her own filth, hands and feet tied, with only gruel force-fed and just enough water to keep her alive. Not enough to quench her steady thirst.

With a sudden swiftness, strong arms lifted her, placed a sack over her head, and dragged her across the floor. She groaned as they heaved her across a large rocky bump on the ground. It tore at what little clothing she wore and scraped her skin raw. The air was thick with the stench of her own filth, making her gag.

"Can't stand the smell of ye anymore," a voice said. A man? A woman? Hard to tell. Did it matter? They were large and dragging her, now tearing away her shreds of clothing, leaving her shivering. Then they lifted her into a tub of tepid water. They scrubbed at her, as she gasped for air. The sack moved in and out against her mouth. Sweat streamed down her face. She imagined fighting against the force that scrubbed. But what good would it do? She could barely lift her arms. She'd be gone soon. Why struggle?

"I don't care," she said in a rough, whispery voice.

The hands scrubbed even harder. "Filthy little harlot."

She wanted to be angry, to rise and pummel the person. A flicker of anger pulsed, but it tickled in her chest and erupted into a laugh.

Someone grabbed her face through the sack and pinched it hard. "You think that's funny, do ye?"

She bit her lip and breathed hard. The sack cut off her air supply. She vowed not to say another word or to laugh or groan.

When they lifted her from the tub, the freezing air hit her, and someone wrapped her in something soft and warm. Her head still spun. The rough cloth chafed her face, adding to her misery. She reached to take the sack off her head. Her hand was smacked away. A hard blow against her head landed her on the filthy floor, where she breathed in the dirt and the soot through the sack. Until she could breathe no more and slipped into blackness.

Sometime later, she awakened in a soft bed that smelled of lilac. If she was dreaming, she didn't want to wake up.

But her eyes flittered open to find a room with a window. Sunlight streamed in. She closed her eyes again. What was this? This couldn't be right. She opened her eyes again, took in a deep breath of the lilac-scented air as hot burning tears of joy sprung at her eyes. The sun. The scent. It was too much goodness. Too much.

She struggled to sit up in bed.

A woman came to her. "Don't get up. Not yet. You need your rest. The fever has just broken."

"Fever?" she asked.

"Yellow fever." The woman smiled at her.

She had no idea what the pretty lady meant. Yellow fever? It struck a chord of fear in her, but she didn't understand why.

"You are recovering, but I thought we might have lost you."

She recalled praying for death. Was that the fever? Was everything she remembered a fever-induced imagining?

She tried to rise from the bed again.

"Please don't," the woman said, softly. "Lay back and I will bring you broth, Josephine."

*Josephine.* Something in her chest bloomed. She was Josephine.

She had a name. If she had a name, she must have a life somewhere. Family? Friends? A life beyond the days of imprisonment.

But she could remember none of it at all.

# CHAPTER 23

When Hamilton had first opened the *Evening Post* office at 77 Wall Street, the Hamilton family had lived at 57 Wall Street. A storm of memories moved through Eliza as she and her sister walked through the front door. The smell of paper and ink and tobacco swept through her. If Hamilton's ghost were living anywhere, it would be at this place, in the creaky, stained floorboards and in the scent of the ink and paper.

Hamilton had loved this place and the people here. Eliza took it all in—the scent, the stacks of paper, the sounds of bustling throughout the building. She had not been here since before his death. In truth, it had been one of the many places she avoided.

She and Hamilton had a simple celebration when the broadsheet was first published. Oh, the countless nights Hamilton sat awake penning his next article. Each morning, he'd read his article to her. She'd offer suggestions, which he mostly took. He'd rush to the office without breaking his fast. He was tormented as he wrote, seeking just the right idea, word, or phrase.

She walked forward to the office of the editor. Also forward through the memories of her Hamilton, so energized he nearly vibrated within these walls. She ran her finger along the wall, imagining that she might revel in that energy once more.

Angelica rapped on the office door. It was flung open to show William Coleman, a friend of Hamilton's and editor of the newspaper. Eliza had forgotten how handsome he was, with blue eyes and a shock of red hair, along with a dimple in his chin.

His eyebrows lifted as he surveyed Angelica and Eliza. "Well, to what do I owe this honor?" William grinned. "Please come in, ladies."

"Thank you so much for seeing us," Angelica said in a playful tone. They had known each other for years.

"Of course!" He gestured toward the chairs. "Please sit." As Eliza sat, he placed his hand on her shoulder. "How are you?" His tone was hushed.

She choked and could not speak without tearing up. She simply nodded and smiled with great effort.

"What can I do for you?" he said as he sat down behind his desk.

Angelica reached over and tapped her sister's hand, in a sisterly sign that she'd do the speaking. Was it that clear how upset Eliza was? She'd thought she'd hidden it. "We are inquiring about one of your regular advertisements. We'd like to learn more about the Women's Morality Alliance."

"Whatever for?" he said and laughed.

Angelica laughed politely.

Eliza did not.

"We'd like to ask them a few questions about their cause." Angelica slipped off her gloves. "Where may we find them?"

"I have no idea. We don't give the names of our advertisers, let alone addresses. But for you two, I'll see what I can find out. I'll be right back. Excuse me, ladies." William stood and exited the room.

Eliza's heart filled with hope. He was going to help them. Perhaps they could get answers about this group.

"Look at this." Angelica lifted a broadsheet from the desk. "This was just out yesterday evening." She pointed to the words, "Reward offered." As Eliza read the text, her heart sped. A reward was being offered for the return of Jo! A hefty sum of $500.

The office door opened. "Ah," William said. "You've seen the reward offered."

"Indeed," Eliza said.

"What do you think of it?" He walked around to his desk.

"It's a brilliant idea, but I wonder where the funds are coming from."

"That I cannot tell you." He leaned forward with the paper in his hand. "I have to ask myself if a reward is going to produce results."

"Why not?" Eliza asked.

He squirmed in his chair and sighed. "It opens the door for shenanigans. This city is full of struggling poor folks who'd do anything to get their hands on that kind of money."

"Let's hope it helps to find her and not bring out the greedy," Eliza said.

He smiled. "Yes, let's hope." He held up a slip of paper. "Here's the name and address of the leader of the Women's Morality Alliance." He slid the paper toward them. "But I am warning you. She is most unpleasant."

Angelica harrumphed, making it clear to Eliza and William that the woman was no match for her.

"Can I ask what your interest is in all this?" William asked.

Eliza glanced at the paper. She did not recognize the name written there: Lucretia Short.

"Certainly," Eliza responded. "We knew the murder victim they rant against."

"So you're going to—what? Confront her?" he asked.

"We seek to understand," Angelica said.

"We also have an inkling that the women in the society might know something about where Jo Ambrose is."

He frowned. "What leads you to believe that?"

Eliza struggled to answer him, as it might reveal too much about Jo's secret identity. She didn't want him to realize that Jo had also been dressed as a man. She also didn't want to mention the notes that she'd found in Rebecca's trunk. The fact that the group had so publicly come out against women living without husbands and women dressing as men led her to suppose that if anybody were to take action against these single women who happened to dress as men, it would be them. And just bringing awareness stirred up interest from others, who may not have the best intentions and take action against vulnerable unmarried women.

"Just call it women's intuition," Angelica said flippantly. "And we won't tell her where we learned her whereabouts."

"Thank you." William stood to usher the women out of his office when the door was flung open.

"Sir, we need you in the newsroom," a young man said.

"I will be right there, after I escort these ladies out."

"No need," Angelica said. "We can find our own way. You are such a busy man. Thank you for seeing us."

Eliza looked William in the eye. Something was exchanged between them at that moment. An acknowledgement of missing Hamilton? Of their deep and abiding love for a man violently taken from them? "Thank you." Her voice was a whisper.

Once on the street, the sisters walked arm in arm to find their carriage and McNally. The streets were not as busy as usual. People stayed in when snow clung to the ground. But this was a busy section of town. This area housed all the newspapers, and the courthouse and government offices were just around the corner. They walked through the thick of it toward their carriage. They moved past the house where Eliza and Hamilton had lived, squeezed in with their children. Eliza warmed as she remembered. She might afford rent at a house such as that once she sold the Grange. Her heart sank at the thought. There was no other way.

Eliza longed to see Alice, René, and Paulette, but first she needed to see Lucretia Short—and for that she girded her loins.

# CHAPTER 24

Lucretia Short lived in a row house on Maiden Lane. A wreath of holly and pine adorned her blue door, and someone had shoveled the snow off her front stoop. A knocker sat in the center of the door.

A tiny woman answered the door, peeked her head around it, and raised her eyebrows at Eliza. Then she opened the door. "Mrs. General Hamilton, please come in."

"This is my sister, Mrs. John Church. May we see Mrs. Short?"

The woman's face crumpled in confusion. "I don't know who you mean. This is the Braithwaite home."

Eliza and Angelica eyeballed one another, baffled. Angelica pulled out the note William had provided.

"I am so sorry. This is the address they gave us." Angelica showed it to her.

"Yes, it's where you are. But I'm Anna Braithwaite."

"Do you know Lucretia?" Eliza asked.

"I do not." Her jaw twitched.

Angelica sighed. "Well, we'll need to find the Women's Morality Alliance another way. He obviously gave us the wrong address."

Anna's head tilted. "You're looking for the WMA?"

"Yes, we wanted to speak with them about their advertisements." Eliza wrapped her scarf closer to her neck in preparation of going back outside to fight against the bitter wind.

"Aye. I've seen those advertisements," Anna muttered. "I just don't understand why they'd be giving this address."

"No, they did not give it to us. Someone else did. Are you a customer of the *Evening Post*? Have you purchased an ad?"

Anna's eyebrows knitted. "No. Perhaps my husband did. He is not home. I can ask him."

"It's not important," Angelica said. "Do not bother him. We simply need to go back to the source. He obviously copied the address wrong."

But William Coleman was a man of detail. It was odd if he'd transcribed an address with the wrong street and number. Perhaps a number could be off—but even that was a stretch.

"Do you know your neighbors? Could Lucretia be one of them?" Eliza asked.

"I don't know the household right next to mine." Anna pointed to the left. "The others I know and take tea with from time to time. I do not know a Lucretia."

The sisters exchanged glances. "Thank you," Eliza said. "You've been most helpful."

"Are you well?" Anna asked Eliza. "I'm so sorry you lost your husband."

Eliza held up her head. "I am well. Thank you for asking."

"There is something foul going on," Angelica said the moment they left the house. "They gave the paper the wrong address."

"Yes, but maybe it's a clue to the correct address." Eliza tilted her head toward the house where Anna had said she did not know her neighbor.

"Indeed," Angelica said, walking toward the place.

The door of the neighboring house was swung open by a woman wrapped up in a thick shawl and scarves. As the woman hurried off, Eliza could not get a good glimpse of her face. But when she turned her head, Eliza detected an eye patch. It was the herbalist, Mrs. Johnston, from Johnston's Apothecary. What was she doing there? Delivering medicinals to someone? Eliza's pulse quickened. Lucretia? Or was she there for the WMA?

What mischief was this? It was too coincidental. Eliza stopped in her tracks.

"What is it?" Angelica whispered.

"I know that woman," Eliza said and explained to her sister.

Angelica drew her closer. "Well, it seems the pieces of this puzzle might come together."

They walked up to the door. It had no adornment like Anna's door had. Not even a knocker. So Eliza balled up her hand and rapped on the door.

There was no answer, but Eliza and Angelica had just seen someone leaving the home. Eliza didn't think this row house belonged to the herbalist, as she was certain the family lived above the apothecary.

Eliza knocked again.

"Perhaps he or she left through a back door?" Angelica said.

"It's possible." Eliza knocked again.

"Or they are not at home or are refusing to answer the door." Angelica shrugged.

"If she's there, she might be ill. After all, the woman from the apothecary was just here."

Angelica raised an eyebrow. "Which apothecary?"

"I told you already. Johnston's." Eliza tried to get her bearings. She pointed toward the shop. "It's close by. Down that way."

Eliza and Angelica walked arm and arm, navigating patches of snow and puddles. Eliza's feet were icy stumps, and her gloved hands tingled with cold.

Once they arrived, Eliza pointed to the Johnston's Apothecary sign, with its green name painted in swirls and loops. They made their way across the street between carriages and a few people on foot. Eliza wondered where the wild pigs were this time of year. Were they buried in a warm nest somewhere? She was glad they weren't underfoot.

Angelica opened the door to the apothecary, with Eliza trailing her. The woman they'd seen earlier was indeed behind the counter, talking in hushed tones to another woman, who held a linen bag in her hand.

"Can I help you ladies?" a man said from the other side of the counter.

"Thank you," Angelica said. "But we need to speak to your wife."

The woman overheard them and lifted her finger as if to say, "one moment."

The man nodded and moved away, likely figuring it was a woman's concern. Most men did not want to bother themselves with women's health issues, even men who were healers.

After the other customer had wandered off, Mrs. Johnston smiled at Eliza and Angelica. "Mrs. General Hamilton."

"This is my sister, Mrs. John Church."

"Pleased to make your acquaintance." She smiled, revealing even more planes and angles to her shadowy face. She reached up to adjust her eye patch. "How can I help you?"

"We're searching for Lucretia Short," Eliza said.

The women's smile vanished. Her mouth formed a line of displeasure.

"We thought we saw you coming out of her home. And we tried to gain entry, but she would not come to the door."

"That household is down with the plague," the woman said in a whispery voice, clearly not wanting to cause any concern. The city seemed to be in a reprieve from the disease, but it kept rearing back. "They won't be answering the door anytime soon."

"I am so sorry to hear of it," Angelica said.

If the house was down with the yellow fever, there would be no talking with Lucretia. They'd have to find another way to gather information about her and the WMA. Eliza leaned toward the herbalist. "How well do you know her?"

She shrugged. "Enough to bring her herbs and tinctures. She is a good customer."

"Do you know anything about the Women's Morality Alliance?" Angelica asked.

The woman frowned. "Only that it's something I want no part of."

Eliza and Angelica glanced at one another. "We agree then. It is our understanding that she oversees the group."

"She did. But I fear she won't oversee much soon. The household is very ill, and she has the worst of it." She craned her head to glance at another customer who had entered the shop. "Now, if you'll excuse me."

"Certainly." Angelica wrapped her arm around Eliza's shoulder. "Let's be off."

Eliza's heart sank. She'd wanted to find Jo and to find answers about Rebecca's untimely death. But each path she took seemed to lead nowhere. She was uncertain where to go next or whom to speak with.

Eliza drew in a breath and let it out slowly. "Yes. I need to return tomorrow for Rebecca's burial. You can join me if you like."

"I would not miss it, sister. Shall we proceed as planned?"

Eliza nodded.

They found the nearest cab stand, aware that McNally would not take them where they wanted to go.

# CHAPTER 25

"I'm not so sure about this, Angelica," Eliza whispered while in the cab to Murphy's.

"You've been to such places before."

"Yes, but I was dressed as a man then. No reputable woman would enter a place like Murphy's."

Angelica cocked an eyebrow. "You are Mrs. General Hamilton. Nobody is more respectable than you."

"My point exactly." Eliza looked out the window. They were getting close. Their plan was for the cab to leave them about a block from the establishment. "It's not like when we were girls sneaking our mother's perfume. We're grown women."

"Let's recall why we're doing this," Angelica snapped. "We need to see what this place is about. It's where Rebecca played cards. She spent a lot of time there. Her killer might be within its very walls."

"And how are we to spot him?"

"If I'm right, he'll spot us." Angelica paused. The cab rattled and swayed. "And maybe someone here knows something about Jo."

"James said that nobody knew a thing. He said he never wanted to go back there." Chills traveled up and down Eliza's spine.

"James is such a mama's boy," Angelica said.

Eliza smiled. That was true. "So we slip inside on the pretense of getting warm. Feign ignorance of what the place is, that we're not allowed in by the very nature of our sex, and glean whatever details and information we can. And then we slip out, as if we were walking out of a bakery or milliner's."

"Precisely." Angelica rapped on the cab roof. "This is fine. Leave us here, please."

They stepped out into the cold. The wind howled down Water Street like a beast loosed from the harbor, biting at their cheeks and clawing through their cloaks. Eliza drew her cloak tighter as she and Angelica, approached the entrance of the shabby Murphy's. Women were not permitted, but today, necessity overrode convention.

"Let's hope they take pity before they ask questions," Eliza murmured. She rapped on the polished door. It opened with a creak.

A liveried steward blinked at them in confusion. "Madams? This is not—"

"Forgive us," Eliza said with breathless urgency. "Our carriage turned over a few blocks away and we've walked the distance in the wind. Could we warm ourselves for just a moment?"

The steward hesitated. Behind him, a round-faced man in a brown velvet waistcoat peered over his shoulder. Recognition lit his expression. "Mrs. General Hamilton? As I live and breathe. You've caught us unprepared, but—yes, come in. For heaven's sake, let them in, Mullins."

*Recognized immediately. Of course.* Eliza wondered how this would come back to haunt her.

They stepped into warmth and cigar smoke. Men crowded around gaming tables and brandy carts. No other women were in sight. Heads turned. Some stared. Eliza kept her chin high. They were shown into a front lounge with a roaring fire and settees. Angelica settled close to the hearth, visibly shaken but observant.

Eliza's eyes swept the room. Off to her right, a man slid a small black book across a table to another, receiving a heavy coin purse in exchange. The second man flipped it open briefly; the pages were filled with tight, neat columns. She tried to get a glimpse of the details, but all she could make out were rows of initials and names of places, Albany, Brooklyn, New Jersey, Pennsylvania.

What was this place?

There was a card game in the corner, and the participants hadn't even looked up when she and Angelica had entered. Eliza had expected that their presence would cause a stir. But these men were intent on their cards.

A door opened off to the right. A man emerged, then turned to say, "The Albany woman secured for Tuesday. The rest, keep quiet until the bidding."

Were they bidding on a *woman*? A prickling sensation traveled up Eliza's spine, and she turned to Angelica. "Did you hear—"

"I did. They're not just gambling, Eliza." Her voice was tight and her mouth barely moved.

Rebecca played cards *here*? Did she not see what else was happening? René had said this was the only place she played. Eliza searched her heart and could not fathom why a woman, even dressed as a man, would support such a cause. Was it possible that Rebecca was so intent on the cards she didn't realize what else was happening here?

Eliza turned to the fire, spreading her hands out. This was definitely a seedy establishment. Women were being bargained for—perhaps for the sacred act of marriage. "We should leave as soon as we can."

"I quite agree."

The man with the velvet jacket came over to them with brandy. "This will warm your bones."

"Thank you so much. We can't stay long," Angelica took the glass from him. "Our carriage should be ready soon."

"I see." He handed a glass to Eliza. "Anything else I can get you?"

"I wondered if you might be able to help us," Angelica said. "We're looking for a friend. Josephine Ambrose."

"I doubt any friend of yours would be here," he said, jittery.

"But there are other women here, somewhere." Angelica pointed to a woman's glove on the table next to the settee.

He opened his mouth, as if to speak, but closed it again. "I think it's best if you drink your brandy and move along. I'm sorry." He lowered his voice. "I'm trying to be accommodating, but this is not a safe place for you."

"I see," Angelica said. She took a sip of her brandy, then set her glass on the table. "Are you ready to brave the cold, Eliza?"

Eliza was already on her feet. She was very ready.

* * *

Once outside, they realized that they'd forgotten to ask the cabby to wait for them. The nearest cab stand was several blocks away.

"Now what?" Angelica looked around.

Eliza had more knowledge of this part of town, as the Widow Society was nearby. "We walk."

"Walk? It's so cold!"

"We can stop in at the Widow Society. We can warm ourselves there. I've been meaning to stop in." Eliza kept in close touch with the women at the Widow Society, but not as much as she once did. Now that she was a widow herself, she had less time and she lacked the resources to help them.

Angelica rolled her eyes. "Very well then. Which way?"

"Follow me."

Finally, Eliza and Angelica reached the Widow Society. Warmth enveloped them as they walked in the front door. Mrs. Schumacher, the matron of the place, looked up from behind a new-to-the-establishment desk. "Mrs. General Hamilton! How lovely to see you!" She stood and came from around the desk.

"Lovely to see you." Eliza walked over to the desk. "This my sister, Angelica Church,"

"Pleased to meet you." Mrs. Schumacher shook Angelica's hand and then embraced Eliza. "It has been far too long."

Eliza noticed a stack of pamphlets on the desk.

"A good woman dropped these off just now." Mrs. Schumacher handed one to Eliza. "I hear you and Mrs. Graham are getting close to having the orphanage. Very good news!"

Eliza glanced over the pamphlet, and dread came over her when she realized what it was. "Mrs. Schumacher, do you know the WMA?"

"Ja, I do. The woman said they help widows to find marriage. And you know some of our population here would welcome a second chance at marriage."

"She said that to you?" Angelica said.

Mrs. Schumacher's eyebrows hitched, "Yes, of course. What is the problem?"

"We've been trying to find information about them. They took out some harsh ads and wrote a condemning letter in the paper about our friend Rebecca's death," Eliza said.

"We wanted to learn what they are about," Angelica said. "They don't seem to want to speak with us."

"I see. Is this Rebecca you speak of Rebecca Dickens?"

Eliza nodded. "She was unfortunately dressed as a man when her body was found."

The fair Prussian's face reddened.

"I'm so sorry. I didn't mean to blurt it out like that," said Eliza.

"It's not that. I knew Rebecca and I know Alice, of course. Is it illegal that this group is matchmaking?"

"We don't care at all about their matchmaking, unless they are forcing women to marry. There's something sinister about their point of view, which they made very clear. They think the only role for women is to marry. Anything else is unnatural and ungodly. And they wrote horrible things about Rebecca. Then Josephine went missing, in search of Rebecca. She was also in disguise as a man. Do you see the connection?"

"Josephine is missing? I feel sick," the matron said. "The WMA have been here many times before. I thought they were offering an option for these women. You appreciate their circumstances. Sometimes another marriage is just the thing to keep them off the streets. But now I worry that I've sent them off into bad situations."

"You had no idea and maybe the women who were married are happy."

"I think it's good that you know now. When we know, we can act in better ways," Angelica said.

Eliza asked for more information about Rebecca and Jo. Mrs. Schumacher told them everything they already knew. Their stories were so similar to other widows and orphans.

"Was the WMA handing out pamphlets and recruiting when they were here?" Eliza asked. "Could they have met either Jo or Rebecca here and targeted them?"

Mrs. Schumacher appeared to be thinking. "Not when Jo was here. But Rebecca was here when they started recruiting. She made it very clear that she was not interested in marriage."

"How so?" Angelica asked.

"She sparred with one of the women. Lucretia. Told her to mind her own business. That just because a woman was not married did not mean she was going to hell. She also told Lucretia that in her opinion the people going to hell were those who judged others too harshly," Mrs. Schumacher said, grinning. "I'll never forget that."

"Interesting. Thank you," Eliza said. Rebecca was no wilting flower. That she knew Lucretia and that they had words made Lucretia seem guiltier. If she herself did not commit Rebecca's murder, she probably knew who did. And how was Jo caught up in this web? "It's so good to see you. I have a trunk full of items I've been meaning to bring you, but it's still at my house. I will bring it soon. But we really must be going. Is the cab stand still the next block over?"

"Yes, but where is your driver?"

"Probably seething at Trinity," Eliza said.

# Chapter 26

The scent of pine greeted Eliza when she walked into her house. She and Angelica went to the parlor and there it was—a tall pine tree. "What is this?"

"Just like when we were children," Angelica said. "I asked the boys to find one."

"You are nostalgic these days." It had been years since she had a tree in her home for the holidays. Her parents had a small tabletop one as often as they could, an old Dutch tradition. A few times, they had a tall tree brought into their home, which was pure delight for the Schuyler children. Others in the Dutch-American community often came to their home for holiday celebrations.

The smell filled her home and brightened Eliza as childhood memories surfaced. Her mother's voice singing a hymn as she arranged the branches just so. Her father's laughter on Christmas Eve, after drinking too much advocaat. She had spat out her first drink of the creamy alcoholic beverage. She'd hated it so much she swore she would never have another. But years later, as an adult, her taste changed and she loved it.

It was late; the children were in bed, or at least off in their rooms, and Eliza and Angelica had missed dinner. Mrs. Cole had prepared plates for them.

"What a day we've had," Angelica said. "I keep going over everything in my mind."

"Me too. I feel as if I have all the pieces to a puzzle but have no way of pulling them together." Eliza bit into her bread.

"I know what you mean." Angelica buttered her bread. "We need to find out more about the Women's Morality Alliance. Do they know anything about the bidding at Murphy's? Seems like they could be working together."

"I agree, but since we know their leader is ill, maybe we should strive to find another person in the group."

"They are so vocal, yet so secretive."

"Cowards." Eliza set her fork down. "Hamilton used to rant about people like this. If they feel their beliefs are right, why stay so hidden?"

"Maybe they are afraid for their safety. Maybe they've been hurt due to their views." Angelica took a sip of wine. "Everybody is entitled to their point of view, I suppose."

Which reminded Eliza of Hamilton. His conversations about freedom for all religions and points of view. "You're right. But I draw the line when someone gets hurt."

"And as Mrs. Schumacher said, maybe they are providing a service to some women. Those out of options," Angelica said.

"If only I could believe those marriages might be happy ones."

"Between the WMA and Murphy's, I warrant people are making money from marrying women off to men seeking wives," Angelica said.

"Whether they want to be married or not," Eliza said.

"The question is did they have anything to do with Rebecca's murder?" Angelica said. "And why would they kill her? Simply because she was unmarried? That makes no sense. Because she was dressed as a man?"

"Let's not forget she was being threatened for both of those matters." Eliza drew in a breath and let it out slowly. "If not by Lucretia, then I warrant it was one of her lot."

The candle on the table flickered. Eliza's worry muddled her thinking.

"I suppose we should make an early night of it." Angelica pushed her plate away. "Rebecca's service is quite early in the morning. And we've had quite a day."

It was hard not to imagine that Rebecca would come knocking at Eliza's door any minute to claim her death was a ruse. But Eliza had seen her body in the dead house. An image that taunted her while she was trying to sleep.

"It seems odd that two women from the same house, in the same concern, who live together have befallen such terrible circumstances." Eliza finished the last drop of wine and stood. Her sister followed suit.

"I agree. But even given all of that, I'm sure they keep a part of themselves private."

"Like Rebecca and her card playing."

"Yes. Even though they knew Rebecca liked to play cards, I warrant none of them were aware she was going to Murphy's to do so."

Which probably hurt them further. Eliza recognized the sting of that kind of betrayal. She'd found out a great deal about Hamilton after his death. She was unaware of his whereabouts the day he was killed, only to be told hours later that he was wounded.

Still, when you love someone—either as a friend or as a spouse—what could you expect? To discern everything about them? Each waking thought, each deed? Were there parts of herself that she kept hidden? Shame filled her when she considered how angry she'd been because of her husband's actions. One should not think or speak ill of the dead.

Even now, almost a year and a half later, she still struggled to sort through her emotions toward her husband. Anger. Disappointment. Fear. But finally, she settled on love. As always.

# Chapter 27

Alice didn't care who was knocking. She was too tired to reply. Too tired to attend Rebecca's funeral that day.

Her back thundered with a pain pressing her down as if a sack of flour were on top of her, pinning her down with a crushing weight of exhaustion. Why bother moving? She had brought each woman into this house, offered them sanctuary. Now, they were being subjected to relentless abuse, faced with the threat of death, or being snatched of the streets. They were being bullied and murdered. Or had disappeared. What was wrong with the world? What was the point of it? The hard work. The relationships.

She'd laid there for hours and hours trying to sort through it. To piece it all together. Rebecca disappeared and died shortly after they'd started getting notes pinned to their door. Vile notes accusing them of God knows what. Who wrote those notes? Were the writers and killers the same ilk? Could it be that simple—find the note-writer, find the killer?

And now Jo was gone, disappeared a week ago while searching for Rebecca. Where was Jo? Alice often relied on her instincts to navigate life, to handle people, to make decisions. But now, her instincts failed her. Fear dampened all of them.

Alice considered Jo's idea of dressing as a man a brilliant one. It always had been before. She'd encouraged Rebecca to do the same.

But then the paper had mocked her when they found her body. Crushing humiliation swept through Alice on Rebecca's behalf.

Life was full of loss. Sometimes, death seemed a relief from the relentless struggle, especially for women without family, exposed and unprotected. Alice had tried to teach the women in her care how to stay safe, how to avoid unwanted attention. She'd assumed she had succeeded. But she had failed them—failed Rebecca, failed Jo. Who would be next?

When her bedroom door opened, Alice rolled over to see who it was.

It was none other than Mrs. General Hamilton. Eliza. If anybody understood Alice's suffering, it would be her. Eliza had not attended Hamilton's funeral. Eliza sat down on Alice's bed. It creaked beneath her slight frame. It was a creaky bed, lumpy too. Alice longed for a new bed, but there was always something more pressing—rent, food, clothes. A mattress seemed a luxury.

What was Eliza doing here?

"Alice." Eliza's voice was a whisper. "Your friends need you."

Alice closed her eyes.

"Your friends downstairs need you. You are their leader, what holds it all together." She paused. "It is the burden of leadership. You must swallow your pain and be there for them."

She was right. Alice's intuition sparked. A tingle of acknowledgement. "But I am so tired."

"I know. But you can rest after." Her voice was soft as silk. "Let me help you." She stood and untangled Alice from her bedclothes and held out her hand to help lift her from the warmth. A chill swept over Alice; she wanted her quilts. She desired to return to the warmth and rest of her cocoon. But something in Eliza's stance, in her large brown eyes, took Alice by surprise. Would Eliza Hamilton never stop surprising Alice?

Alice took her hand and allowed her friend to lift her.

"Now let's get you dressed."

"No need. I'll dress myself. I'll be right there."

And she would be. For here was Eliza Hamilton herself. A woman she admired for many years before she called her friend. Now she stood before her.

You just never knew about life.

# Chapter 28

The sky grew darker gray as they lowered the box containing Rebecca's body into the ground. Eliza and Angelica clutched each other as the icy wind circled them. The warmer weather was giving way to winter again. They'd broken ground just in time to bury Rebecca. And from the looks of it, several other fresh graves waited. Eliza shivered. She'd been to several spring burials, in which loved ones had been forced to wait throughout the winter months.

The bitter wind whipped at the mourners' black clothes, making them seem like a flock of ravens gathered around the open grave. The frozen ground had been stubborn, requiring extra payment to the gravediggers. More coin spent to acknowledge a woman's death than had even been spent investigating its cause. Above them, the leafless trees creaked and swayed, their branches casting shifting patterns on the snow, like nature's own lace—a final tribute to Rebecca's art.

Eliza barely perceived the minister's words, as she watched Alice from across the grave, swaying as if she might topple into it and atop the coffin.

The group walked back to Pearl Street for a small reception.

"Who is that?" Angelica whispered to Eliza as they walked.

She discerned who her sister was talking about. A tall, dapper fellow with blond hair, shiny brown eyes, and a square chin. He followed along to the house.

"I do not know." Eliza held her sister closer to her. The wind was biting. She recognized one other person there: Constable Schultz. He was familiar with all the women who lived at the house on Pearl Street, as he'd helped Eliza with the dreadful business involving her son. They'd given her a place to stay when she was in danger, and Schultz checked in with them from time to time. It was decent of him to attend, especially in this gray, stony-cold weather.

A note was attached to the door when Eliza and Angelica arrived. Eliza suddenly recalled Schultz taking a note off the door last Sunday. She tore it from the door and held it in her hand, planning to give it to Alice or René. But the constable was there, like a sudden gust of wind.

"May I have that note?" he asked.

"I believe it belongs to the women of the house." Eliza glanced in the direction of the oncoming group.

"Aye. But they don't need to read that note today." He looked her straight in the eye. She handed him the note.

"What is it?" Angelica asked.

"'Tis nothing to concern yourselves with." He slipped it in his jacket.

Eliza's skin prickled. Who was pinning notes to Alice's door? And why was Schultz taking them? Eliza and Angelica stole glances at one another before entering the home. What was going on? Was someone writing untoward words to the women in the house? Were they threatening?

Seized with more than a measure of curiosity, Eliza found her way to Schultz in the crowded front room. Schultz spotted her and, as if sensing her plan, turned away. He understood her too well. Shame swept through her. When they'd first met, she had only been trying to help her son. Of course, he must understand that. She wasn't being a busybody then nor now. She cared about these women, wanted to find answers about Rebecca's death and locate Jo as soon as possible. Eliza followed Schultz and sidled up to him.

"Mrs. General Hamilton, I cannot speak with you now."

"Why not?"

He leaned toward her. "I am watching someone, and I don't wish him to know it."

Him? Eliza scanned the room. Four men were there, including the constable. One was Paulette's husband, or at least that's who Eliza assumed he was. The other two men were strangers to her—the tall, dapper man and one other man who stayed to himself. He was short of stature, round at the belly, and wore rimmed circular glasses over his large dark eyes. Perhaps he was a friend of Rebecca's.

So Eliza assumed it was one of those two men that Schultz was watching. But why? Did he surmise that one of them had placed the note on the door? Or that one of them knew where Jo was? Or worse, that one of them killed Rebecca? Eliza's heart sped up. She might be in the room with a killer—they all might be in the room with the killer.

"You've gone pale, Eliza. Are you feeling well?" Angelica asked.

Schultz's eyes never left the crowd jammed into the room. Eliza attempted to follow his gaze.

"I'm fine." Eliza leaned into Angelica and whispered what Schultz had told her.

"He can't just say that without telling us more," Angelica said. "Constable Schultz?"

He turned his head.

"What is going on here? I demand you tell us. It's upsetting Eliza and I won't have it."

Schultz glanced at Eliza, then back at Angelica. He shrugged. "She seems fine to me."

"That's because you don't know her like I do." Angelica folded her arms across her chest.

Schultz lifted one eyebrow. "Madam, I am a constable. I am not swayed by such charms."

"You are unbearable!" Angelica said.

"That's exactly what my wife said this morning." He turned his face back to the wake and walked away from the sisters.

Angelica and Eliza stayed for the duration and after people left Rebecca's wake to help clean up. After the dishes were done and the floors swept, they readied themselves to journey back to the Grange.

"Thank you both for coming," Alice said.

"We wouldn't have missed it." Eliza slipped her gloves on.

"Has there been any word?" Angelica asked.

Alice's face fell. "None."

"What do you know about Lucretia Short?" Angelica pressed.

Alice's eyebrows knitted. "I don't recognize the name. Who is she?"

"She is in charge of the Women's Morality Alliance," Eliza replied. "They've been taking out those advertisements railing against unmarried women."

A bubble of laughter escaped from Alice. "No wonder I do not know her. What poppycock."

Eliza judged it best not to press Alice further. She appeared as if she might topple any minute. If Lucretia was aware of this household, and if she was writing those notes, by any slim chance, Alice was unaware.

"Who were those gentlemen who attended the wake today?" Eliza asked.

Alice frowned. "The blond man was Ramsay. I don't know who the other was. Maybe a friend of Paulette's husband."

"Ramsay?"

"He owns Murphy's, and he was here to collect a debt that Rebecca owed." Her voice was harsh with disdain. "Just buried and the man only cares for money."

Eliza's heart quickened. "Is he hoping to get the money from you?"

Alice poked her chin out. "If he did, he now realizes he will not get money from any of us. We are not her relations. Her debt was her business."

Eliza considered asking Alice about the reward, but this wasn't the time. She'd had to nearly pry the woman from her bed. Alice had managed to attend the service and hosted the wake and that was more than enough for her.

Angelica stole a glance of concern at Eliza. "Be careful, Alice. Such men can be dangerous."

"Unscrupulous," Eliza said.

Alice shrugged her shoulders. "I've handled worse than him." Eliza didn't ask what she wanted to ask, but Angelica cleared her throat, and the question spilled out of her mouth.

"Could he have killed Rebecca?"

Alice paled. "I've been over and over it in my mind. I don't think a man killed her. She was poisoned." She paused. "Men are creatures of violence. She would've been strangled or stabbed if a man killed her."

"So you think a woman killed her?" Eliza asked.

"Aye. I do."

"Do you have any idea who?"

"Someone who knows how to use arsenic." Alice's voice was flat with worry.

"That could be anybody," Angelica said. "I could figure it out if I needed to."

"But would you know the correct dose needed to kill?" Alice's eyes met hers. "The correct dose to kill and not just to make some-one sick?"

Angelica said nothing.

Eliza's limbs heavied with dread. "We must go. McNally waits for us. He's not too happy with all our back and forth. And tomor-row is church, so he will grumble even more."

She hugged Alice, and then the sisters left to find Eliza's carriage.

As they left, Alice trailed behind and a woman approached her at the door stoop.

"What are you doing here, Lucille?" Alice said, almost yelling.

Eliza and Angelica turned.

"May I come inside and speak with you?" The woman was tall and stately, dressed in a black wool cloak and fur hat.

"No, you may not. Get along now. I've no wish to speak to you. Not now. Not ever." Alice walked back into the house and shut the door. Lucille glanced at Eliza and Angelica, before ducking down and disappearing into the alley between houses.

"Was that *the* Lucille?" Angelica leaned closer to Eliza.

"It must be." Eliza slipped her arm through Angelica's. "Let's go."

"How does Alice know her?" Angelica asked.

"Who knows? Alice's business takes her all over the city." But Eliza had been wondering the same thing. Lucille's Gentleman Club had quite the reputation, as did its purveyor.

"Isn't that where Rebecca was found?"

Eliza nodded. "In the alley behind the establishment."

"And she has the audacity to show her face here, to Alice? No wonder she sent her away."

As Eliza mulled it over, she wasn't surprised by any of it. But then again, these days very little surprised her.

# Chapter 29

Eliza spotted Ramsay, the man Alice had mentioned, as they approached McNally at the carriage. Ramsay had left the gathering an hour ago and yet remained just outside the small courtyard alley that led to Alice's home.

Eliza elbowed Angelica. "Look who's still hanging about."

"He's up to no good," Angelica said. She didn't take McNally's extended hand to help her into the carriage.

"What can I do for you?" McNally asked.

Eliza considered her options. She pointed to the carriage. "Can we get inside and pull around the corner?" She gestured in the general direction.

"Grand idea," Angelica whispered.

McNally lifted a wiry copper eyebrow. "And what will you be doing?"

"Watching that man over there," Eliza whispered.

"Why?" McNally tilted his head. Eliza recognized that tilt, the one that said, "What are these ladies up to now?"

Eliza leaned forward and spoke in a hushed tone. "We think he might go inside after the others leave. He's after Rebecca's debt."

"Who?"

"The woman whose wake we are here for."

"Very well. But it's getting late in the day, and we are coming back in the morning for church," he pointed out.

Eliza took his hand and slipped into the carriage. "And?"

Angelica took his hand, hefted into the carriage, and sat close to Eliza to keep warm.

Eliza stole a glance out the window. Ramsay was still lurking. McNally pulled the carriage around the block and parked it at a spot where they could see Ramsay, puffing on his hands to keep them warm, tipping his hat to the few people who strolled by. Winter in the city was not as busy as in the other seasons. It was time to hunker down and keep warm, and it was Advent. Eliza said a brief prayer to herself. She liked to spend this season in prayer, contemplation, celebration, and with her family.

McNally dismounted from the carriage. The lack of his weight lifted the carriage. He was a big man with thick arms and legs. Hamilton had handpicked him to be Eliza's driver, and mostly McNally did a good job, but he sometimes became impatient with Eliza. Eliza tried to overlook it, since the man hadn't been paid in quite some time. She was hoping her promised monies would come through soon and she could pay the help. But it wouldn't be enough to save the house.

McNally poked his head inside. "He's not going anywhere."

"He's waiting for everybody to leave so he can go inside and assault those women. They do not have the funds to pay him whatever Rebecca owed," Eliza said.

"It's not their concern." Angelica's eyes were ablaze. "They are not her relatives."

"What sort of debt is it?" McNally asked. "It seems indecent to bother these women during their mourning."

Sometimes McNally irritated Eliza, but he was a proper sort in his own way. She warmed. "We don't know. But Rebecca played cards at his establishment, Murphy's."

This time both of McNally's eyebrows lifted. "Aye, I heard of the place."

They sat for a few minutes and watched the passing people without being seen, keeping an eye on Ramsay.

At last, a group exited Alice's home.

"I think that's everybody," Eliza said.

As soon as the last of the crowd drifted away. Ramsay walked toward the house.

"Let me handle this. Stay here, ladies," McNally ordered.

Before Eliza could say no, he took off across the street and disappeared inside the courtyard.

"What is your man doing?" Angelica asked.

"I suppose he will have a word with Ramsay." Eliza cupped her gloved hands tight and placed them on her lap. "Or perhaps he will simply enter Alice's home to express his condolences, and his presence there will make Ramsay slither away like the snake he is."

"Well, well, Eliza, you impress me with your powers of observation, yet again, along with your rather colorful language. Hamilton would be proud."

Eliza laughed. "Indeed."

The minutes they waited seemed like hours. A group of people stopped on the corner and seemed to discuss which direction to walk in, obscuring the view. After a few moments, they walked off in the other direction.

A few moments later, Ramsay emerged from the courtyard, peeved. He walked off toward a carriage and disappeared into it.

Soon after, McNally bounded across the road with a joyful countenance. He had a pie in his meaty hands, which he handled to Angelica. "Alice sends her regards and says they have more food than they can ever eat."

"What happened?" Angelica took the pie and placed it on the seat next to her.

He shrugged. "Nothing. I just stood there until he left." A grin spread across his face. "He's a small man. In every sense of the word."

Eliza beamed. "Well done!"

"At your service," McNally said. "Now, let's get you ladies home safely."

# Chapter 30

Josephine sat on the edge of her bed and took in the room. She had been kept in other rooms until now. The woman told her it was a sick room, a place where people with yellow fever were kept and cared for. But little about her circumstance made sense to her. She supposed the fever had taken a toll on her, as it was hard to form a complete thought, let alone remember her life before the dank and dark room of her recent memory.

How long had she been ill?

Why hadn't her family cared for her?

Did she have a family? Friends?

According to the woman who brought her meals, they were searching for her family. They had found her wandering the streets barefoot and in rags, sick and half mad, and had taken her in to care for her. Waves of gratitude moved through her. At least she was still alive.

She understood nothing of healing and medicine. But she certainly hadn't been taken care of. Until after her bath. Until they lifted the blindfold from her eyes and she watched the streams of sun coming through the window.

She closed her eyes now to force her brain to recall walking through the streets before they found her. The only sharp image in her mind was the plump hands holding a cup of tea. The cup was dainty, with pink flowers painted on it. As hard as she tried to remember something specific, nothing came forth. It was like there was a brick wall between what came before this house and this room, with the yellow walls. Before her illness.

Her head throbbed.

Josephine lay back on her bed and watched the dust particles dance in the sunlight. She closed her eyes again. Sometimes, if she relaxed, entertaining images came to her. Seemingly unrelated to her life, or what she surmised was her life.

Visions of delicate embroidery and lace patterns played in her mind. What did it mean? Lace? It made no sense. But then again, nothing did. Has the fever changed her forever? Wiped all coherent memories and thoughts from her mind? She gave up fighting against the lacy patterns in her mind and enjoyed them. Then words came to her, along with the patterns. *Star leaf, daisy, Queen Anne, spider web.* They played in her mind and made her fingers twitch, which prompted her to examine them. They were sinewy. Her palms were etched in lines, and her fingers were long, the tips of them rough. Was she a craftswoman? These were not the hands of a fine lady. That she recognized. Not like the hands engraved in her memory—soft, white, plump, handing her the bitter tea.

The tea was so bitter it was unlike anything else in her memory. Most unpleasant. She could almost taste the metallic flavor in her mouth, even now.

She further studied her hands. These hands were her hands. She was not a woman of leisure. Yet here she was, dressed in a fine orchid muslin, simple, but fine. She was in a room with a bed and mattress with linen sheets, well-stitched, pillowcases with embroidered violets, and a mirror on the wall opposite her bed. She dared not take more than a glimpse of herself from time to time, for though mirrors never lied, she didn't recognize one thing about her reflection.

The door swung open. The woman who brought her food smiled at her. "Dear Josephine, we have found your family. We will make haste tomorrow morning to get them to you as soon as we can."

Her family? She had a family! And she would go to them tomorrow! Impatience swirled around her. She stood. "I'm ready! Why don't they just come and get me now?" Josephine asked.

The woman's smile turned into a frown. "We need to make certain before we send you off to them. We are still making inquiries. The mistress of this house will handle the matter. Not before."

"Make certain of what?"

The woman ignored her and left a plate of bread and butter on a chair, then left the room, shut the door, and locked it.

The sound of the lock reached out and twisted in Jo's chest.

# Chapter 31

When darkness came over Eliza, as it had done often since Hamilton's death, she sat in his study, the place where his mind and heart came together to string ideas together with words. All the words. Her Hamilton loved words. Sitting in his chair now provided a modicum of comfort.

She found it difficult to concentrate on the papers from the orphanage. But she must. Not knowing where Jo was, or if she was dead or alive, was like living on the edge of a broken piece of glass. It was distracting. Finally, she refocused and finished with the papers. She would find someone to deliver them to Isabelle.

Eliza had suffered so much loss in the past few years, but she was finding her way, through prayer, and turning outward to help others as much as she could. Her plans for Hamilton's biography. Her plans with Isabelle to start an orphanage. Tending to her family. These were things that mattered, that buoyed her, so as not to dwell in the vast dark sea of grief.

But not knowing Jo's whereabouts was torture.

She turned her mind to other unpleasant deliberations, but in this space, she could help others. She unscrewed the inkwell; the scent filled the room. It had been many months since she'd used it. Memories of Hamilton flooded through her, as he had often smelled of ink. She reached for a piece of paper, dipped her pen into the well, and wrote. She must inform Rebecca's relatives of her passing. It was the least she could do. They weren't close but should know she was gone.

Rebecca's things were still in the room with Eliza. What was left of her things, that is. A life came down to a trunk full of mismatched items. Letters. Commonplace books. Drawings of dresses.

Eliza finished writing the letters and went into the trunk to find the addresses of Rebecca's cousin in Williamsburg and her brother somewhere in Manhattan. She dug in the trunk, found the letters, including one with a return address for Rebecca's cousin. She set it aside and searched for something with Rebecca's brother's address. After much searching, she found a scrap of paper and set it aside with the letter. As she placed the things back in the trunk, her hand brushed up against an oddly shaped muslin bag. She pulled it out.

The drawstring was pulled tight. She worked at opening it.

"What are you doing?" Angelica asked as she entered the room.

Eliza's heart almost leapt out of her body. "I thought you were asleep."

She sat on the floor next to Eliza. "What is this?"

"Rebecca's things. I was supposed to drop them off at the Widow Society, but a storm came, and I've not gotten to it. I wrote a letter to her cousin in Williamsburg and her brother, who lives in the city, to inform them of her death."

"Shouldn't he have known before her burial?" Angelica asked.

"Her friends said they didn't speak. Which led me to believe he'd been unkind to her. They were not in touch."

"Family!" Angelica said.

Eliza wondered if Angelica was considering their own. With them and their brothers in a legal standstill over their father's land. Eliza wanted no part of the argument. Angelica did not have need for the money, as she did. But indeed, there was a principle involved.

Eliza still worked at opening the bag.

"What is that?" Angelica asked.

"I don't know. I just discovered it in the trunk."

The bag finally opened. Eliza dumped the contents onto the floor. She studied the items. Raven feathers with a red thread tied around them. A tiny scroll of paper, wrapped in red ribbon. Dried lavender and sage, also tied together with a red thread. Two iron nails. And a deep black stone. Angelica reached for that while Eliza unwound the scroll.

"I think this is jet, what they make jewelry from. It is lovely." Angelica held it to the candle's flame, and they watched as the reflected reds, ambers, and purples gave the black stone a dark glow.

"What does any of this mean?" Eliza held up the tiny paper bearing a scribbled design, the likes of which she'd never seen.

"I'm no expert, but I'd say Rebecca believed herself cursed, and these items were for protection." Angelica placed the stone back on the floor.

"Why would she believe such a thing?" Eliza asked herself, more than Angelica.

"Maybe someone told her she was cursed."

"Did she gather these items herself? How would she even know what to gather?" Eliza wondered.

"She probably did not," Angelica said. "'I've seen old women in London and Paris selling these charms. I warrant she purchased it after being told she was cursed. Swindled."

Eliza mulled over what she had learned about Rebecca since her death. "She played cards. Hamilton told me that sometimes card players are superstitious. There are lucky items, like certain shirts or hats, that they believe will help them win. I wonder if people sell these things in the city."

"If they are being sold in London and Paris, I'm certain they are being sold here."

"I've never seen such things."

"They probably are not being sold in typical shops."

Eliza placed each item back into the bag. When she and Angelica were young women, the city was much smaller. They had explored almost every street and alley, and developed a handful of favorite, reliable shops and establishments. Now there were places like Murphy's and charm sellers somewhere in the city. There was more available than she'd ever dreamed. Sadness twirled through her body that someone like Rebecca spent her well-earned money on trinkets with no meaning.

* * *

Later, Eliza left her younger children at home with Angelica, and the rest of her family went to church with her. Trinity Church loomed against the gray morning sky, its spire disappearing into low clouds. Inside, the familiar scents of beeswax candles and aging wood wrapped around Eliza like a well-worn shawl. The church held winter at bay but just barely. Sunlight barely filtered though the frosted windows and cast a rainbow pattern across the pews, while brass footwarmers tucked beneath ladies' skirts sent up barely visible waves of heat. The pews—assigned by social rank and wealth—told their own story of New York society. Up front sat the Van Horns and their ilk, the ladies' silk ribbons and velvet cloaks a sharp contrast to the plain wool garments in the back rows filled with working women.

Eliza was delighted that her boys were home, and they sat on either side of her. The Trinity congregation noted it, she was certain. She found comfort within its walls, though it had taken a while for her to come to this place, as her husband lay in the graveyard, his life stolen from him, from them. It had been hard to return to the comfort of this church.

After the service, Eliza took each of her sons' arms as they left the hall. They stepped out into the now bright winter day. The sky was so blue it hurt her eyes to gaze at it. The sun warmed her face, even though a chilly breeze blew against it. Trinity's congregation usually milled about in the courtyard, though not many did so that day because of the cold. So Eliza and her kin made their way to the line of carriages to search for McNally.

"Mrs. General Hamilton," a voice behind her said. She turned to find Brigid, the weaver who lived with Alice.

"I'm sorry to disturb you," Brigid said.

"What is it?" Eliza's stomach turned. She feared something was wrong with Alice or the women sharing her home. "Is everybody well?"

The young woman grinned. "We've heard from Josephine. At least we think we have."

Eliza gasped. James and Alexander, who were almost in the carriage, ran to their mother. "What is it?" James asked.

"We must hurry and go with Brigid. They've received word from Josephine."

"What? The missing woman?" James said.

"Aye. It's the woman she's been staying with that we've heard from. Not Jo herself," Brigid explained. "Alice wants you to read the letter she received. She'd like your counsel."

Eliza startled. "Why?"

"She'd just feel better having your opinion."

"I'll go with you, Mother," James said.

"I'll stay with McNally and the others," Alexander said.

"Shall we take the carriage?" James asked.

"Heavens, no. We shall walk. It's not far," Eliza said. She believed one should always walk when one could. She hated all the carriage traffic in the city. As they turned to go, Eliza caught Angel's eyes, gazing out of the carriage. She would be fine, she told herself. Alexander managed Angel well. Angel had good days, such this one, where she almost seemed well. Other days, she was lost. Eliza did not like to leave her alone.

As they scurried along the river toward Pearl Street, Eliza's steps grew lighter. Jo! They'd heard from her! Josephine was alive and well!

Brigid's gait slowed outside of the courtyard. Eliza wondered why she wasn't more excited. Why did she not fly back to the house?

"I have a bad feeling," Brigid said. "I can't shake it. I know it might sound stupid to the likes of you both. But something isn't right."

"Whatever do you mean?" Eliza stopped walking. What could possibly be such a concern for Brigid when then was word about their friend? After a week of not knowing if she was dead or alive!

"You will see when you read the letter," Brigid said and continued on. Eliza and James followed.

What might be the worry? Eliza and James followed Brigid into the house and then downstairs into the kitchen, where Alice sat at a table.

"Good day," Alice said to them. "Thank you for coming." She held up a folded letter. "We've had news of Jo, as I'm sure Brigid told you. But it's odd." She unfolded the letter and slid it across the table. "I'm an old woman, not as sharp as I once was. Please look it over for me."

Eliza and James leaned over the table and read the letter:

> *We have been taking care of a young woman who fits the description of your Josephine. She was ill with yellow fever and had been quarantined. There's a farmer in Pennsylvania seeking a wife and willing to pay double your offered reward. We believe it a beneficial situation for her, given that she was in an unnatural state when we found her, and that she has no memory of you. But we will negotiate the terms. Please respond and leave your response at*

*Johnston's Apothecary, with a man named Samuel. He will get it to us.*

*With esteem,*
*X*

Eliza's mouth dropped open. "Married?" What was this? Were women all over the city being forced to marry like this?

"This is obviously a scheme to get more money from you," James said.

"If that is all they want, I will find it somewhere." Alice raised her chin.

Brigid, standing against the wall, groaned.

"What is it?" Eliza asked.

"How do we know if we give them money, they will return her to us and not send her to marry a man she doesn't know?" Brigid asked.

The conundrum silenced the room.

"Should we get the constable involved?" Eliza asked.

"Heavens, no," Alice said. "Then you can be assured we will never see her again."

"We need more time," James said. "Can we buy more time?"

Alice's head tilted in interest. "How so?"

"Write back to them and ask if you can see her. Tell them you need to see her before you give them any money," James said.

"What if we never hear back?" Brigid asked. The question hung in the air.

"The choice is to do that or send the money and risk not seeing her anyway," Eliza said.

Alice smacked her lips. "'Tis exactly as I supposed."

"Our Jo would not wish to marry a farmer in Pennsylvania!" Brigid said.

"Not our Jo as we know her, but if she was truly ill, maybe something has happened to her," Eliza said.

"How many people get over the fever in such a short time?" Alice queried. "If something has happened to her mind, it has nothing to do with that."

Eliza studied Alice. She was nearly herself again. Eliza admitted that she had been wondering if she'd ever see the old Alice again. Sharp. Witty. She was sitting straighter, and her eyes were lit with passion.

But now this. What was going on with Jo? Was it really Jo these people held? She'd hate to see another heartbreak in this house. In her own heart, as well. Should she get her hopes up? If Jo were ill, it would not be an easy road ahead.

Eliza shivered, even as she stood next to a fire. She contemplated her own Angel, who had been broken when her brother died. She had never been the same. Eliza and Hamilton had consulted with physicians and specialists, to no avail. Eliza prayed that was not the case with Jo.

* * *

"Do you have a plan?" Eliza asked while Alice finished the letter to be carried to the apothecary.

"I do."

"Mother, we really must go," James said.

"In just a moment, James." She turned to Alice. "What is your plan, and can I help?"

"My plan is to take the note to them and come straight home."

"Sounds like a good plan," James said.

"But Brigid and Mary will watch to see who the letter is delivered to," Alice said.

"I can do that," Eliza said.

"Absolutely not," said James.

Eliza frowned. He was her son, not her father.

"Your son is right." Alice stood. "Eliza Hamilton is too noticeable."

Eliza's heart sank. She couldn't argue, despite wanting to help. "Isn't there anything I can do?"

Alice walked over to her and looked her straight in the eye. "You've done so much for us. And we thank you for it. But the best thing you can do now is go home and be with your family. We can handle this."

Eliza searched her friend's face for any hint that she might budge from her position. "Very well. We will leave, under the condition that if you need us, you will send word."

"What will you do when you see who gets the letter?" James asked.

"Depends on who it is," Alice said. "We will figure out our options then."

"Let us know when you know," Eliza said and wrapped Alice in her arms.

Back in the carriage, Eliza's son brooded as they headed to Harlem where the Grange sat. Eliza was impatient with his moodiness, refusing to acknowledge it.

James sat up with a sudden movement. "Mother, I am not sure you should be involved with these women. They get into some dangerous matters."

It was true. But all of life posed danger. It just did. Didn't her son recognize that, after losing both his brother and father to duels?

"I care about your well-being. And your children need you," James continued.

"I know that!"

"I don't mean to denigrate you, but your attention being focused on these women instead of your family is perplexing. Especially since it's Advent."

Eliza did not respond. Had she been ignoring her family? Were they not safe, clothed, and well cared for? The circumstances of

Rebecca's death and Jo's disappearance were extraordinary—and something she had not planned for when she imagined a lovely Advent and Christmas with her family.

He sighed. "I worry they take advantage of your good nature."

"I've known Alice for a long time, through the Widow Society." She paused. "The women who live with her are creating a life together. It might be hard for you to imagine. You, a young man from good circumstances. But they are vulnerable in ways you cannot—nay, should not imagine. I admire them. I love them as my friends."

"They are not in your sphere."

"Who is? Do you imagine your mother to only be capable of taking tea with the likes of Mrs. Van Horn?" In truth, the move to Harlem had suited Eliza, as there were fewer and fewer opportunities and obligations to call on others. She dreaded the whole society thread of her life. Hamilton used to call her his social soldier, as she maintained her family's reputation. But she considered no such obligation anymore. "I appreciate your concern. But I am not a child and will do as I want."

James slumped back into his corner.

*Very well, then.*

* * *

"How infuriating!" Angelica said when Eliza told her the news about Jo.

"Indeed." Eliza bounced little Philip on her lap. The boy squealed with pleasure.

Angelica's eyes slanted, the way they always did when she was scheming. "They want more money. Otherwise, they'll marry her off to a stranger. Who knows if he even exists?"

Little Philip suddenly tired of his mother and ran to James as he entered the room.

"We need to do something," Angelica said.

"What? I feel like you do. I want to help. But Alice and her friends insist I don't. I'm waiting to hear who the person is. Alice will send word. Then I suppose they will figure out what to do from that point."

"They should go directly to the constabulary," James said. "These women should not be taking matters into their own hands."

Eliza and Angelica exchanged glances. Men underestimated women's capabilities. Eliza did not have the constitution to argue with her son further, as a delicious Sunday dinner was waiting for them.

"The service was lovely this morning. I'm sorry you stayed here, Angelica," Eliza changed the subject. If she allowed herself to dwell on what was probably happening right now in the city with her friends, she might scream.

"I had a wonderful time with your children, whom I don't see often enough," said Angelica.

"Is everything as well as it should be with your husband?" Eliza had meant to ask that earlier. She considered it odd that Angelica left her family in London.

Angelica shrugged. "I suppose. I hardly see the man. And my children are grown and have their own lives. As I said, I was seized with nostalgia for our Christmas celebrations when we were girls."

Angel walked into the room and sat next to Eliza on the settee. "Dinner is almost ready, Mama."

"Good. I am starving," Eliza said.

Angel was having a good day today. She seemed normal and carefree. Eliza whispered a prayer that it would continue.

# Chapter 32

Alice walked into the apothecary with the letter in her hand. She'd done harder things than this in her life and was disappointed in herself that she was so nervous. But there it was. Her knee clicked and pinged with a shot of pain as she walked toward the long counter. Behind it were shelves holding labeled jars of dried and powdered herbs and plants. Echinacea. Licorice root. Willow bark. Several mortars and pestles were lined up along with a few scales of different sizes. Alice tried to name the scents in the place. Clove? Eucalyptus? She gave up. The scents mingled too much to identify.

The apothecarist behind the counter was speaking with someone in hushed tones. Alice had never liked this apothecary, but in truth, she didn't like many of them. She'd grown her own medicinal plants and had learned how to use them. Most women did. Her old friend Lucille maintained a steady relationship with a woman herbalist close to her establishment, as was necessary. Of all places for their Rebecca's body to be found! Alice and Lucille had been acquainted with one another for many years, both relying on the mercy of the Widow Society. Even though Alice had tried to teach Lucille how to make lace and she was an apt student, Lucille had found another way. Alice had never understood her choice. And she was not completely certain that Lucille truly knew nothing about

Rebecca's death, as her body was found in the alley behind her establishment. Lucille should know more about what happened in her own alley.

A man came out from behind a curtain that divided the public space from the private. He must be the woman's husband. He approached Alice. "Can I help you?"

"I am here to deliver this letter," Alice said. "Are you Samuel?"

He nodded. "I'll be happy to forward it."

Alice bit her tongue as she handed him the letter. She wanted to tell him that whomever the note-writer was, they were up to no good with her Jo. But she supposed it was best to not cause a scene here and now. Mary and Brigid were perched outside, and they would find out who the note-writer was. Alice forced herself to smile. "Thank you. We are eager to conclude this business. Good day to you, sir."

"Good day."

Alice turned and walked away. She glimpsed the woman behind the counter, turning her head. She had a patch over her eye and an angular face.

Alice tightened her scarf around her neck and situated her hat closer to cover her ears. The wind was biting, and she had to walk several blocks back to her warm little house on Pearl Street. She dared not search for Mary and Brigid, lest she give them up.

She walked by a boy selling papers and at the other end of the street was another. Alice smelled the roasted chestnuts before she spotted the young girl selling them on the corner. She dug into her pocket and pulled out a coin. The girl could not have been over nine years old.

"I'll take a sack, young lady," Alice said and handed her the coin.

"Thank you," the girl said.

She was thin, too thin, with threadbare gloves. Alice took the chestnuts and then slipped off her gloves and handed them to the girl. "Take these. I have another pair at home."

"But—"

"'Tis no problem for me. I am almost at my warm home. I warrant you will be here until you sell all your wares. Please take my gloves."

The girl smiled, revealing nubby brown teeth. "Thank you, lady."

Alice walked off, eating her roasted chestnuts, her hands not minding the cold.

She'd go home and await word from Mary and Brigid. A slice of something like light entered her old heart as she pecked at her chestnuts. Maybe by this time tomorrow, they'd have Jo back.

# Chapter 33

The next day, Eliza received word from Alice while she was sitting beside the fire with the family. She nearly tore the note open and read:

*Dear Mrs. General Hamilton,*

*I hope this day finds you well. I regret to tell you that nobody came to receive the letter yesterday. This leads us to believe that the shop owner is the person who has Jo, or the letter was delivered in the night long after Mary and Brigid left, though it was quite late before they gave up. Another possibility we considered is that the whole thing is a ruse. Nobody has Jo at all and they just want money. We've not heard more from the note-writer.*

*Yours,*
*Alice*

Eliza harrumphed and slammed her fist on the arm of the chair.

"Mother? What is it?" James asked, looking up from his book.

She handed the note to him, and he read it over. "You must get the constabulary involved." He closed the book.

"Whatever for?" Angelica asked as she also now read over the note. "They do nothing but muck about."

"Maybe I should see Trist again. Maybe he has news." Eliza folded her hands in her lap.

"I'll go with you," Angelica said.

"I'm not fond of Mother being involved in such a concern," Alexander stood and walked over to be closer to the fire.

"Your mother is a grown and free woman and will do as she pleases," Angelica said. "While it is charming that you care so much for her, you need to leave her be."

"These are dangerous people. If it's true that they have Jo, then they have kidnapped her. What kind of person does that?" Alexander said.

"Not a person that I want my mother or aunt to associate with," James said.

As her sons postured, Eliza's mind was busy at work. What did she know about the Johnstons, the family who owned the pharmacy? While she wracked her brain, Angelica and her boys quibbled.

"Right, Eliza?" Angelica poked her with her elbow.

"I'm sorry. I wasn't listening." Her younger children were happily busy with games and books, while their older brothers scrutinized her.

"What I said is that these women are your friends. What has happened to them is no fault of their own. If they are in danger, we must act quickly."

"It's Jo who is in danger," Eliza said. "The more I consider it, I fear she did not have yellow fever, as Alice suggested. It would've been the quickest recovery I've ever heard of."

"Besides, I read that it's no longer a problem in the city," James said.

"There are sporadic cases. It's certainly not as bad as it was this summer," Eliza replied.

"So, the question is, what are they up to? Did they just grab her off the streets, deciding to get money somehow from her or her relatives?" James asked.

"No. They didn't reach out until a reward was posted. They did not know that would happen. Even I was shocked," Eliza said.

"Mama, I want to go outside and play." William stood from the floor where he'd been playing.

"It's freezing. You may not go outside," Eliza said. "But you may go upstairs to your room. All of you."

After the younger children and Angel left the room, Angelica spoke. "They were going to sell her to a farmer in Pennsylvania. That's what they planned to do. A marriage brokerage of the worst kind."

"Hard to fathom," James said. "That they'd pick up a woman off the streets—"

"Wait. They probably weren't aware she was a woman. She was dressed as a man," Eliza said as she grabbed her napkin and twisted it.

Silence rippled across the table.

"She was searching for Rebecca, who was also dressed as a man and who ended up in the grave," Eliza said.

"Sound to me like someone doesn't like women who dress as men," Angelica said. "And that brings us back to the WMA."

"What is that?" James asked.

"The Women's Morality Alliance. They've been running advertisements in the newspaper," Eliza explained.

"What kind of advertisements?" James asked.

Eliza stood, brought the newspaper to the table and flipped to the back page. "There."

James read and then said, "Just a group of busybodies."

"Who made them in charge of what women wear, how they act, who they love?" Angelica said.

"They released a statement about Rebecca, which was unpleasant at best. They are more than busybodies," said Eliza.

"Who is in charge of this group?" Alexander smirked. "I shall have a word with them."

"A woman named Lucretia Short. But we've yet to find her. We tried to pay her a visit, but she didn't answer the door. The herbalist said she was sick."

"Look at this advertisement." Angelica pointed to the paper and read, "'Need a wife? We have plenty of good, upstanding women, ready to marry. Please contact us.'"

"That is the same advertising box number as the WMA," Eliza said, peering over Angelica's shoulder.

"We must make haste." Angelica stood.

"Wait. Let's stop and consider this," James said. "I agree that you should go to Trist with the information you have, Mother. But I don't think you'll get anywhere with the WMA."

Eliza glanced around the room and tried to gather herself. Her eyes landed on the silver wine holder that President George Washington had given her late husband. It was the most valuable thing in the house. She was determined not to sell it, as it was such a thoughtful gift from a man she and Hamilton both loved. Oh, how she wished Hamilton were there! What would he do in these circumstances?

"I agree," Alexander said. "A bunch of busybodies who consider themselves the arbiters of women's morality. It's quite ironic, but I doubt they'd respond to the women sitting across the table from me."

"It matters not to me whether they wish to see me," Angelica said. "If I wish to see them, I will."

A woman who was certain of her place in this world, Angelica rarely took no for an answer. Even when they were girls, Angelica had an air of confidence. Eliza learned much from her older sister, though she could not say she had always agreed with her forward nature.

"What if James and I were to go?" Alexander said. "Let us go into the city. You two go to the constabulary and check in on Alice. And we will go in search of a wife."

James laughed his father's laugh. So much alike. He resembled Alexander at that age. "Brilliant, brother."

Eliza wasn't so sure. "You are Hamiltons. Will they believe you are looking for wives? That you need a brokerage?"

Alexander grimaced. "We can try."

"Agreed. That's all we can do," said James.

Her boys, now young men, were involved in this treachery. And how could she stop them when she herself was in so deep?

"Mother, you'll kill that napkin." James held out his hand. "Please give it to me."

She handed it to him and then glanced at Angelica, who was grinning. It was always the case, even when children, that Eliza took her anxiety out on napkins, tablecloths, and pillowcases.

"This matter will be resolved." James said reached for his mother's hand. "You have my word."

# CHAPTER 34

When McNally returned from dropping off John, William, and little Eliza at school, the rest of the family spilled into the carriage, leaving little Philip behind with Mrs. Cole, who loved keeping him. Children often missed school because of the weather, but today, despite the cold, they'd attend. They'd then soon be off for the Christmas holiday.

It was difficult for Eliza to contemplate Advent and Christmas with Rebecca's death and Jo's strange disappearance. But she needed to plan them, wanting her children to experience a joyful holiday. The Christmas menu and decorations needed to be done. The children loved helping with that. Or, at least, they always had before. And she expected they would not be celebrating Christmas at the Grange next year. She had to sell the house for which she and Hamilton had worked so hard. There were no two ways about it.

Angelica sighed. "It's such a long journey. If it wasn't important, I'd suggest we all stay home and play backgammon."

"Not at all, Aunt. Not if Mother's involved." Alexander Jr. grinned. "Either she's the best cheater in the world or a brilliant player. I can't decide."

"Alexander! Your mother is no cheater!" Angelica quipped and playfully swatted at him.

"Not all of us had Benjamin Franklin as a teacher of the game," he said.

"I don't know where I was when all of that was going on," Angelica said. "I remember him being at our home, but I didn't have the least bit of interest in playing backgammon."

Eliza warmed, recalling the summer Mr. Franklin had stayed with them. Angelica had been more interested in attending parties and picnics. Eliza tired of them and sought refuge with Mr. Franklin, who also tired of parties and picnics from time to time. He likely hadn't been well then. But, as a girl, she believed he'd stayed behind at the house just for her.

"Let's discuss the plan," Alexander said.

"We already know it, brother," James said. "You are not a drill master here."

"Still," Alexander said. "You and I are going in search of wives. Mother and Aunt Angelica are going to the constabulary, and then we shall all meet at Alice's home."

James rolled his eyes and turned his head to peer out the small window. "We're almost there. Shall we go over the plan yet again?" he said in a mocking tone.

Eliza waved her sons off.

"This winter cold is serious business. I'm glad we're packed in here," Angelica said.

The carriage came to a quick stop. McNally dismounted, and the carriage sighed. He opened the door. McNally was red from the crisp air. Eliza reckoned she'd knit him another scarf. One would not be enough for this cold winter. "Sorry for the abrupt stop. I just realized we are at the constabulary."

Eliza exited the carriage and Angelica followed.

"Where to?" McNally asked James and Alexander after the women had departed.

"We are going to the newspaper offices, then to whatever address they give us," Alexander said as Eliza and Angelica slipped through the doors of the constabulary.

* * *

The constabulary's office bore little resemblance to the ordered institutions Hamilton had envisioned for their new nation. Papers spilled across scarred wooden desks, while constables in various states of dishevelment wandered in and out, some still wearing last night's rum on their breath.

Once again, the scent of the constabulary assaulted Eliza. She covered her nose by repositioning her wool scarf. She stole a glance at Angelica, who had bemusement on her face as the constables all stood when they recognized them.

One constable approached them. "How can we help you?"

"We want to see Sergeant Trist," Eliza said.

"Ah, he's just back. Please follow me."

"No need," Angelica said. "Mrs. General Hamilton knows the way. Thank you."

The man appeared startled, but he stepped aside. The sisters found their way to the back office, and Eliza knocked on the door.

"Come in," Sergeant Trist yelled.

Trist stood upon seeing both Schuyler sisters, now grown women with husbands and children, enter his office. Trist's desk, at least, showed some attempt at organization. A carefully maintained ledger recorded deaths deemed worthy of investigation—a dismally thin volume that spoke much about which lives the city valued. The weapons confiscated from street criminals hung on the wall like grim trophies, while a notice board held sketches of wanted criminals, some so water-damaged their features had blurred into anonymity.

"Mrs. General Hamilton, Mrs. Church, please take a seat," Trist said. After they were seated, he sat down behind his desk. It dwarfed him. "I take it you're here about your missing friend." He leaned forward. "We've no word."

"But we've had word," Eliza said, working her gloves off her hands, finger by finger.

His mouth fell open. "What? What have you heard?"

Eliza told him everything they'd recently learned.

"What do you think?" Angelica said when Eliza was done. "Can you help us now?"

"With everything you've told me . . . I need to sit with this information. It presents an interesting dilemma. Oh dear, I wish Mrs. Rhodes would've come to us immediately on hearing from the kidnapper."

"Kidnapper?" Angelica said. "Is that what you imagine?"

He drew in air and let it out slowly. "If they cared about getting her back to her family, there'd be no halting of communication. They want more money."

"Or they will send her off to marry a bloody Pennsylvania farmer," Angelica said. "What nonsense."

Trist opened his mouth and closed it, as if he thought better of what he had wanted to say. Then he cleared his throat. "There have been cases where young women were 'sold' into marriage, of course. It's not unheard of."

"This is 1805, sir. Not 1705. I surmise it is highly unusual," Angelica said, even though she and Eliza both had been to Murphy's and seen otherwise. Of course the sisters had to keep that to themselves.

He shook his head. "I wish I could say it's true. These are adults wanting to better their lives. Or in this case, a group of people who imagine they are helping women who have no other options."

Eliza's heart sank. She had known many such women as a volunteer at the Widow Society. In truth, she heard whispers of women seeking marriage through the newspaper or an agency. But she never learned about specifics. "But this young woman has options. She is a skilled craftswoman involved in a thriving concern. I do not believe she wishes to marry. Can they force her?"

"If she doesn't wish to marry, then why doesn't she just go home?" he asked.

"They are holding her against her will, of course," Angelica said.

"Can you be certain? It's been, what? Ten days?"

"She went looking for Rebecca—and we know what happened to Rebecca," Angelica said. "Perhaps Jo is dead too, and once these people learned about the reward . . ."

"Precisely why I'd have suggested not doing such a thing," said the sergeant.

It was exactly what the newspaper editor had said to Eliza. It was the wrong move to make. "Fine," Eliza said. "So Alice made a mistake, but now we are here, seeking your advice."

He nodded. "With everything you've told me, I'm telling you to leave this matter in my hands. Some of these people, who may be involved or not, are dangerous. You have my word, ladies. I will do my best to track her down and bring her home."

Alice had said Trist did not care, that he would do nothing. Eliza wasn't sure she believed him. "Has there been any word on who killed Rebecca Dickens?" Eliza asked.

"I'm sorry. Nothing yet."

"Please keep us informed," Angelica said.

"I'll do my best. Did you tell me it was Johnston's Apothecary they dropped the letter off at?"

"Yes. Why?" Eliza asked as she slipped her gloves back on.

"Just making sure I understand everything. My wife swears by their headache elixir. I'll stop in there later today."

Maybe he did care. Maybe Alice was wrong. That didn't happen often, though.

# Chapter 35

Eliza and Angelica made their way to Alice's home. Alexander and James were already there, along with René and Alice, sitting on the settee.

"So now that we are all here, let's compare observations," Alice said and smacked her lips. She eyed Eliza. "You went to speak with Trist?"

Eliza slipped off her cloak and hung it on a hook. "Yes. I know you don't like him, but we need him to investigate this matter."

Alice grunted. "It's not just him I don't like. The constables only pay attention when you give them money."

James coughed. "That's absurd!"

"It is not," Alexander said. "I've heard talk at school. The system is corrupt."

"Whatever your take on them is, Trist said he will investigate, and I plan to hold him to it," Angelica said as she sat down next to Alexander Jr.

"What did you find out?" Eliza asked her sons.

"The WMA is helping men to find chaste and wholesome brides. It's part of their vision. They think all women should be married and having children," James said.

"It's against God's will if they remain single and childless," Alexander added.

"That's not surprising," Alice said.

"But they did not want to work with the Hamilton boys," Alexander said and straightened his collar.

"What? Why not?" Eliza said.

"They only work with men in desperate need of wives, apparently," James chimed in. "And we obviously are not."

"Did you meet Lucretia? We have not been able to track her down," Eliza said.

Alexander and James glanced at one another. "Yes, and she's a dour, plump thing. Hard to believe she's a threat to anybody," said James.

"Well, certainly not to you," Angelica stated. "But to a young woman? Her ideas are poisonous. Did you raise suspicions?"

"I don't think so. We handled ourselves well," James said.

"Do you think she has our Jo?" Alice asked.

"The girl who brought tea slipped me a note," James said. "On it was the name 'Ramsay.'"

"What?" Eliza exclaimed. "Is it some kind of treachery?"

"Ramsay may have Jo. He may be the marriage broker. The girl was making eyes at him." Alexander nodded to his brother. "She was quite interested in my dear brother and listened in on the conversation, I'm sure."

"It's highly unusual for a woman in her position to take such a risk. What was she up to?" Alice asked.

"We don't know. But we have the Ramsay name. He owns Murphy's and if they have Jo and are trying to sell her into marriage, we're uncertain what we can do."

"Do you have the girl's name?" Angelica asked. "We need to speak to her."

"Aye," Alice said. "But that might bring great danger to her. She's already risked plenty."

"We don't have her name in any case," Alexander said. "I'm not even certain I'd recognize her again."

"So what do we do next? All we have is half-answers. Nothing to really chew on to save Jo," Eliza said.

The room went silent.

"I have a friend who works in the Ramsay house," René spoke up. "I will make inquiries."

"But should we go to the constables?" Eliza asked. "This seems like a matter for them."

"Not yet. If Ramsay gets wind of it and they have Jo, they might kill her," Alice said.

"Or worse—send her to Pennsylvania." René shuddered.

Eliza's tumbling reflections moved from the WMA to Ramsay to the constabulary. Was he paying the constables to ignore the happenings at Murphy's so it could thrive as a seedy establishment? She didn't want her sons to figure out she'd visited the place. She highly suspected Murphy's was a part of brokering marriages in the city. "We need to do something. We can't just sit here with all this. None of it is quite making sense. Not knowing who is paying whom off to look the other way. And in the meantime, Jo is still missing. We've had no further word from the person who has her."

The room silenced again.

"I will find out from my friend what is happening at Ramsay's home. She will know if Jo is there." René stood and walked toward the door. She slipped on her cloak and pulled a hat on over her hair. "Today is her day off. I know where to find her."

"Be careful," Alice called after her. She turned back to Eliza and her family. "Thank you all so much for helping us figure this out."

"Can you please start the story from the beginning so we might understand better?" James asked.

Alice repeated the tale to her eager audience. The Hamilton men were not amused.

# Chapter 36

That Ramsay was aware of where Alice lived worried Eliza as she left the house on Pearl Street. She hoped that McNally had frightened him enough that he wouldn't return.

"Will you be all right?" Eliza asked Alice as they were leaving.

"As all right as I ever am," she replied. "I have deliveries to make in the morning. After that, I shall rest for the day. Maybe we will have word tomorrow."

"I hope so," Eliza said.

The foursome gathered in the carriage for the two-hour journey back to the Grange. Snow was starting to flit about in the air.

"I hope that René can find out something from her friend who works at the Ramsay house," Eliza said.

"That would be the best of all worlds. Why mess about with the constable or WMA, when we can go straight to the source?" Angelica crossed her arms, trying to keep warm.

"I warrant if Ramsay has her, then we should go to the constable," James said. "It's not safe for any of us to approach the situation."

"But—" Eliza began.

"Mother, we absolutely can't have you involved in such a dangerous situation. Can't you see that?" James said.

Angelica harrumphed and gazed toward the curtained window.

Eliza knew her sons were just being sons. But they had no idea what she was capable of. They were unaware of her escape from death after she had been kidnapped off the streets of the city. And she considered it best to never tell them. And yet there it was on her tongue, but she held back. Perhaps she might tell them someday, but not now.

Angelica knew all, of course. She was her closest sister, her confidante. And Angelica was a force to be reckoned with.

"I understand. But you realize that I care for these women. They are friends. I want to help them." Eliza pulled her scarf tighter around her neck.

"I understand, Mother. You have such a big heart. Father did too. It's impossible for you to turn your back on those in need," James said. "But the orphaned children you cared for posed no threat. This does."

"On so many levels," Alexander said. "Ramsay is a dangerous man. He has no scruples. I want you as far away from him as possible."

"I have no intention of going anywhere near him. Rest assured."

"Do you presume your mother daft?" Angelica whipped her head around to glare at them.

"Of course not. We are her sons and worry about her safety. Yours too," James said.

"You are not women who frequent card houses and other places when men gather. You are genteel," Alexander said. "And so are ill-equipped to handle men like Ramsay,"

Eliza and Angelica scrutinized one another and laughed. "Genteel" was not a word they used to describe themselves, even as girls. Eliza disregarded society. She'd much rather be outdoors in the fields and forests, with her native friends, who also liked to explore, to track, to run. This was something Hamilton appreciated about her. They both disdained the workings of society, though they had learned to use them for the benefit of his career.

Her sons just rolled their eyes, and to Eliza's amazement, they sat quietly for the rest of the journey.

Back at the Grange, the four of them gathered around the fireplace. The fire was crackling and hot. Shapes danced in the flames—an owl, a heart, a snake. Eliza and Hamilton used to call out the shapes they found in them, back when they had time to do so. But once the children came, Eliza would often fall asleep while they were watching. Many times, it was with a babe at her breast. He had wanted children—and she was only too happy to give them to him. Being a mother was both her life's joy and sorrow. She'd never get over Philip's death. She didn't believe any mother could get over the death of a child. You just learned to live with it—and take comfort in knowing that with God's grace you would be joined in heaven.

She watched Philip's brothers, who were now older than he had been when he was struck down in a duel, and said a prayer to herself for their health and safety. She had two fully grown sons who were home and visiting for the holiday. The holiday, however, was the furthest thing from her mind. She pondered Rebecca and Jo, distracted by their circumstances.

Angel played the pianoforte, its notes striking chords in Eliza's heart, mind, and spirit. Waves of gratitude swept through her. This was her family. Here and now. Anything could change at any minute. Eliza wished life could stop so she could savor each of these moments, but it marched on, sweeping her along.

Eliza moved away from the fire and sat on the settee. Little Eliza sat next to her. The boys played a game. Little Philip, now almost four, was attached to his brother John most days. And John loved playing with him. The undecorated Christmas tree sat between the two windows in the room. Its pine scent filled the air.

Jo was out there with God knows who! And could be killed or sent off to a place where they would never see her again. How was she going to bear it? How was Alice bearing it? A knot formed between Eliza's rib cage and spine. Then again, maybe the person who wrote to Alice had no real knowledge of Jo. But that was naught to hope for. That would mean there was no thread of possibility.

"I can't stand it!" Angelica said. "There should be something we can do."

"Nothing." Eliza tapped her fingers on a nearby table. "We wait. Just like Alice and the others. We've done all we can do." Or had they? Eliza's attention turned to Rebecca's trunk. "There is the trunk. It belonged to Rebecca. I was supposed to take it to the Widow Society, but we didn't make it because of the snow."

"And?" Angelica said.

"Maybe if we go through it together, it will yield a clue to Rebecca's life that we can hold on to while we search for Jo. Perhaps there's something I missed."

"Excellent idea. What have you learned so far, Mother?" James said.

"She had a brother, whom she disassociated from. She had a cousin in Williamsburg who wanted her to live with her family, but she didn't have money to send to purchase the fare. She had several popular books, so Rebecca must've loved to read . . . and there was an odd bundle of things—"

"Witchery," Angelica said. "They were tokens of protection. That surprised me."

"Witchery?" James asked.

"We reckon she guessed someone put a spell on her or that she was in danger," Angelica explained.

A chill ran through Eliza's body.

James frowned. "If only she'd gone to the right people to help her and not some strange cunning woman on the street."

"Indeed," Eliza said. "She also had a lovely commonplace book. With clippings of dresses pasted, along with drawings, which I assume were hers."

"She was a dressmaker?" James asked.

Eliza nodded.

"They know all the ladies' secrets, don't they?" James asked.

Angelica laughed. "They know many of them."

James smacked his knees. "Let's see what's in the trunk and what sense we can make of it."

Just then Mrs. Cole entered the room. "Dinner is ready."

"Thank you," Eliza said. "It looks like the trunk will have to wait."

⋆ ⋆ ⋆

After a dinner of baked oysters and potatoes, the younger Hamilton children continued with their games and Angel went back to the pianoforte, as Angelica, Eliza, James, and Alexander gathered around the trunk, sorting letters, books, clothing, and trinkets.

"Is this what you were talking about?" James held up the bundle tied with red string.

Eliza nodded.

"Such nonsense." He set it aside.

"He's right. We should just throw it away. It won't do the ladies at the Widow Society any good," Alexander said.

Eliza appreciated the sense in that. "It obviously meant something to her, but she is gone." Her stomach knotted.

"Who's saying that it's nonsense?" Angelica took the bundle. "If she believed it helped her, then maybe it did. The mind is a powerful thing. European women fashion these things. Quite a market for it. I don't know where to find one of these here."

"I'd start at the apothecaries," James said. "Sometimes the women there know of such things."

Eliza's eyes went to her sister. Had they missed something? Were one of the women at the apothecary involved in Jo's disappearance? Eliza immediately considered Johnston's Apothecary, as that was the place Alice had taken the letter. Many apothecaries served as places where letters were delivered; that was not unusual. But nobody had come.

"Could it be the reason nobody showed up at the apothecary was that they are the people who are holding Jo?" Eliza said.

"I thought the same thing, just now," Angelica said.

"Highly unlikely. As business owners in the community, why risk everything to get involved in an underground wife market and a kidnapping?" James said.

"More likely Rebecca bought this from one of them. Let's find out why. That might lead us to finding Jo," Alexander said.

"And Rebecca's killer," James said.

"Are they one and the same?" Angelica asked.

"They must be." Eliza opened the commonplace book and paged through it. The scent of thick paper and ink wafted out. "If Rebecca needed help, whoever helped her knows more about her than we do."

"And somehow she gets killed," Angelica said. "From the same trouble."

"And her friend Josephine goes in search of her," James said.

"And finds out too much?" Eliza said. "I'm not sure this line of narrative makes sense to me. We think Jo is still alive. If what you're saying is the case, then Jo would be dead. Why would they allow her to live?"

"Because she is pretty and young and can make them money," Angelica said.

There it was. But Eliza's mind flipped and flopped. Did it make enough sense to accuse someone? And whom would they accuse?

"What is this?" James said, holding up one of the books. "The pages are wavy or something." He pulled them apart. His mouth fell open. "It's birth papers."

"What? Whose?"

"Rebecca Dickens was a mother," he said.

Eliza's heart sped. "What?"

"By my calculations, the child should be about twelve years of age," James said.

"Rebecca was quite young when she was killed. She must have been not more than a child when she gave birth. Who was the father?" Eliza pressed.

"None is listed. It says he's deceased," James said. That was the way with illegitimate births; fathers would often be listed as deceased.

Eliza's head swirled into lightheadedness. A child! Rebecca had a child. She must have given him up to a family. Had the women at Pearl Street House kept this from her? Or were they as ignorant as she about this matter?

"Best to let sleeping dogs lie there," Alexander said. "If we want to find Jo and save her, let's not get distracted by other mysteries."

"Agreed," Angelica said. "She clearly wanted to keep the child secret. It's unrelated to Jo."

But a knot formed in the pit of Eliza's stomach. Was it intuition? Fear? Concern for the child?

"Let's hope the child is in a happy household," James said.

This was too much for Eliza to ponder. She and Hamilton had taken in so many children over the years. It was hard to imagine giving one up. But she had seen it in her work at the Widow Society—young women who had been taken advantage of, having their babies and giving them to another family to raise as their own. A selfless act.

Oh, Rebecca! A stinging hot tear formed in Eliza's eye, trailing down her face. James handed her a handkerchief.

"That's enough for tonight. Time for a good night's sleep," he said.

But after the boys went to bed, Eliza and Angelica penned a letter to Rebecca's cousin in Williamsburg, Virginia. She might be the only person who could tell them Rebecca's real story and what had happened to the child.

# Chapter 37

Eliza had disjointed and fitful dreams. More images than dreams. Vile notes. Newspapers. Charms. Ramsay.

She hadn't found time to ask Alice and René about the notes. They were aware of Rebecca's brother. The cousin, maybe not. They most certainly were unaware of Rebecca's baby. The child would be around twelve years old. Who would she have given the baby to? Eliza doubted Rebecca would have given him to a family member. She was probably filled with too much shame to tell anybody in her family that she was with child. Eliza understood little about adoption, as Hamilton had attended to such matters when they adopted Fanny. Fanny was the daughter of a Revolutionary War colonel who was a friend of Hamilton. They were friends of the Antill family and had been named godparents to several of their children. So, when Colonel Antill's wife died, and he became undone, Eliza and Hamilton took Fanny in and raised her as if she were their own. Eliza sighed, as it had been quite some time since she'd seen Fanny.

Eliza rose from her bed, her sister barely stirring, and lit a candle. She opened the door quietly and walked down to Hamilton's library. His leather chair still held the impression of his form, a ghost shape Eliza avoided disturbing. Eliza sensed his presence strongest here, among the bookshelves and scattered papers, where even the dust dancing in the morning light seemed to carry the echoes of his voice. She imagined him here now, strategizing, theorizing, that brilliant mind working through each puzzle piece. But this mystery was hers to solve—with no guidance from him.

Eliza found a sheet of paper and wrote a list of her ideas about finding Jo. Time pressed on her, as it did for everyone. Though clearheaded in the morning, she forgot things later in the day. As she wrote, the sun rose higher in the orange sky. Sounds of movement upstairs alerted her that her children would be downstairs at any moment. She continued writing, stopping only to gaze over the horizon as a fog settled in the hills and valley between the Grange and river.

"Mama. You know Father doesn't want you in here." Angel stood in the doorway.

"Your father is dead, dear Angel. He has no cares anymore." Even as she said it, a swath of disbelief moved through her. He'd been dead for over a year and she'd been at his bedside when he passed. Yet a measure of her believed that he might somehow still be alive. Somewhere. That it all had been a nightmare.

"No, Mother, I'm sure I visited with him last night. He said not to go into his office. He said for you to leave well enough alone."

Eliza's breath caught. If she believed in ghosts, she might take her troubled daughter seriously. But she did not. "Angel, your father did not visit you last night. He died last year, remember?"

Angel ran to her mother and fell into her, wrapping her arms around her. "I know, Mama. But he's still here!" she cried.

Was Angel's mind getting worse? Eliza fretted. It seemed as if one moment she was sound and reasonable. The next, she was a child again. What would Eliza do if her daughter became pregnant without a husband? She shuddered at the idea that someone would take advantage of Angel's addled state. She kept Angel close, never allowing her to go out without a chaperone. Still, men had been known to find a way.

"Angel, let's see what Mrs. Cole has fixed for breakfast this morning." Eliza stood.

"I'm not hungry." Angel said.

Eliza held her daughter by the hand and pulled her toward her. "Well, let's sit down to eat with the family in any case."

* * *

After breakfast, while the family gathered around the fireplace in the main room, Mrs. Cole brought Eliza a note. "The messenger was just here," she said.

Eliza opened and read the note from Alice:

*We've been watching the Ramsay household. René has a friend who works there. He'll be out of town tomorrow. We are planning to search the house for Jo this afternoon.*

Alice and the others planned on entering Ramsay's house without his knowledge. It was ill advised to enter someone's home, even to search for someone. The constable should be the person who took these matters in hand. Alice and the others should understand that! If they got caught, they'd be imprisoned. She read over the note again.

"What is it?" Angelica asked.

Eliza handed her the note. As she read it, Angelica laughed. "They are incorrigible."

"They are going to get into trouble if they're not careful."

"I'm sure they will be, and they have a friend inside of the house. It will be fine, Eliza."

"What if it's some kind of treachery? Someone luring them in?"

Angelica's smile turned downward. "I hadn't considered that."

Eliza stood. "Mrs. Cole, can you tell McNally to ready the horse and carriage?"

"What are you doing, Mother?" Alexander Jr. queried.

"She's going to stop her friends from doing something foolish, if we can get there in time," Angelica replied. "I'll go with her."

"Boys, please keep the children today. There's no school now until after the new year," Eliza said.

"One of us should go with you," James said.

"That's unnecessary," Eliza responded.

She slipped into the library and picked up her notes and the vile letters that were amongst Rebecca's things. She shoved them into her reticule. It was time to confront Alice and her companions. She must tell them about Rebecca's child. Someone in that house had to know more about Rebecca than just her talent with lace and dresses. There was much more to the woman than met the eye. It was hard to believe she had not mentioned any of her past to them, in moments of closeness and camaraderie.

Eliza and Angelica swiftly prepared for the cold journey into the city.

"They don't trust the system," Angelica said after they were in the carriage. It was as if she'd read Eliza's mind.

"Who can blame them?"

# Chapter 38

Alice waited for René to ready herself. While she waited, she picked up needles to work out a lace pattern she'd been envisioning. Loop through there, up through the loop.

Would she have Jo back today?

René's friend did not give them cause to expect Jo was in Ramsay's house. But she did say there were rooms in the house he forbid the servants to enter. He must be hiding something. And maybe, just maybe, it was Jo. He was out of town and would be back tomorrow. So they must hasten.

What was taking René so long?

Alice kept her fingers busy and tried to focus on the new pattern. But she couldn't find peace, neither in her mind nor her actions. Should she hope to find Jo there in Ramsay's fine house tied to a bed ?

It was better not to hope. She'd learned that repeatedly. But, at the same time, one must strive. One must survive and help others along the way too. Where was that wisdom that came with age? She was exasperated with her disjointed rumination. Better to focus on the task at hand.

In, out, loop. In, out, loop.

She tried to not look at the letter from Lucille again. It sat there with her words spread across the paper: *You must know I'd never harm one of yours. I recognize it looks suspicious. You have my word I know you well, old friend. It will take you some time, but eventually, you'll see.*

The audacity! Lucille didn't know her anymore. It had been more than a few years and presumptuous of her to assume Alice had not changed. How did Alice know that Rebecca's death was not caused by one of Lucille's vulgar guests? Lucille should be figuring that out and dealing with it herself!

Alice held up what she'd been working on. It stretched out in a tangled mess. She cast it aside. She should know better than to try something so intricate when she could not focus. Alice could not imagine their Jo being married to anybody, let alone a farmer. Jo loved the city, loved her freedom to move about dressed as a man. She rarely went out dressed as a woman; it was too prohibitive, she said, and she much preferred the comfort of men's clothes.

Perhaps Alice should try it someday. As she mulled it over, she reconsidered. She imagined pants would not give her any more comfort than her skirts. She recalled the day Eliza first wore pants. The way Jo taught her to walk in them. Alice chuckled.

"What's so funny?" René said as she entered the room.

"Just remembering the day we dressed Eliza as a man."

René cracked a smile. "Not something I will ever forget." René lifted the lace Alice had been working on. "What's this?"

"It's a mess is what it is. I can't focus."

"'Tis no wonder," René said. "With so much going on."

Alice grunted. "And now we prepare for . . . what? To search a man's home without his permission on the off chance that Jo is inside?"

"Well, it's something. We know Rebecca owed him money. Maybe he snatched Jo off the streets, supposing he'd get the money owed to him by selling her into marriage."

It held a certain logic, but one full of too many ifs and imaginings. Alice's hopes were dashed.

"And Rose did say that thing about the rooms they are not allowed in. We need to search those rooms. Maybe Jo is there."

Alice took in René's hopeful stance. "Maybe."

"Are you ready?" René asked.

"As ever I will be." Alice stood and walked to the door to pile on her winter things.

A sharp rapping came at the door. Alice opened it to find Angelica and Eliza.

From the expressions on their faces, she was unsure if she should invite them inside. But of course she did.

# Chapter 39

Eliza held up the letter she'd received from Alice. "You can't do this."

Alice narrowed her eyes. "Do what?"

"Go into Ramsay's house without his permission," she said. "You could get into so much trouble."

Alice continued putting on her hat and scarf. "Who's going to know? He's out of town and the servants are sneaking us in."

"What if he comes back?" Eliza asked.

Alice searched Eliza's face. "What if?"

"He could have you arrested," Angelica said flatly.

"Well, now. I supposed he could, but I doubt he's a man who wants to get the law involved in any aspect of his life."

Angelica glanced at Eliza. "She has a point."

Eliza frowned.

"We have one opportunity. Let's not waste it bickering," René snapped. "We must go.'

A rush of shame and worry moved through Eliza as her heart raced.

"We'll come with you," Angelica said.

Eliza hadn't considered it, but they could help keep Alice and René safe. "What is the plan?"

"The plan is to search his home floor by floor, room by room. We are scanning for any clues to her whereabouts," Alice said.

"We could use your help. The more, the better. We can get in and out quicker. It makes us all nervous. But my friend is certain he is not to return until tomorrow," René explained.

Eliza couldn't believe she was following Alice and René out the door into the freezing air. She'd come here to talk them out of this plan and now she was going to be a part of it.

Stopping on the walkway, Alice peered at Eliza. "Time is crucial. He may have Jo somewhere in his home. To me, it's worth the risk."

"Can't your friend simply search the house herself?" Eliza asked René as she struggled to keep up with them.

"She has. And she sees nothing out of the ordinary. But we may spot something she wouldn't know to look for," René said.

The women continued to walk, passing a boy selling papers, a girl selling chestnuts, a woman selling wreaths. Past Trinity Church, where Eliza's husband lay in his grave. An alley led them to the back of a home. René sped her gait, then stopped and knocked on the door.

Eliza's breath was measured.

"We are not breaking in. We are being let in," Angelica reminded her.

"There's not much difference," Eliza said.

A woman in a maid's uniform opened the door. "Quick," she said. "Get inside." She was a tiny wisp of a woman, with strands of gray hair flying out from beneath her cap.

"Thank you so much for allowing us to do this, Rose," René said.

Rose sized them up quickly. "I suggest two of each take a floor and meet back here when you are finished. Be quick about it."

They were in a storeroom on the bottom floor of the townhouse. They followed her through the kitchen, where a cook stood in front of a hearth, tending a fire. She barely regarded them.

Eliza shivered. She was not happy they were here. The group snaked through a hallway and went upstairs. Dim and slightly dusty, the rooms on the main floor of the house appeared as if a bachelor lived there. The furnishings did not match, and one chair had a tear in it. There were no paintings or decorations on the walls. Eliza hoped that they found Jo today but shuddered at the idea of her being here.

"Alice and I will search this floor," René said.

"It's expansive, as he bought the neighbor's and made two houses one," Rose said.

Eliza and Angelica headed to the stars. "I guess that leaves us the second floor." Angelica said as she grabbed Eliza's hand.

The stairs wound upward until they reached the second floor, which had four bedrooms.

"There's not much here. I suppose we look under the beds, and in the wardrobes and trunks," Eliza said.

"Let's search for any items out of place. For example, a hair ribbon. Because a bachelor has no need for one," Angelica said.

"Clever," Eliza said. "I'll take these two rooms."

The sisters separated, and Eliza opened the door to a room with two trunks and nothing else in it. That alone was odd. Even the fireplace had no logs in it. The room smelled as if it hadn't been lived in. She searched behind the curtains and investigated every inch of the almost empty room and trunks. Nothing suspicious anywhere. Even though she observed nothing leading her to believe that Jo might be in this house, the two empty trunks unnerved her. It was the way they seemed to be just left in the middle of the floor with the lids open. Why was there nothing in the trunks? Why hadn't Ramsay pushed them to the wall, arranged them nicely in some manner?

Eliza moved from one room to the next. She listened for Angelica, but her sister was tiptoeing through the other rooms. The next room contained a bed and an enormous wardrobe. The bed was nicely made, with a fine blue spread. Eliza pulled back the cover to reveal clean sheets. She crouched, peering under the bed. There was something there. She strained her arm out to grab it and pull it to her.

It was a locket. Eliza strained to recollect—did Jo wear such a thing? Alice would know. She lifted herself from the floor and rushed to the door, but stopped dead in her tracks when she heard a voice. A male voice.

Ramsay was back, and he was heading for the room! Eliza scanned the room for a place she could hide and her eyes landed on the wardrobe.

# Chapter 40

What had she done? How was Eliza going to get out of the wardrobe with nobody discovering her? The thick air in the cramped wardrobe threatened to suffocate, even as she tried to control her panicked breaths. The scent of stale clothing clung to her, mingling with the acrid tang of fear that coated her tongue. Sweat dripped down her back, tracing cool paths along her spine as her heart pounded against her rib cage like a trapped bird. The pulse in her neck throbbed against the collar of her widow's weeds.

Through a crack in the door, Eliza watched Ramsay's shadow move across the room, his expensive boots creaking on the floorboards. The taste of fear was metallic in her mouth, sharper than any she'd known since her own abduction. This time, her children might truly become orphans. She pressed herself further into the shadows, willing herself to become one with the darkness, but the stifling confines of the wardrobe offered no refuge.

Ramsay's voice echoed through the room, a low rumble that sent shivers along Eliza's spine. She strained to make out the words. The muffled sound of laughter cut through the silence like a knife. She needed to escape before Ramsay discovered her hiding place. But how? She was trapped.

Tears pricked at the corners of her eyes as she fought to hold back a sob. Constable Schultz's warnings echoed in her mind, a haunting refrain of caution that she had ignored. She had been reckless, driven by a blind determination to uncover the truth at any cost. But now, as Ramsay drew closer, she grasped the true price of her folly.

She clung to the hope that she'd be rescued by Angelica or any one of the others skulking about the house, but the silence that enveloped her like a shroud told her she was alone. There was no one coming to save her. Her children's faces came to her mind's eye. Would they ever see her again? Would they ever forgive her for being as foolhardy as their father and leaving them to fend for themselves? With each passing moment, she realized she was on her own, left to face the consequences of her actions in the darkness.

Ramsay's footsteps drew nearer. He approached, leaned against the very door she was right behind. He was inches away from her. She held her breath and prayed.

A harsh rapping came at the bedroom door. "Sir, I am sorry to disturb you." It was Rose, coming to her rescue. "You have a visitor," she said.

"It can wait. I need rest after my journey," Ramsay said.

"Sir, it is Angelica Church."

What? What was Angelica doing? Sweat dripped down Eliza's back.

"Angelica Church? What business does she have here?"

"It's about a debt owed, sir," Rose said.

"Very well," he said, clearly annoyed, but intrigued. "I'll be right there."

Eliza held her breath until he left. Then she cracked the wardrobe door open. She clung to the locket in her hand. How to get out of this room? With a shaky hand she wiped the sweat from her brow. She walked toward the door, unsure if she should open it. Her legs wobbled. She stopped and drew in air. In and out. She was grateful to be out of the wardrobe. But what next?

The bedroom door opened, and an arm waved her to come forward. It was René. "Come this way," she whispered as she grabbed Eliza and led her through a small door and down a narrow staircase. Eliza's legs continued to shake even as she made her escape. She willed herself to continue, when all her body wanted was to rest.

Reaching the bottom of the staircase, Eliza saw she was back in the kitchen, where Alice waited for them. But where was Angelica?

"We must go," René said. "Angelica has the matter in hand."

"I will not leave my sister." Eliza stood, unmoving.

"Very well. We shall wait for her outside then," René said.

René, Alice, and Eliza left the warmth of the kitchen and huddled in the alley outside.

"What happened?" Eliza finally asked. The crisp air snapped her back to her senses.

"He came home early because of an expected storm," René said. "Angelica thought quickly about the debt owed to him and distracted him."

Money had no meaning to Angelica, or at least not like it did to Eliza, who had to scrimp and save. But she hoped her sister was not paying Ramsay. She herself had refused to take money from her sister—it sometimes was a bone of contention between them.

"I found nothing," Alice said. "Not Jo. Not anything."

"I found something." Eliza held up the locket. "Is it Jo's?"

Alice reached for it and studied it, her breath forming puffs around her. "It doesn't belong to Jo. She was dressed as a man. If it were hers, she wouldn't have been wearing it. Where did you find it?"

"Under his bed. I did a very thorough search," Eliza said.

"Of course," Alice said.

"Maybe we can figure out who it belongs to," René said. "And then maybe she'd have answers for us."

"If we can't figure out who it belonged to, maybe a jeweler knows something about it," Eliza suggested.

In the meantime, Angelica still hadn't shown herself. Eliza and her companions stared at the kitchen door, waiting for Angelica's appearance. A voice came from behind them.

"What is everybody looking at?"

All three of them jumped. It was Angelica.

"Angelica!" Eliza said.

"I left from the front door, of course," Angelica said. "I'm glad you all made it out safely. What is that?" She pointed to the locket.

Alice handed it to her. "Eliza found it under Ramsay's bed."

Angelica cocked an eyebrow and pursed her lips. "That is no ordinary locket. I know the jeweler. You see? This mark right here. It's Franco. I have several pieces from him."

"What luck!" Alice said. "Let's go to him now. Shall we?"

Eliza's legs had stopped shaking, and she breathed steadily as they walked out of the alley. She pictured Angelica's reaction when she learned that Eliza had hid in a wardrobe. In truth, Eliza was unsure her mouth could even form the words.

# Chapter 41

Franco's was on Fifth Avenue. By the time they arrived, the women's faces were raw from the windy, plummeting temperature, even though they were wrapped in scarves. Eliza reached up and patted her nose to make certain it was still there.

A wooden sign hung above the entrance of the shop proclaimed *Franco Jewelry* with a red gemstone painted next to it. Alice pushed open the door and walked in, and the others followed into the narrow, elongated shop with wooden floors. The room was lit with oil lamps and candles, which made the jewels on display glisten.

Eliza had never been to a jeweler. She owned little jewelry, all of which had been given to her.

"Mrs. Church!" A man with a shock of black hair tumbling around his face and down almost to his shoulders, came from around the corner and kissed Angelica's cheeks. "It's been too long!"

"I agree, Franco," she said and then introduced the others. "We've run across this locket and wondered if you could identify the owner for us."

Franco studied it and opened it. "There is nothing inside. I know of this piece, but it had likenesses inside." His Italian accent had a musical quality.

"We found it and want to return it," Eliza offered. "Perhaps it was stolen?"

He hesitated. "I can return it myself, if you don't mind."

"Why bother?" Angelica asked.

"She might not appreciate your involvement. She is a loyal customer."

*A loyal customer, so she must have money. And if she had money, she most likely also knew Angelica.*

"More loyal than me?" Angelica said and batted her eyes.

"No, Mrs. Church. I can assure you. You are my best customer," Franco said, his Italian accent breaking through. He sized up the women standing before him. "Very well. It belongs to Mrs. Van Horn."

Eliza's heart stopped for a second. Mrs. Van Horn. She was the last client Rebecca saw and Jo questioned in search of her. Then Rebecca went on to the apothecary and later when Mrs. Van Horn told Jo that, she followed. Eliza's head spun. She lifted her eyes to see both Alice and René peering at her. Angelica didn't realize what she had exposed, the connection between the necklace, its owner and the murdered woman, along with the missing woman. Somehow, Mrs. Van Horn's necklace ended up in Ramsay's room. Was it too simple to imagine that it could have been Jo or Rebecca who left it there?

Eliza's stomach wavered. "Thank you, Mr. Franco. We must be going. We'll get the locket back to her. She is an acquaintance of mine."

"Very well." He handed it back to her. This time, the locket felt warm in her hands. "Please give her my best." He noted the ring on Eliza's finger. A mourning ring that her father had made for her. "That's a lovely piece."

"Thank you. A gift from my father."

"You wear it well. You must visit me sometime. I can create something gorgeous for you. Something to bring out those large dark eyes,"

Eliza's face heated. She didn't like his attention on her.

"Some other time, Franco. We really must go." Angelica rushed her away.

"We must visit Mrs. Van Horn," Angelica said, after they stepped out into the raw weather. "Now."

"She doesn't live far from here," Eliza said.

Alice stopped, weary. "You two go ahead. We will meet you back at our place."

"A marvelous idea," Angelica said. Mrs. Van Horn would be unnerved if Angelica and Eliza entered her home with two complete strangers.

The wind whipped around them, causing the women to run off in each of their respective directions with a spring in their step.

Mrs. Van Horn's butler let Eliza and Angelica in. They remained in the foyer for several minutes, warming themselves before she appeared.

Mrs. Van Horn entered the room with a flourish. "Eliza! Angelica! My dears! You look frozen to the bone. Please come in!"

They were swept into the parlor with kindness and concern, immediately sat, and tea was brought to them.

Eliza could weep with joy as the heat from the teacup warmed her. She hadn't appreciated how cold she was until her body warmed. She studied the room, which was lavishly decorated with Christmas decor. Of course Mrs. Van Horn was of Dutch heritage, like Eliza and Angelica were. Hamilton despised what he called their "quaint" Dutch traditions but went along with it for Eliza.

The drawing room's opulence—gilt mirrors, imported wallpaper, Turkish carpets—seemed to demand a particular kind of conversation, all social niceties and careful abstractions. But beneath the rustle of silk skirts and the delicate clink of bone china cups, Eliza sensed currents of fear. Mrs. Van Horn's fingers trembled slightly as she poured the tea. Eliza noted that her costly lace cuffs were Rebecca's work.

"We just came from Franco's," Angelica said as she sipped her tea. "We found a locket, and I recognized his work."

"A locket?" Mrs. Van Horn said. "Where did you find it?"

"That's not important. What is important is that he said it belongs to you," Angelica said. She held the locket up.

Mrs. Van Horn's face drained of color. "What? What is this? I don't understand . . ." Her face twitched with emotion. Then she looked at Eliza and Angelica, as if catching herself. "I-I believed I'd quite lost it." She took the locket from Angelica and sank into herself when she opened the empty locket.

"Lost?" Angelica said. "A fine locket like that?"

"Well, what I mean is . . . That is . . . it was stolen from me. I was robbed," she stammered, clearly making up her story as she went along.

"Robbed?" Eliza said. "I did not know that you'd been robbed. Usually such matters are in the papers."

"Really?" Mrs. Van Horn said, as if she was only half listening. "I never read them anymore."

"What happened?" Angelica asked.

"It was in broad daylight. A young man came up and yanked it right off my neck."

"How terrible. Were you out alone?" Eliza asked.

"Yes, I was on my way to the dressmaker's." Every word that came out of her mouth did not sound true.

"Who is your dressmaker?" Angelica asked.

Mrs. Van Horn opened her mouth, then closed it.

"I ask because I'm always seeking a good one," Angelica said. "I don't know how long I may be visiting."

"I go to several," Mrs. Van Horn stated. "But I'm quite sure the one I went to that day was Mimi's." She looked at Eliza. "Do you know it?"

Eliza shook her head. She wore only one sort of dress now: her widow's weeds. "I don't." But she suspected she and Angelica would visit there before they headed back to the Grange.

Angelica continued the ruse. "Where is she located?"

"Her shop is on the bottom floor of her home on Maiden Street," Mrs. Van Horn said, without conviction. "There is a row of houses there amongst the businesses."

Eliza knew it well. But she couldn't recall a place called Mimi's. But those were the same houses she and Angelica had visited earlier when they were searching for the WMA.

# Chapter 42

After warming themselves in Mrs. Van Horn's home, Angelica and Eliza ventured back out onto the cold streets.

"We need to walk over there." Angelica pointed to Maiden Street. She fiddled with her gloves. Puffs of air streamed from her mouth.

"But Alice and René are expecting us." Eliza stopped walking.

Angelica tugged on her arm. "Then we must be quick about it."

The streets were nearly empty because of the cold. Most people were inside, where Eliza herself preferred to be. Instead, she stood at the corner of Maiden Lane and Pearl Street, trying to decide which direction would be likely to hold a dressmaker's shop.

"Did you give that Ramsay your money?" Eliza asked.

"Yes. It was not that large of a sum for him to make such a problem over it. I've told you time and time again that we have resources and you know I'd love to help you."

Eliza was desperate but not that desperate. She'd just have to find her own way. It's what Hamilton would have wanted.

"Why would you do that? He has no claim to a dead woman's money," Eliza said.

Angelica waved her hand as if to dismiss the question. "It gives our friends a bit more safety. I worry about them."

Put like that, Eliza could not argue.

"You go this way, and I'll go that way." Angelica gestured. "We'll circle around and meet up." Her sister barked orders as if she were a commander. But she'd been doing that her whole life.

Eliza walked off, peering for any signs of a dressmaker's shop. She noted the house where she and Angelica had tried to find Lucretia Short. It was dark inside with no movement anywhere, whereas the homes around it were bustling with light and movement. She moved along. If the residents were truly sick with plague, the house's stillness was understandable.

She moved further away from where she expected to find a business. As she walked along, she spotted a few Christmas wreaths on doors. This was clearly a residential neighborhood. There'd be no businesses here. Eliza turned down the next street, heading for the meeting spot with Angelica. Soon enough, her sister barreled toward her.

"I have news," Angelica said. "I found Mimi's. I talked to her. She said she has not seen Mrs. Van Horn in at least a year."

"Then Mrs. Van Horn is lying." The back of Eliza's neck tingled.

Angelica looped her arm through Eliza's. "Let us go to see Alice and René. They may know this dressmaker."

They hurried along, Eliza trailing her sister. How was the wealthy, well-connected Mrs. Van Horn entangled in the disappearance of Jo and Rebecca's murder? There must be a reason the woman lied to them. When Eliza had first told her about Rebecca's death, her reaction was dramatic. It was as if she cared for them. Most women in the Van Horn circle cared little for any person working for them. She was hiding something. Mrs. Van Horn and Rebecca clearly had a relationship beyond the concern. But what was the nature of it? How did that come about? She tried to frame the relationship between Rebecca and Mrs. Van Horn. But she had no details, so she couldn't. She wondered if Alice or René would.

As she and Angelica approached the front door of Alice's home, a piece of paper pinned to the door flapped in the chilly wind.

Another note? Eliza unpinned it and a breeze blew it away from her gloved hand. Angelica caught it and, in doing so, the note unfolded. She read it and her face grew pale.

"What is it?" Eliza asked.

Angelica showed the note to Eliza:

*Die, unnatural wenches.*

Eliza gasped and tucked the note into her pocket. "They should not see this! It's awful. That's all they need with everything else going on." She had witnessed Constable Schultz taking a note off the door and tucking it in his pocket the day he came to talk with them about Rebecca's case. He must know about this harassment. Eliza contemplated the tiny enclave of houses. Did anybody see who did this? It might have just looked like a friend pinning a note to the door.

"Eliza, compose yourself." Angelica knocked on the door. "We all need a clear mind. We'll deal with the note later."

Eliza nodded.

René answered the door. They were ushered in, took off their winter attire, and sat on the settee.

"What did you find out? Anything?" Alice asked.

"We went to find a dressmaker named Mimi. Mrs. Van Horn claimed she was on the way to see her when she was robbed of her locket," Angelica said. "But the dressmaker said she hasn't seen her in over a year."

"Mrs. Van Horn knows something," Eliza replied. "Do either of you know the nature of her relationship with Rebecca?"

"As far as I know, Rebecca delivered linens to the household," Alice said.

René cleared her throat. "Rebecca was friendly with many people. Maybe they struck up a friendship of sorts."

"They must have." Eliza leaned closer. "But doesn't it seem unlikely?"

"Aye," Alice said. "I agree. We are friendly with the customers, of course. But we do not become overly close."

"Given that she knew Rebecca as a man, I doubt they'd have had a past connection," Angelica said. "So, whatever the relationship was, it was through your concern. Through the delivery service."

"She saw Rebecca as a man. Knew that he delivered things." René set her cup down.

"Not just anything, but fine linens," Alice said. "She wasn't making deliveries for extra money."

Eliza's brain clicked. "Alice, you're brilliant. Would Rebecca help someone by delivering an item not handled by the concern?"

Eliza always needed someone to deliver her messages. If someone delivered to the Grange, she might ask if they could drop something off for her on the way back to the city.

"That's a smart idea, Eliza!" Angelica said. "It's a real possibility."

"Rebecca was busy making deliveries for us. I doubt she'd have had the time to help someone else," René said.

Eliza was unwilling to let her theory go. It made sense to her. Mrs. Van Horn and Rebecca had developed a trusted relationship of sorts. She may have asked Rebecca to handle something for her. Which is what sent her into the bad part of town. It was intriguing that Mrs. Van Horn would need a messenger to go to Water Street.

They had been thinking about this all wrong. It wasn't a card game that took Rebecca there. It was delivering a message for a friend. Eliza was certain of it. As to what the nature of the message could be, she had no idea.

In that moment, Eliza's childhood friend, Two Kettles, a native, came to mind, Known for her tracking skills, she had taught Eliza a few things. But they were in the city. There'd be no broken twigs and bent grass. And the snow had come and gone twice, most likely erasing any physical evidence of Jo or Rebecca's path. Her contemplation circled and landed back on Mrs. Van Horn. It always came back to her, much to Eliza's regret.

# Chapter 43

As they sat around Alice's kitchen table, Eliza finally asked the question. "Did you know Rebecca had a child?"

Alice leaned back against her chair; her eyebrows shot up in surprise. "What?"

"We found birth papers among her things," Eliza said.

"But she was only twenty-four. When did she have the child? I've known her four years," Alice said.

"According to the document, she had the child twelve years ago," Angelica said.

René's face bloomed into a bright red.

"René?" Eliza said.

"Yes, I knew she had a child, but she gave him up to a family, a wonderful family, one that could give him what she could not," René said.

Alice's mouth dropped open.

"Do you know who the family is?" Angelica asked.

"No. I'm sorry. That I do not know." René clutched her hands on the table and glanced at Alice. "I only found out by accident. I didn't mean to keep it from you. I just felt it was best left alone. Private business."

"Do you know who the father is?" Angelica asked.

René's chin trembled, and she shook her head.

A prickling sensation traveled up Eliza's spine. René was lying. She regarded her troubled state. But it was best to leave it alone for now, and she didn't want to push an already weary René. They had other matters to attend to.

Angelica pulled out the slip of paper from Rebecca's trunk, which Eliza had given her to carry, and placed it on the table. "What do you know about this?"

Alice and René read over the note.

"Where did you get this vile note?" Alice asked.

"Also among Rebecca's things." Eliza folded the note. "She was being harassed. Did she ever tell either of you about it?"

"Not at all. I know we'd gotten a few notes, but nothing like this," Alice said. She grunted. "Seems I didn't know our Rebecca as well as I supposed."

"Why didn't you take your notes to the constabulary?" Eliza asked.

"I steer clear of them. They are no help to me," Alice said.

Eliza pulled out the note she and Angelica had found on the door earlier. "This was pinned to your door. Perhaps she'd been finding them first and gathering them so you all wouldn't know."

Alice and René read over the note. René gasped.

"You found this today?" Alice slid the note back over.

Eliza nodded. "And I saw Constable Schultz pull a note from your door and place it in his pocket the day of the wake."

Alice bit her lip. "This house is being harassed, and I didn't know of it!"

"Who would do such a thing?" René asked.

"That's something we need to find out," Angelica said. "Can Brigid or Mary watch your door, like they did the apothecary?"

"Leave that to us. We will figure this out," Alice said, chin lifted. "No constables."

"If our Rebecca was being harassed—if these notes were for her, might they have gotten to her and killed her?" René asked.

Eliza placed her hand over René's. "Perhaps."

A rapping came at the door, and René went to answer it. It was McNally to fetch Eliza and Angelica. It was getting late and, with the setting sun, even colder. Angelica and Eliza readied for the journey, both women hugging Alice and René. The sisters then moved from the warmth of the tiny home into the bracing air. They huddled in the carriage to help keep warm.

Nothing more could be done now. They considered seeing Schultz but changed their minds. They had no proof of anything. What they had—the locket found beneath Ramsay's bed—they'd gotten illegally. Eliza's face heated at the idea of Schultz knowing what she had done.

"What are you thinking so deeply about over there?" Angelica said.

"You might guess what."

"We've reached an impasse. I cannot figure out our next move," Angelica said. A note of weariness tinged her voice. A pang of guilt popped in Eliza. Angelica had come for Christmas, and what did Eliza give her? Murder and intrigue.

"Why are the kidnapers taking so long to reach out about Josephine?" Angelica mused.

"The only thing I can imagine is that they are contacting the groom-to-be, waiting for his response." Eliza could not imagine Jo as a bride, let alone a farmer's wife.

Jo moved like a breeze through New York. She was a vibrant part of the city, acquainted with society families and more aware than Eliza herself about the happenings in their households. A skilled lace maker, having lived with Alice and the others for years, Jo's freedom was hard won, and she relished it. She'd never give it up and move to a Pennsylvania farm, waiting on a husband and working her fingers to the bone.

Gratitude swept through Eliza. She's never had to consider utilizing a marriage broker. She had been born into a good family and had many suitors. But many women hired a broker or placed an advertisement in the papers seeking a husband. It served a purpose. Marriage, some believed, was a business partnership. Many women's economic status forced them to marry for financial security, denying them other experiences. Eliza understood that.

But thank God for love. Even though her love had brought her more pain than she could imagine, it also brought her joy.

But that was not Jo. She was an independent woman.

"What could Rebecca's relationship be like with Mrs. Van Horn?" Angelica said. Their minds seemed one again.

"I guess we could simply ask Mrs. Van Horn."

"That's not wise. If she were up to no good, she would have time to cover her tracks."

"Well, René said she'd ask around," Eliza offered.

"That might lead us somewhere. She knows the servants, and we all know servants talk."

The carriage swayed, and the sisters both slid to the other side.

"Your driver is ill-mannered," Angelica said with a grin.

Eliza brushed lint off her cloak. "Is that what you call it?"

Sometimes McNally was a bit impertinent, and his driving skills were rough. Patches of snow and ice still lingered on the road. Perhaps he was doing his best. Many drivers would not venture out. But McNally did, even though he grumbled about it.

Eliza herself did not care for leaving the house in winter, but circumstances prevailed. She tucked her arms closer to her body, wishing for warmth. "I despise this cold."

"It never stopped you when you were a child. Mother tried to keep you inside and you'd not have it," Angelica said.

"I remember. But since I've grown, I've lost my taste for it."

"I prefer the splendor and warmth of spring in Paris," Angelica said.

Paris. Eliza had never been but learned about it from her sister. Their friend Lafayette was doing well there. The idea warmed her.

"I'm sure you do," Eliza replied.

When she was a girl, she'd read about other places and longed to visit them. Much had changed for her. She didn't like the cold. And all she wanted was to keep the Grange, which she'd give a million Parises for. It would be taken over by the bank soon. And there was nothing she could do about it. Even with the sale of her father's property, she wouldn't have enough money to save it.

The Grange came into view then. High on a hill, looking out over the city and the river. Its soft butter color stood out amongst the earth and patches of grass and snow. The Grange. It meant so much to Hamilton—and still so much to the whole family. It was a place he designed with heart. And each family member sensed that.

# Chapter 44

A woman Jo had never seen before appeared in her room and dressed her after much scrubbing. The woman then took a brush to her hair, and she cried from the pain of it. What was happening?

The woman sharply barked an order. "Stand up and walk over to the window."

Josephine did as she was told. Her lavender dress swished around her legs as she moved. So uncomfortable. So . . . wrong.

The woman cracked a smile. "Good. It is time for you to meet Mr. Harvey. He's downstairs having tea."

Downstairs? There were stairs? She didn't recall them at all. In fact, she didn't remember even getting to this room.

"Mr. Harvey is a marriage broker. There is an amiable gentleman in Pennsylvania searching for a wife."

Why would he be talking with her? She had no need for a husband—did she?

Josephine watched the woman open the door. She would walk through it to . . . what? A man to check her over to see if she'd be a good match for his customer? She followed the woman down the stairs. Josephine tried not to gape at the lavish furnishings around her. The settee covered in white silk. The oriental rugs on a marble floor. Heavy, lush crimson drapes. She was certain she'd never been here before.

A portly man sat in a chair, sizing her up with his gaze. He smiled at the woman. "You were right. She is beautiful."

Beautiful? Was she?

The woman gestured to Josephine to sit on the settee. "Tea will be ready soon."

"Very nice to meet you, Josephine," Mr. Harvey said.

She smiled politely. She had not spoken a word in a long time and was unsure her mouth could even form them. She sat on the settee, afraid she might slip off as the fabric was so slick and cool.

"My client is eager for a wife. He's rich, tall, and handsome. He's Prussian, so you may be learning his language. Can you do that?" he said with a gentle voice.

She smiled again.

"Do you speak?" he asked. "You've nothing to be afraid of. It's a carefully made arrangement. Between your mother and I."

Mother? Josephine comprehended nothing, as she sat on the settee gazing at the man, trying to figure out what had happened to her. She had more questions than answers. Why was she in this place? Why was this man talking about marriage? But one thing she did know: That woman was not her mother.

"M-mother?" Josephine stammered.

He smiled. "You spoke."

She wanted to scream. Why did he believe the woman was her mother?

"Not my mother," Josephine said.

"Pardon me?"

The woman entered the room with a tray of tea and a decorated cake. Yellow icing. Pink icing, sugary pink roses. Swirls and dots.

The man seemed confused as the woman poured the tea and sliced the cake. Josephine's mouth filled with the smell of the lemony cake. Water sprang in her mouth. She stuffed her mouth with it, unable to resist.

The man gaped at her. The woman handed her a napkin.

"Josephine, really," she said with mock indignation. "Must you eat your cake like that?"

Josephine barely looked up from her plate before her stomach sickened. She set the plate down and lifted the tea to her lips. As she did so, she spotted the pink flowers on the cup. The same swirling flowers. She dizzied, and her hand teetered and spilled the tea.

"Goodness, aren't you a nervous little bird?" The woman stood, red-faced.

"What is wrong with her?" The man set his own cup on the table. "My client will not have a wife with ill manners."

"Your client is a farmer." The woman's voice was flat.

"He's a gentleman as well." He tsked. "This won't work at all."

Josephine licked the icing from her fingers. She eyed the rest of the cake, glanced at the woman, then the man. She reached for the plate with the cake, stood, and ran for the front door.

# Chapter 45

Everybody had a secret self. Alice did. Sometimes she had several. Sometimes she remembered them.

This Rebecca and Mrs. Van Horn thread of the story perplexed her. She imagined the simplest thing to do would be just to ask Mrs. Van Horn herself. But she was certain she would refuse to see the likes of Alice, an old lace maker not in her social circles. That is why René's friendship with a member of the staff was vital.

Alice herself did not know Rebecca well. Rebecca was orphaned and living at the Widow Society and made lace well. But Alice didn't make a habit of prying. Often the past was best left in the past. That Rebecca had a child at such a young age . . . of course she would not talk about that with just anybody. Alice did not know Rebecca's secrets during her short life. And now she never would.

But sometimes the past was an important piece to understand the present. Like now. What part of Rebecca's personality drew Mrs. Van Horn to her? If she was running an errand for her, what made her trust the young "man"?

On the one hand, Alice was glad to know those who represented the concern were held in such high regard. On the other hand, had she not trained them well enough to know there was no good reason to go to certain parts of town? She herself went there, as nobody bothered a woman like her. Her invisibility became a cloak that allowed her to move about the city unbothered.

Alice stretched out her leg, with a crack and pop of her knee. Her mother's knee used to do the same. If only her mother could be aware of the life Alice had fashioned for herself in the New World. What would she think?

Alice laughed. Her mother had hated the man she loved, mostly because he was Jewish. But there was also the fact that he was not in the right social sphere. But Alice loved him and left her home and country behind so that they could be together.

And here she was now. She was the unlikely friend of Eliza Hamilton, a woman she respected and loved. A woman who, in many ways, had not been given an easy life, despite what some may presume. In the center of Eliza, there was a strength you didn't get from an easy life.

Mrs. Van's Horn face played in Alice's cluttered mind. Did she have secrets? What were they? And did they reach Rebecca's ears?

Did Rebecca and Mrs. Van Horn know one another from a previous part of their lives? Did Mrs. Van Horn ever volunteer or help at the Widow Society?

That was something she could certainly find out. She stood, knee cracking, feet a bit swollen, and grabbed her cloak, scarves, and hat, and left. Maybe she'd be back before nightfall and could hear what René found out—and maybe she'd have something of her own to say. She opened the door and edged herself forward, one creaky step at a time.

* * *

By the time Alice arrived at the Widow Society, she needed to sit. Her bad foot pulsed with ache. She took the first chair she found in the front room of the place that held so many memories—both bad and good.

A stout woman whom Alice didn't recognize entered the room. "Can I help you?

"I'd like to see Mrs. Schumacher. I'm Alice Rhodes."

The woman nodded. "She'll be right with you."

Alice's foot throbbed as she waited. She took in the surroundings—mostly the same, with the announcements pinned to a board and the same rules: no imbibing, no bringing men into the establishment, and church attendance was required. Ah, those Sunday mornings squeezed into a pew at the back of the church!

Mrs. Schumacher entered the room and rushed toward Alice. "Alice! How wonderful to ss you! And looking so well!"

"Thank you."

"What's wrong?" Mrs. Schumacher took a seat.

Alice told her that Rebecca was dead, and Jo was missing.

"Ja, Mrs. General Hamilton was here and told me. You've not found Josephine?"

"No. We are trying to find out what happened to Rebecca and are working to find Jo. And I have questions for you," Alice said.

"Certainly." Mrs. Schumacher's Prussian accent was pronounced as she spoke. Her chin quivered.

"Did one of your benefactors, Mrs. Van Horn, know Rebecca?"

"I believe so," she said after a few seconds. "But let me check a few records. I'll be right back."

Alice's head spun with possibilities. If they knew one another here, perhaps that solved the mystery of why Mrs. Van Horn was so fond of Rebecca. Could she have recognized her, even disguised as a boy? Did Rebecca go against the rules of the House of Pearl and reveal herself to Mrs. Van Horn? There was much to consider.

"Yes." Mrs. Schumacher bounded into the room. A large-boned woman, who was full of fire, she dropped into the chair next to Alice. "It's as I remembered. Rebecca and her mother came here, and Rebecca's mother was very ill. Mrs. Van Horn took great care of her mother, but she still died. Rebecca stayed to help with chores." She paused. "She had nowhere else to go."

"How long was she here before she came to live with me?"

"About three years, I think."

Alice had no idea how she'd find out if Mrs. Van Horn recognized Rebecca when she was dressed as a man, but it might explain her reaction to Rebecca's death.

Mrs. Schumacher leaned in. "How is your foot?"

"Hurts like a beast."

"I keep some whiskey in my quarters for medicinal purposes. Could it help?" Mrs. Schumacher stood and reached out her hand.

"I believe it would." Alice took her hand and followed her to her room. Just a shot would take the edge off the pain of her foot. But nothing would help the pain in her heart.

# Chapter 46

Eliza and Angelica arrived home in time to brew a batch of advocaat for an after-dinner treat. Both Schuyler sisters used to sneak the drinks from the "adult" batch when growing up. Their mother always made two batches of the sweet frothy drink—one with brandy and one for the children, with more vanilla and no alcohol.

As Eliza cracked the eggs, Angelica poured in the sugar and brandy. Eliza wished for a lighter heart. Her mother always had said to hire happy cooks, or else their sadness might spill into the food. Eliza usually didn't believe old wives' superstitions. Yet she always hired happy cooks.

She just couldn't get her mind off Jo and Rebecca.

"What did you hear from Isabella Graham? I know you were working on something with her. Something about children?" Angelica licked spilled drops of brandy from her fingers.

"She is caring for six orphaned children. I asked if I could take one or two—"

"You have no business!"

"Wait. Let me finish." Eliza cracked the last egg and stirred. "She refused to let me take a couple. We're finding a bigger place to take in more children. The city is running over with orphans. A few other women are interested in helping."

"Wonderful! Let me know if you need funding. I'd love to help with that."

Eliza continued to stir. Not everything was solved with money. It was something Angelica never believed. "That's generous of you. Thank you. I will let the others know. We plan to meet in the spring."

"So, Rebecca and Jo were both orphans. Correct?" Angelica asked.

"Both were daughters of women in the Widow Society, and both lost their mothers. Jo was quite young, as I understand it. Alice was also living there, and she spotted Jo's talent for lace making."

"Shall we have a taste before dinner?" Angelica didn't wait for an answer and poured them each a small glass. "But I recall it was Rebecca's mother that died, and Alice took her in?"

Eliza held the brew to her lips and sipped. "Yes. Though, to be quite honest, I don't pry. These are women whose stories are heart-breaking, and they may not appreciate my questioning."

"So, we know Rebecca had a baby and gave her up to some-one. Was she still with her mother then? Because many women would turn their daughters out in such a state."

Eliza chilled. She didn't want to say the words, but they came out, hesitantly. "Unless she was so young that she was still in her mother's care when she became with child."

The sisters sat in silence, drinking, absorbing the heaviness of that possibility.

"The way I figure, that's what happened. Some men are such beasts," Angelica said.

Eliza's breath stopped. Hadn't René said Rebecca's brother had hurt her, and she had nothing to do with him? Could it be? She dared not consider it.

"Eliza? You've gone pale. What is it?"

"My thoughts are very dark."

Angelica's eyebrows lifted. "More reason to share."

"When I mentioned to René that I'd learned Rebecca had a brother, she told me Rebecca has nothing to do with him. That he'd hurt her badly."

Angelica leaned toward Eliza. "Could it be?"

"René must know." Eliza took another sip of the advocaat.

"We shall ask her. Maybe she knows where the child is as well."

"Then why did she not tell me when I asked?"

Angelica shrugged. "It's not something we speak about, is it? I mean, you and I are sisters, and we still don't like to talk about it." She paused. "I warrant it's better if we do. Shoving such things aside will only hurt us more."

Mrs. Cole walked into the room. "Is it finished?" She took in the two jars of advocaat—one for the children and one for the adults.

"Yes, and we've had a taste." Angelica held up her glass.

"I see." Mrs. Cole folded her hands. "I'll take care of them."

She reached for the jars holding the eggy brew, placed a linen towel over them, and took them outside to chill. "Or else I shall have two drunk sisters on my hands." She winked.

Eliza laughed. For a moment, her heart lifted. It was a familiar scene with her sister in the kitchen making the drink their mother had taught them to make. Angelica had crossed the sea for moments like this. It warmed Eliza to anticipate her children drinking the same traditional brew later that night. Hamilton's first taste of it did not go well. He'd spit it out. She laughed out loud. "Hamilton hated it."

"I remember," Angelica said. "But he tried to drink it so as not to be rude to Mother."

After laughing about the memory of Hamilton's distaste, the sisters calmed into seriousness.

"What next, dear sister?" Angelica asked.

"We need to talk to René."

"Shall we visit the brother and confront him?" Angelica said.

"Only if we have to." Eliza's stomach soured.

Later that evening, after the children were in bed, Eliza, Angelica, James and Alexander Jr. drank the advocaat. Angel plucked at the pianoforte. Eliza sat on the settee and sipped her drink while going through the mail she'd missed earlier that day.

Angelica held up the ribbon she'd fashioned into a bow for the Christmas tree. "Several dozens of these bows would look lovely on the tree."

"Let me help you." Alexander sat on the floor with Angelica next to the fire. The floor was Angelica's preferred seat when she was alone with her family in the evenings.

Eliza flipped through the letters and calling cards. One large envelope from the bank stood out. She knew what that was. It was her final notice.

"What is it, Mother?" James asked. He had always been too sensitive to her moods, even when he was a boy.

"I need to find another place to live. Somewhere in town, I should think." She tried to sound lighthearted. But they all understood what the Grange meant to her.

They all stopped what they were doing.

"What? It's not the end of the world. I shall be able to live on my allowance in town with the children," Eliza said.

"I wish you'd let me help you." Angelica fiddled with the gingham bow.

"I wouldn't hear of it," Eliza said. "Don't you all look so sad! Worse things could befall this family. We will have a roof over our heads and food in our stomachs. Some don't have that. I refuse to wallow in self-pity." Rebecca and Jo were examples of worse things that could happen. She carried them with her through her every motion tonight.

"Well, at least let us help you find a place while we're here." Alexander twisted his ribbon into a bow and held it up.

"That would be lovely," Eliza said.

"Is there any news about Josephine?" James asked.

"None," Eliza said quickly. She didn't want her sons to know she'd gone into Ramsay's house to search for Jo. She caught Angelica peeking at her, but she couldn't meet her gaze, or her sons would pick up on the secret.

Angelica said, "We haven't heard from those claiming to have her."

"Have you gone to the constable?" Alexander asked.

Eliza's face heated. How could she tell the constable what she had done? Even though it had resulted in a fascinating clue for her to unravel. "Not yet. No."

Angelica leaned forward. "A servant in the Van Horn residence found a locket in the Ramsay house and brought it to René, Alice's friend."

Angelica was such a clever liar.

"She wondered if belonged to Josephine, but it does not. Instead, it belongs to Mrs. Van Horn."

"She said it was stolen from her." Eliza set aside the mail. She couldn't think anymore. Was it the advocaat? She took another sip. The brandy warmed her.

"But we went to her dressmaker who said she had not seen Mrs. Van Horn in a year," Angelica said.

"So, we figure she has a secret," Eliza added,

"This is brilliant," James said. "You two are quite the investigators." He held his glass up as if to toast them.

"You need to leave this to the constables," Alexander said. "I don't like the idea of you endangering yourselves. Honestly, there is this unsavory Ramsay character, the WMA, and now Mrs. Van Horn. It seems unseemly, and maybe dangerous."

Eliza recalled almost being caught at Ramsay's. He was right. Yet, how could they go to a constable when they had obtained the necklace illegally?

"Really, Alexander!" Angelica said. "We know how to take care of ourselves. More than you know, perhaps."

Eliza's eyes met Angelica's. "Do we?" She laughed.

Angelica laughed too. Both were a little lost in the moment, with the drink, and Eliza's troubled daughter playing music in the background.

# Chapter 47

The next morning found Eliza, Angelica, and Eliza's older sons in the small barn. When Eliza's sons were home, she often gave McNally a break from his barn duties. She reasoned it especially fair now, since she hadn't paid him in over a month. Even though it was frigid, Eliza enjoyed the barn; its earthy scents comforted her, taking her back to her youth when things were uncomplicated.

"I received a note from my friend Cedric," James said, while mucking the stalls. "He has several houses to let. I thought we might go into town today to see them."

As Eliza brushed Peacock, Hamilton's favorite horse, her heart sank. She was losing the Grange. She would have to find a place for her and the children soon. But if they were to move to town, she could sell the horses and the carriage.

Angelica, brushing another horse, placed her gloved hand on Eliza's for reassurance. "You don't have to choose today. We can just see what's available."

"Better while we are all together, I should think. And Cedric can be trusted." James took his shovel and its contents outside.

"Of course." Eliza's heart raced and her stomach turned. If only she could stay in the home she and Hamilton had worked so hard for.

"I'll stay with the children," Alexander said. "Imagine us all piling into that carriage!"

"We've done it before." James came back into the barn.

Three hours later, they had viewed one house, which was on Wall Street, near where they used to live. Even during winter, the street was busy. Eliza doubted the children, used to playing outside, could adjust to this smaller home on a busy street. And in the back of her mind, she was also considering suitable places for the orphanage. It would not do, for the same reason. Children needed space to run and play.

"I understand your concerns. You might like the place on Maiden Lane better. It has a small garden in the back," Cedric said. Cedric and James had gone to school together, yet his pale skin and stout stature made him appear much older than James.

"Maiden Lane?" Angelica's eyes widened, glancing at Eliza.

"Yes, it's become quite a nice neighborhood. The market is close by, and the streets are only busy on market day," he said.

Of course, it was also where the mysterious Lucretia Short lived. Whose house supposedly was down with the plague. As luck would have it, as they got close to the house for rent, Eliza realized it was nearby Lucretia's. She would finagle a way to shed her son and pay Lucretia a visit.

"The house and yard are lovely," Eliza said. "I'm just uncertain." She had lived in worse places than this. If it were just her, there'd be no problem, but she was concerned for the children.

"You will know where you want to live when you see it," Angelica said.

"No bother. It gave us a chance to catch up," Cedric said. "I shall let you know if any other suitable houses come on the market."

"Making other stops today? If so, I will have a drink with Cedric," James said.

No finagling was necessary.

"Of course. Let's meet at Alice's place in an hour," Eliza said.

Eliza and Angelica stood and watched the young men walk off. "Which house was it?" Angelica asked.

Eliza spotted the wreath she'd seen on Lucretia's neighbor's door. "It's that one," she said.

They began walking toward the house. "Wait," Eliza said. "What are we going to say?"

"Leave that to me," Angelica answered. She knocked on the door.

Finally, a red-cheeked, short, round woman came to the door.

"Lucretia Short?" Angelica asked.

"Yes, who's asking?" Her eyebrows lifted high over her brown eyes.

"I'm Angelica Church. and this is my sister Mrs. General Hamilton."

She did not open the door further to invite them in. "Pleased to make your acquaintance. I am quite busy. Is there something I can help you with?"

"We'd like to learn more about the Women's Morality Alliance," Angelica said.

The woman squinted at Angelica and shifted her gaze to Eliza. "What do you want to know?"

"How does it help women? You see, my sister is involved in many charities that aid women," Angelica said.

The woman poked her chin out. "We are more concerned with the souls of women."

"What method of recruitment do you use?" Angelica persisted.

"Women come to us," she said.

"Why do you place so many adverts in the paper?" Eliza queried.

"We need to let them know we're here, don't we? Now if you don't mind." She started to shut the door.

"Actually, I do mind." Angelica's foot stopped her from shutting the door. "As a representative of the WMA, I figure you should take the time to speak with two interested parties."

Lucretia's face was so red, Eliza thought it might burst.

"How does tomorrow sound, say one o'clock?" Lucretia said.

"Perfect. I'll see you then." Angelica allowed her to close the door. "What an impertinent woman."

Impertinent, yes. Also nervous. She was hiding something. Who was in her house?

"Maybe we should find a bench," Eliza suggested.

"Whatever for? I'd much rather go to Alice's."

"Let's wait and see who comes out of her house."

Angelica's right eyebrow lifted. "Yes—let's."

# Chapter 48

Josephine awoke to the murmur of voices echoing through the church hall. A rough blanket had been draped over her, but it did little to warm her aching body. Her mind was heavy, as though weighed down by a fog she couldn't shake.

The air was thick with the scent of candle wax and aged wood, a comforting contrast to the icy wind outside that she had escaped from. Somewhere in the distance, the faint echo of footsteps reminded her she wasn't alone in this sanctuary.

How did she get here? The memories came in fractured pieces—the lemon cake, the biting cold, and the sweeping relief as she stepped into the warmth of this church. She'd almost cried when she found it. But now, as the chill returned to her bones, she gathered she had nowhere else to go.

Her stomach growled. Maybe she shouldn't have eaten the whole cake. But she smiled. It had been tasty, and here she was in the warmth of a church. It couldn't be all bad.

Except.

Except now what? The warmth of the church was a temporary relief, but it did nothing to fill the gnawing emptiness inside her. She had no memory of where she'd come from, no sense of belonging.

She had nowhere to go. No home that she recalled. They said she had a family, but Josephine doubted a family existed as they had never come for her. A tear stung her eye. She quickly wiped it away, unwilling to let herself break. Not here. Not yet. She must find her way. She must find her purpose. Her place.

She tried to focus on evoking a family. A person. A thing. Before the woman in the house. Before the bitter tea in the flower cup.

She held up her hands and studied them again. She must be a craftswoman. Her hands told a story her mind had forgotten. These were hands that had once known purpose, had created something delicate, something beautiful. But what? She closed her eyes, willing the images to come into focus, but like the patterns she almost glimpsed, they slipped further away the harder she tried.

What could she do now? She couldn't stay here indefinitely. Her shoes pinched her feet, and the lavender dress—though beautiful—was woefully thin for the bitter winter. She shivered, pulling the blanket tighter around her. Where else could she go? She had no cloak, no home, and no memory.

She was lost. Weariness swept through her. She sank onto the bench. With great effort, Josephine rolled onto her side, the narrow bench barely holding her weight. It creaked beneath her. She didn't know what to do, or where to go, but for now, she let exhaustion pull her back into the safety of sleep, hoping that when she woke again, something—anything—would make sense.

# Chapter 49

"Well, I guess we can safely say Lucretia lied to us. There are no visitors," Angelica said.

"Either that, or they are staying very long. And we both know there's no yellow fever."

"I'm cold and need a cup of tea. This is getting us nowhere. Let's go see Alice," Angelica said. "Maybe she has news."

"I suppose you're right." Eliza stood. Then Lucretia's door opened and out came Ramsay. Eliza sat back down, pulling Angelica with her. When Angelica spotted Ramsay, she turned her head.

"God," she whispered. "I don't want him to see me."

But it was too late.

"Mrs. Church!" He headed in their direction.

Angelica turned her head and smiled politely. "Mr. Ramsay. Do you know my sister, Mrs. General Hamilton?"

Eliza extended her arm. He took her hand and shook it. "Very nice to meet you. Of course, I know of you and the unfortunate loss of your husband. My condolences."

Eliza took him in. Tall and fit, with s square chin and brown eyes, he oozed charm. "Nice to meet you."

*Now will you please leave?*

"It's a cold day to be sitting on a park bench," he said. "May I escort you ladies to warmth?"

"Thank you for your kind offer, but we are enjoying the cold air. We've never liked to be in stuffy houses," Angelica said. "Have a good day, Mr. Ramsay." She said it in such a dismissive tone he had no choice but to move on.

"Ladies," he said, tilting his hat. He walked off.

"He doesn't seem like he could kill someone," Eliza said with a low voice. "He seems soft."

"I agree. But I'm sure he knows how to hire someone to kill for him." Angelica stood. "Let's go. We'll be late meeting James."

"But Lucretia is home alone now. Should we try to see her?"

"I don't think she'll open her door to us, do you?"

"We can try," Eliza said and walked toward the door, Angelica on her heels. But no amount of knocking could persuade Lucretia to open the front door.

"She's gone. Probably left through the back door. Some spies we are," Angelica said.

"Either that or she just doesn't want to see us. But why?"

"She summed us up at first glance. She could tell we were feigning interest in the WMA." Angelica slipped her arm through Eliza's.

"Maybe we should find someone who looks the part. But even as I say that I'm not sure what that is," Eliza said.

"Why is she so difficult?" Angelica wondered.

"I've wondered the same. If she and her group stand for good behavior, why is she not hospitable? Surely that's one of the tenets of good behavior."

"Indeed."

The sun warmed their skin, even as the bitter air did not. They walked briskly toward Alice's home, trying to keep warm, while the wind howled between the buildings like a hungry beast, shifting drifts of snow, stinging Eliza's face. Could Jo be here, somewhere in this frozen maze of streets? The notion drove Eliza forward, despite her numb feet.

Around her, New York had become alien and threatening. Familiar storefronts transformed into looming shadows; alleyways gaped like open mouths.

The cobblestones were treacherous with ice, forcing the sisters to pick their way between piles of horse manure and frozen puddles. Around them, vendors' cries echoed off buildings.

"Hot chestnuts!"

"Fresh oysters!"

The cries mixed with the clatter of cart wheels and the barking of stray dogs. The bitter wind carried the mingled scents of wood smoke, rotting fish from the docks, and the ever-present tang of human waste that even winter could not mask.

Eliza slipped on an icy patch, holding on to Angelica to keep her upright.

"Are you all right?" Angelica asked.

"I just slipped. It's fine." Eliza righted herself and sighed. She couldn't wait for the spring, though it was a long way off.

They made it to Alice's, where Eliza rapped on the door. Alice answered with René, both lively and happy to see them.

"Come in!" she said. "Warm your bones."

Eliza, Angelica, and Alice sat down in the tiny room.

"What brought you here on this cold day?" Alice asked.

"I'm searching for a house to let. We may have to move from the Grange," Eliza said. Her face heated with the shame and horror of those words coming from her mouth.

"Oh, I see."

"How are you, dear Alice?" Angelica focused on her.

"I'm grand," Alice said. "I found out something yesterday. Something about Rebecca and Mrs. Van Horn."

Eliza's attention pricked up. "And?"

"They may have recognized each other from the Widow Society. Mrs. Van Horn took an interest when Rebecca's mother became ill. She found a doctor for her, even though it did no good," Alice said.

"So, you think she might have recognized Rebecca, even when she was dressed as a man?" Eliza asked.

"It's possible she did not. But she could have. Maybe she didn't outright recognize her, but their familiarity made her feel comfortable with Rebecca, even if she did not realize it."

"Did you learn anything else at the Widow Society?" Angelica asked.

"I'm afraid not," Alice said. "We all know their stories. There is nothing more to add."

But Eliza noted a measure of sadness on Alice's face. Was it because the place brought up such bad memories for her? Or had she discovered something she didn't wish to share?

"When we were there, we found out that the WMA has been recruiting both members and women wishing to marry from the Widow Society," Eliza said. "We also found out that Rebecca told them she had no interest in marrying. In fact, she and Lucretia had words."

"Really?" Alice's eyebrows shot up. "Now, that is something. Rebecca was never cross."

René walked in the room. "The question still remains—what was the nature of their relationship and did she hire Rebecca to deliver something?"

"And if so, what was it?" Angelica persisted.

"My friend working for Mrs. Van Horn is trying to find that out," René said.

What was Mrs. Van Horn hiding? And then there was Lucretia Short, who would not even open the door to her and Angelica. She wondered if those two were familiar with one another. Now that they had learned that Ramsay was acquainted with Lucretia, the entanglement provided much to mull over. Mrs. Van Horn. Lucretia. Ramsay. What was the connection?

Maybe there wasn't. Maybe Eliza was imagining things, as she had done so many times, always a problem to her parents and, later, Hamilton. But her instincts told her otherwise.

# Chapter 50

The next day, while Eliza and her family were stringing together candies for the Christmas tree, Eliza received a visitor: Constable Schultz.

"I'll see him in the sitting room," Eliza told Mrs. Cole as she tied a knot in the string and handed it to James. "This string of stars is finished."

Little Eliza held up a paper star she made. "Look, Mama!"

"It's beautiful. How many more will you make?"

The girl glanced at her papers. "As many as I can,"

"I shall return soon. I'll be in the sitting room." Eliza hated to leave the happy tableau.

"Shall I come with you?" Angelica said.

"If you wish."

"Why is a constable here to see you?" Alexander Jr. said as she was leaving the room.

"I have no idea. But I'll let you know." Eliza kept walking.

Constable Schultz stood when she and Angelica entered the room.

"How nice to see you," Eliza said. Angelica, on her heels, said nothing.

"Mrs. General Hamilton," Schultz said. "Mrs. Church."

"Please sit. Is everything all right?" Eliza gestured to a chair.

Schultz perched on the chair and nodded. "I'm here for two reasons."

"Yes?

"We've had a sighting of your friend Josephine."

"What?" Eliza's hand clutched her chest. Angelica grabbed her shoulders. "And?"

"A gentleman came in yesterday. A marriage broker in town to pick up a wife for a farmer in Pennsylvania."

Eliza nodded. "Yes, yes?" They had known about the Pennsylvania farmer and that he'd offered more money for Jo. But they'd not heard a word since.

"He read about the reward being offered and figured she was the young woman he met two days ago. He said she was . . . how should I say . . . she had the mind of a child. Barely spoke, ate cake as if she were an animal."

"That doesn't sound like Jo. That couldn't be!"

Angelica clasped her hand. "We don't know what's happened to her."

Eliza's breath left her. "Where is she? We must go to her now."

"We can't." Schultz gazed at the floor and then back up at Eliza and Angelica. "She escaped."

"What? Escaped where?" Angelica hissed.

He cleared his throat. "There was a tea. A meeting. He was representing the gentleman in Pennsylvania, and she walked out."

"Just walked out?" Angelica repeated. "Where is she now?"

"We don't know." His Prussian accent was pronounced. Eliza recognized his nervousness. "We know she spent the night at the country church, St. Paul's, the night before last. She's wearing a lavender dress." He paused. "She has a blanket, but no cloak or hat."

"Why leave the church? Why did she not go home?" Eliza twisted at her dress. "I don't understand."

"The minister of the church approached her, and she ran. He tried to catch her, but she was fast," he said.

Fast. That sounded like Jo, but nothing else did. A lavender dress? The mind of a child? Eliza reflected on her own daughter, broken by her brother's death. Never again the same. Had something like that happened to Jo?

"Why did she not go home?" Eliza repeated the question more to herself than to Schultz.

"It seems as if she might not remember her home." Schultz stared at the floor again. "I am sorry to tell you this news. But we are searching for her."

Eliza's heart raced. "What about Alice? Have you told her?"

"Ja. She knows."

Eliza could not find words. Jo escaped from the marriage broker and the people who had kept her. She was somewhere in the city. The cold, cold city. "What can we do?"

"There is nothing for you to do but wait." He stood. "I need to get back to the search. Good day, ladies." Schultz left the room.

There was nothing for Eliza to do but wait. The one thing she was never any good at.

"What shall we do?" Angelica paced in front of the floor-to-ceiling windows.

"Where would we begin to even search?" Eliza said.

"We know she was at the St. Paul's church. We could start by searching around there."

"I'm sure the constables are considering that area."

"He said she was there the night before last."

"She could be anywhere by now. She's fast and wily."

"We need to think like her. She's scared and maybe doesn't remember her home. Her name even. Where would she go?"

"She went to the one place I'd figure she'd choose. A church."

"There are other churches," Angelica said.

"Mother," Alexander Jr. walked into the room with James. "We're joining the search for Josephine."

"What?"

"We ran into Schultz in the foyer. He told us what's happening. Two more men could help the cause," James said. "We should be back by nightfall."

Eliza's heart exploded with pride. Her boys were helping to find Josephine. She searched for words as she embraced them.

"Please be careful," she said finally, as they walked out into the bracing evening.

"Well," Angelica said. "That is that. We can't search for her now. Your boys would not allow it. Nor would Schultz."

"If we can imagine a likely place she'd be, I'd go there as quickly as possible." Eliza's heart sank.

"Let's sit and consider what is around the church. Establishments. Homes. That kind of thing. Maybe we can come up with something."

Eliza and Angelica sat and listed all the homes, churches, and establishments they could remember that were in the area where Jo had last been seen. Mrs. Cole brought them the newspaper and the mail, which had been getting delivered late in the day. Eliza supposed it might be because of the weather.

As Eliza took the stack from Mrs. Cole, the word "murdered" jumped out at her from the newspaper. Eliza unfolded it and read aloud: "'Lucretia Short, Head of the Women's Morality Alliance Found Murdered in Her Home.'" Eliza gasped and dropped the paper.

Angelica lifted the paper and read it over. "Oh dear." She read more. "Eliza, the reason she didn't answer the door is because she was lying dead in her house."

"Ramsay!" Eliza said, heart racing. "We must go to the constabulary and tell them we saw Ramsay there."

"They are busy looking for Jo." Angelica stood and paced.

"They must also be searching for Lucretia's killer." Eliza picked up the paper and read over the article. "Wait. It says here she had a meeting with Ramsay that afternoon, which we know. There was a planned meeting with her group later in the day. The next morning, she was scheduled to appear in court."

"Court?" Angelica stopped pacing.

"It doesn't go into why. But she never showed up. So, she wasn't dead when we were knocking on her door."

"Not dead, then. Just rude," Angelica said.

"She was rude, and from what we know, opinionated, and not intelligent," Eliza said. "But she didn't deserve to die like that."

Eliza prayed for her. As misguided as she was, it was a sad and pointless ending. Just what had the poor woman gotten herself into?

"What about her husband and family?" Angelica asked. "She was always preaching about family. Where is hers?"

Eliza scanned the article further. "Her husband, a minister, has been traveling up north."

"A minister?" Angelica said. "That makes sense."

"I know they often travel from village to village," Eliza said. "But to leave your wife behind? I had always assumed they took their wives with them."

"Poor woman. Murdered in her own home, without another soul around."

Dread filled Eliza. "She's the second murder victim we know about these last few weeks. The other is Rebecca. Our theory was the WMA and Lucretia might have something to do with it since they ran that advertisement—"

"Maybe they did. I'm not ready to let go of that theory. Just because she died doesn't mean she and the WMA are not guilty of another kind of murder."

Eliza grunted. "They certainly are against women dressing in men's clothing."

"And women not marrying. That hasn't changed." Angelica plopped down on the settee next to Eliza.

Eliza held up the list of all the places near the country church, which is what everybody called St. Paul's, as it used to be in the country. Not so anymore. The city had grown around it. Her heart dropped. "Jo could be anywhere. If she has no memory. If something terrible happened to her, applying logic will not help."

"She's probably cold," Angelica said. "She'd find a place for warmth."

"And she's probably hungry," Eliza said.

The sisters studied the list. "There's the bakery," Eliza said. "I've learned they throw out what doesn't sell during the day."

Angelica nodded. "It's not just any bakery, is it? I mean, in Paris they are on every street. But here? Usually, you find baked goods on market day. This is one of what? Two? Or three?"

"But she could not sleep inside the bakery."

"There has to be another church."

Mrs. Cole entered the room again. "Supper is ready. Will James and Alexander be joining us?"

Eliza gazed out the window. Darkness tinged the sky. They'd have to stop the search soon. Who knew? Maybe they'd found Jo by now. "Let's put plates aside for them. I'm certain they will be hungry when they return. But I doubt they'll be home within the hour."

Mrs. Cole smiled and left the room.

"Well, let us eat, put the children to bed, and get back to it," Angelica said. "We will take our theories to the constables tomorrow."

Helplessness swept over Eliza. Others were out searching for Jo, including her sons. She wanted to be with them. Doing something. If they didn't find Jo tonight, she'd join the search tomorrow. If nothing else, she and Angelica could keep an eye out near the bakery or other places where Jo might be hiding.

# Chapter 51

As dusk folded over the city, and the temperatures dropped so low that Alice's breath lingered in the air, the search was called off. Like always, morning would come, and the available men would persist in searching for Jo.

Alice worried about Jo surviving the frigid night. Breathing burned her lungs as she slowly returned to her tiny house, unable to will her frozen limbs to move faster. Where could Jo be? Was she comfortable? Was she safe?

Alice closed the door behind her, shoving the cold away. Tears formed from the relief of the heat, the relief of returning to her home with the women she was creating and living a life with. The house was warm and glowing, like a cozy cocoon, with gold, flickering light and heat from the fireplace. Alice loved her little house and the women she shared it with. That someone suspected them of committing unnatural acts sat somewhere between fear and anger with her. Some people just didn't like to see women going against the same old life patterns.

And what if they were living unnaturally? What did it concern anybody else? House of Pearl provided a service to most of the good houses in the city. They paid their rent, paid for their own food, and paid their taxes. Minded their own damn business. What care did people have in insinuating other things about their lives?

A slight movement in the dark on the settee grabbed her attention. Her eyes adjusted and she made out three figures. René sat on the settee with Mary and Brigid, who rose when they perceived her, still bundled in her winter overcoats and scarves. She wasn't sure she'd be taking them off any time soon, as the cold had gotten into her bones.

"News?" René said, with a note of hope.

Alice shook her head. "It's like she disappeared into thin air. One moment in a house having tea and cake, the next escaped into the city."

"She knew enough to go to a church. I'd say she still has some of her wits about her," René said.

"She must," Brigid offered. "She's out there. We just need to find her."

Alice turned to her. "Have you discovered who left the notes?" Brigid and Mary had watched the house all day.

"No," Brigid replied.

"Maybe it was too cold for the nutter," Mary said and laughed a bit.

The room quieted. Alice slumped back on the settee. "Tomorrow is another day." It was something her mother had always said when they could not accomplish as much as they wanted.

"I'll be seeing Maria tomorrow," René said. "Maybe she knows more about the relationship between Mrs. Van Horn and Rebecca."

Alice brightened. "Let's hope. In fact, let's hope tomorrow brings us news and our Josephine." Even as she said the words, she was losing hope for their Jo. How would she survive this cold? Her own limbs were tingling as they warmed, but they were heavy with cold and despair. Were they meant to have hope after the marriage broker had conveyed his information to the constable? Or were they meant to have this sharp, burning fear in their chest?

What cruel thing had happened to Jo? Did she have the mind of a child now? Jo of the sound mind and free spirit. What had someone done to her? How could she, with the mind of a child, survive in this cold, dark city? "She knew enough to go to a church. I'd say she still has some of her wits about her" is what René had said. Those words rolled around in Alice's head repeatedly until they became a living prayer.

Alice was familiar with women who broke easily. Some women were like wild fillies until they were married to the wrong man, who beat them, or might as well have. Some of those women were like the walking dead, broken by the men who were supposed to love and care for them. Figuring they had nowhere to turn, they broke. Some of them were in asylums. Some of them walked the streets. Some took their own lives.

But Jo was not like that. She was resilient. Her father died many years ago, leaving her and her mother destitute enough to be taken in by the good women at the Widow Society. A few years later, when her mother died, Jo was at a crossroads she had never considered. But rather than strike out on her own, she had stayed and helped care for the children in the house and helped with the chores. In the evenings she worked on lace. That was when Alice had spotted her. Alice herself was seeking another situation. She and René had put their heads together and while still at the Widow Society began selling lace until they had enough money to rent a place. But they'd recognized that they'd need more craftswomen to join them.

Jo had been sitting near the fire with her tiny needles, crafting nearly perfect patterns. Her concentrated expression caught Alice's attention. As she got closer to the fire, she'd seen the beauty Jo was creating. Alice had gasped. "My dear. You have an extraordinary hand!"

Jo glanced up at her and grinned. "Thank you. My grandmother taught me."

This moment came to Alice in detail, the pattern of lace Jo was working, Jo's deep brown eyes reflecting the fire. Her eyebrow lifting.

"Do you need a teacher?"

Alice found the remark endearing. When it came to lace making, Jo could teach her very little. But the fact that she wanted to try to teach her? That said a lot about Jo's heart.

# Chapter 52

Eliza and Angelica waited deep into the night for Alexander and James, who both arrived famished and half frozen. They ate from their warmed plates.

"What news is there?" Eliza asked as they were eating.

"We formed groups. One group went north of St. Paul's; the other went south," James said between bites. "She vanished."

"Impossible!" Angelica said. "She must be close by. We're just not searching the right places."

"What about the bakery near the church?" Eliza said.

"What of it?" James asked.

"She'd be searching for food. Maybe she'd be around the bakery somewhere. Searching for scraps of food," Eliza said.

"I believe it's just north of the church. I'm sure we looked there."

Eliza let out an exasperated sigh.

"Mother, the city is growing every day. I barely recognize parts of it myself. There are so many little alleys leading to God knows where—"

"And don't forget the camp around the Collect Pond. It's a maze," Alexander added.

Eliza hadn't thought about the Collect Pond, one of the city's sources of fresh water. People who could not afford to rent a home lived around it in tents and makeshift homes.

"She could be anywhere," James said with sadness in his voice.

It took much effort for Eliza to get out of bed the next morning. She had stayed up late because her sons were out and now she was paying for it. She glanced over at Angelica's spot, where Hamilton used to sleep. Of course Angelica was already awake and probably giving orders to Mrs. Cole on how to prepare breakfast.

Eliza slipped on her robe and headed downstairs, where everybody in the family was already gathered at the table.

"Look! Eliza rises!" Angelica teased.

"Madam," Mrs. Cole entered the room. "Constable Schultz is here to see you again."

Eliza's heart raced. He must have news. "I will be right there."

"You've not had your tea yet," James said. "I will go."

Eliza continued for the stairs. "You may go, but I will be right there."

She dressed swiftly and raced back to the sitting room. James and Constable Schultz eyed her as she entered the room.

"Please sit, Mother," James said.

"What is it?" She plopped down next to him. "What has happened?"

"We have found Josephine," Schultz said, voice quivering.

Eliza leaned closer. Was it bad news? Had she died? Why was he pausing? "And?"

"She is alive, but barely," Schultz said. "She has frostbite, is malnourished, and knows her name, but nothing else, I'm afraid."

A burning need swept through Eliza. "We must go to her."

"Mrs. General Hamilton, she is under medical supervision and is not in any condition—"

"It might be best if we give her a few days," James said.

"But what has happened to her? Does she know where she's been?"

Schultz shook his head. "Nothing."

"Where did you find her?" Angelica had walked in during the conversation, but Eliza's eyes were fixed on the constable.

"A farmer found her sleeping with his cattle in the barn," he replied, eyes cast downward. "I want to promise we'll find who did this to her, but I'm not sure."

Making sure that Jo was safe was top of Eliza's mind. Did it matter who did this to her? The word "justice" popped into Eliza's head. Maybe they'd never find justice for Jo or for Rebecca. But Eliza was not ready to give up. A clue to where Jo had been held must exist. But she didn't trust the constabulary to figure it out, given that they had completely overlooked Rebecca's cause of death. Which prompted Eliza to wonder why they were giving Jo's disappearance such attention. Was it the marriage broker's intervention?

"The important thing is she's alive," Angelica said, "and we should all be thankful. I'm sure she will heal and be her same old self soon."

Schultz could not pretend. Give a smile. A word of encouragement. His gaze shifted.

Eliza spotted the lack of hope in him. Fire burned in the pit of her stomach. "We need to find out who is responsible for this."

"I cannot discuss the ongoing investigation with you. I've said this to you many times." He surveyed James, who shrugged. Schultz lowered his voice. "We had a lead, given to us by the marriage broker, and have questioned another marriage broker. I regret to say nothing has come of it."

"The other marriage broker being the person who had kept Jo against her will," Eliza surmised.

"We have no proof she was keeping her against her will."

"She!" Angelica said. "What kind of woman could do this to another woman? Keep her against her will and force her to marry!"

"Sir, we want further investigation into this marriage broker," James said with a force Eliza had not seen before. "Who is it?"

Schultz held up his hand. "I can assure you the matter is being investigated."

"Very well. We shall find out for ourselves," Eliza said. "Thank you for bringing this news. You are free to go." She did not offer him tea and hoped he perceived it.

He stood, embarrassed. "Mrs. General Hamilton, you know highly I regard you. But my station is . . . all I can say is only a handful of these brokers exist in the city."

"We've been to one already," James said. "And we did not fool her. And she is dead now."

"This time we won't be considering fooling anybody. We will just be searching for answers," Angelica quipped.

Schultz exited the room, appearing defeated. Yes, he had been a help to Eliza since losing her husband. But that he would not tell her the identity of the marriage broker annoyed Eliza. She understood his livelihood depended on keeping a code. But this matter was not about that code. Some things were beyond this world. Some things called out for a different breed of justice.

# Chapter 53

"Eliza, you must eat before you do anything," Angelica said.

But nothing appealed to her. Jo was safe but not sound. How Eliza longed to see her. How she longed to find out who had done this to her.

"Just at least eat a biscuit." James handed her one.

She took the biscuit and buttered it. Lucretia Short was dead. She was the woman in charge of the WMA, and she also evidently ran a marriage brokerage. James and Alexander had gone to Lucretia Short's office, but they were turned away and given a note with the name Ramsay on it. "Ramsay must be one of the brokers," Eliza said, before she bit into the biscuit, not tasting it.

"I figured that because the girl gave me the note with his name. But as I wasn't looking for a wife, I paid little attention to it," James said. "So, if she ran a brokerage of sorts and Ramsay is running one of them, how many others could there be?"

"I don't know, but what I do know is that Mother and Aunt Angelica will be nowhere near Ramsay," Alexander said.

If only they discerned that their mother had already been in Ramsay's bedroom, hid in his wardrobe, found a locket beneath his bed. And their aunt had paid off the debt left by Rebecca. They'd been in his home. But Eliza did not have the fortitude to explain this to her sons.

"So, Lucretia is dead. If she was holding Jo against her will, it doesn't matter, because justice has already been served." Eliza broke the biscuit in half.

"We could ask the marriage broker who went to the police, if he's still in town, if it was Lucretia," Angelica said.

Alexander sighed. "I doubt the constable will give us his name, though we can try."

"I can talk to them," James said.

"It's a grand idea," Eliza said. "But it seems we might have other avenues to explore in the meantime. Angelica and I will visit Mrs. Van Horn today to see if she will be honest with us about her relationship with Rebecca."

"We should also inquire about other marriage brokers in town. Schultz said there were a few. We know of Lucretia and Ramsay. Maybe they were collaborating. How many more could there be?" Angelica asked.

"We will find out. One way or the other," Eliza said. "Maybe Coleman would know. We can stop at the newspaper office and ask."

Eliza wished she'd paid more attention to the marriage market, but as none of her children were ready to marry, she'd not paid it any mind. Perhaps James would be married within the next few years. She was sure she wouldn't need a broker—and she wondered who did.

"I like that idea," Angelica said.

"We have a plan, then," James said.

Mrs. Cole would keep the children and watch Angel while the others went into town.

The two-hour carriage trip was mostly silent. Each was in their own contemplation as they approached Manhattan. Jo was once again top of Eliza's mind.

★ ★ ★

The Van Horn butler opened the door. "Mrs. Van Horn is out today. Would you like to leave your card?"

"Of course," Eliza gave him the card with her name elegantly written on it. "Thank you."

Eliza and Angelica soon entered the newspaper offices in a whirl and headed directly to William Coleman's office. He opened the door when they knocked.

"Hello, ladies. What can I do to help you? Please sit down." He gestured to nearby chairs.

"I'm sorry, Mr. Coleman, but we can't stay," Eliza said. "We are on a mission."

"You know the woman you were seeking the last time you were here is dead." He sat on the edge of his desk.

"We are aware," Angelica said. "But we're here to find out if you know how we can reach marriage brokers."

"What for? Is one of your children seeking a spouse?"

"No. Our friend Jo has turned up. The one who was missing? She was being held by someone who planned to marry her off to a farmer in Pennsylvania." Eliza told him the rest of the story.

His jaw dropped.

"You seem surprised," Angelica said.

"I am shocked. To tell you the truth, this is a great story for the paper."

"Wait a minute," Eliza said. "There is no story if we don't know the marriage broker who kept her."

"You can have your story once we know there is one, not just a report of a half-truth," Angelica said.

"That's fair," he replied after a few moments. "As far as I know, there are four marriage brokers in Manhattan. One is concerned with Jewish marriage."

"So we can cross that off the list."

He nodded. "Though I wonder if any of the other three will help."

"Why?"

"It doesn't sound like this person is legitimate, if they are taking young women off the street and selling them to husbands. It's almost like . . . like . . ."

"Prostitution." Angelica finished his sentence.

His face grew red. "I'm sorry. I don't like to talk about such matters with ladies."

Eliza ignored that and persisted. "Exactly. I'm sure it's illegal. And I must wonder how many young women this is happening to."

"We should start with the legitimate brokers," Angelica said. "Because if other brokers in town are not reputable, they will be more than happy to point us in their direction."

"Very well," the newspaper editor said. He tore off a paper and scratched words onto it with a quill. "Once you know who this person is, beyond a doubt, bring the story to me."

Eliza took the note. "You have my word."

Eliza and Angelica began to walk out.

"Ladies?" Coleman said.

They turned back around.

"Please be careful. I'm sure a person selling young women off to be married is unhinged. They may be dangerous."

Their eyes met again, a silent exchange of respect and fear passing between them. She drew in a breath. "We will be careful."

Eliza read over the list and noted that Ramsay's name was not on it.

As Eliza and Angelica rounded the corner to Alice's house, they witnessed a strange woman at the doorstep.

"Wait!" Eliza whispered and dragged Angelica back. She peeked around the corner. Was the woman doing what Eliza believed she was doing?

She attached a note to the door. Was this the person harassing the women who lived here? Eliza and Angelica stood firm as the woman passed them.

Beneath Eliza's cloak, sweat formed as her heart thundered. She and Angelica fell in behind the older woman. From behind the woman had a respectable guise, with a sturdy overcoat, scarves tucked in, and gloves. Eliza did not expect a harasser to resemble her.

She turned the corner off Pearl Street and then the next. Eliza and Angelica attempted to keep their distance while watching where she went. Should they confront her? Eliza had no way of knowing if the person was dangerous. If appearance was any judge of character, she doubted the woman could harm them.

The woman stopped at a door, fetched keys from her bag, and fumbled around with the lock, then slipped inside. A sign hung outside of the building she had gone into: *Sally Connors, Mantua Maker.*

Eliza and Angelica glanced at one another. "A competitor?" Eliza asked.

"It might be. Didn't you say Rebecca was making dresses?"

"Yes, but not at this level. It was one skill she brought to the group. I don't know how many dresses she had even made."

"I'm sure Alice knows," Angelica said.

Eliza and Angelica stood for a moment, sizing up the shop. "Should we approach her?" Eliza asked.

"I think not," Angelica said. "Let's figure out her relationship with Alice and then report it to the constable."

They walked back toward Alice's house. "How dare she write such vile things and leave her note at the door," Eliza said.

"She may be trying to run them off. It may be nothing more than that," Angelica said.

Pearl Street bustled with pre-Christmas activity. Market women huddled over braziers of hot coals, their faces ruddy as they called out their wares: fresh oysters, still glistening with bay water; chestnuts sending up fragrant steam; oranges from the West Indies that cost a week's wages but promised a taste of faraway places. The cobblestones were treacherous with half-melted snow turned to ice, forcing everyone into an ungainly dance of near-slips and desperate grabs at neighboring stalls. Above it all, church bells competed with street vendors' cries, while the constant clatter of cart wheels on frozen ruts provided a steady drumbeat to the city's winter symphony.

A group of children darted past, their patched clothes and hungry eyes marking them as orphans—the kind that would soon fill Isabella and Eliza's new refuge. One small boy clutched a stolen apple to his chest, while a girl who couldn't have been more than six covered his escape with the practiced ease of the streetwise. Eliza's heart dropped. How many more children would winter claim before spring brought relief?

Before they turned a corner, a lone child dashed in front of them, dropping a bundle at their feet. Eliza picked it up and called after the boy. She attempted to follow him, but he was long gone.

"Goodness, in such a hurry!" Angelica said.

Eliza studied the bundle in her hand.

"What is it?" Angelica said.

Eliza held it up for her to see the feather, small animal bones, and rosemary tied together with a red string.

"What on earth?" Angelica said.

"It reminds me of what's in Rebecca's trunk."

"Ridiculous witchery," Angelica said.

Eliza shuddered. It was purely coincidental that the bundle had been dropped by the clumsy but fast boy. But it left her with an odd sensation.

"Where did he get such a thing?" Angelica said as she tugged Eliza along.

"That's a good question."

"I wonder if someone around here is selling them. I told you the wise women sell such items in Paris and London. I did not know it was being done here now," Angelica said.

"It seems a ridiculous waste of time," Eliza's said. But she couldn't shake the odd, prickling sensation.

"Let's get to Alice's place. I am cold. Aren't you?" Angelica slipped her arm through Eliza's. They huddled together down the street, Eliza still clutching the curious bundle.

Mary was exiting the house, picking up the note from the door, when Eliza and Angelica arrived.

"Hello, Mary. We have news. We observed who pinned that note."

Mary's head tilted. "You did? Who was it?"

"Is Alice home? We want to tell you all at once," Eliza said.

"Alice and René are with Jo. I'm making deliveries, and if the doctors allow it, I'll join them after. They are being strict with who gets to see her," Mary said.

"We'd love to see Jo," Angelica said. "Would that be possible?"

Mary shrugged. "You can check. She's at the New York Hospital."

"Is she . . ."

"She is alive but has lost her memory. They say it may come back."

"We'll pray it does," Eliza said.

"Who's leaving those nasty notes on the door?" asked Mary.

"Sally Connors." Eliza shivered. The temperature had dropped, and Eliza's throat burned from the cold.

"The mantua maker?"

"If that's her. We followed her, and she went into the building. She had the keys, so I'm assuming that's her," Eliza said.

Mary nodded. "She wanted Rebecca to work for her. Rebecca was very skilled." A darkness came over Mary. Eliza reached out and touched her shoulder.

"Oh, for heaven's sake," Angelica said. "Don't tell me those notes were because of spite. Because Rebecca worked here and not there."

Mary shrugged. "It's the only thing I can think of. It makes sense, but it's mad. What do you have there?"

Eliza held up her bundle. Mary backed away. "Where did you get that?"

Eliza recounted the story, leaving out that Rebecca had a similar bundle in her trunk. "Where would one get such a thing?"

Mary shuffled her weight from right to left. "There's only one place I know. There's a woman who works at the apothecary . . . she sometimes sells spells to people."

"Which apothecary?"

"Johnston's."

"Why would any self-respecting apothecarist dabble in such matters?" Angelica queried.

"No, she's works for them. She's not an herbalist. She makes delivers and helps clean, that kind of thing."

The wind whipped and whistled in Eliza's ears.

Before Mary walked away, she said, "Oh, please let me talk to Alice before you go to the constable with Sally's name. She will want to handle the matter. I must be off."

Eliza nodded.

Angelica stared at her pointedly. "Where to now?"

Eliza wondered the same thing. They'd found who had been writing the notes but had also been asked to keep quiet about it. They probably could not see Jo. There was only one place left to go: the apothecary.

# Chapter 54

"Are you sure we can't take her home with us?" the kindly old lady said.

The man in charge shifted his gaze from Jo to the kindly old lady. "We must keep her here for a few days. We do not know how she's going to react if she gets her memory back. That could be any day or—"

"Not at all." The lady finished his sentence.

Jo struggled to remember the stoop-shouldered lady with soft brown wrinkled eyes. She moved fast, belying her age, and was quick-witted as she spoke with the doctor. She leaned over Jo. A locket dropped out from beneath her clothes. Something about the locket niggled at Jo.

Her hand swept across Jo's forehead. "We love you," she said. "We'll hunt down whoever did this to you."

But Jo, snuggled into a comfortable bed with warm blankets and soft sheets, was unsure of what she meant. Who did what to her?

Tears formed in the woman's eyes. "We need to gather information from you. We must uncover the truth to find the person who hurt you."

Jo's thick, dry tongue could not find words. She tried to take her mind back. Lemon cake. A man across the table. A plump woman with soft hands. Teacups with pink flowers. Bitter tea.

"Tea," Jo said.

A different woman joined the older woman. "She was having tea and cake with the marriage broker when she ran off."

The old woman straightened. "We need to find this marriage broker."

The other woman, also kindly, but younger, with black hair falling out of her cap, placed her hand on the other women's shoulder.

"Bitter tea," Jo said.

"Was she poisoned?" the older woman said.

"If she was, I've seen no trace of it yet. We've been most concerned with exposure and trying to save her fingers," said the doctor.

"You must do everything you can. She's a lace maker and needs her hands to earn a living," the old woman said. "Though we will care for her no matter what."

The woman's voice soothed Jo. She wanted to wrap herself in the warmth of it. Instead, she closed her eyes and concentrated. She was a lace maker. It made sense. She imagined patterns, not words. But sensed those words. Her hands twitched. She was a craftswoman, as she had suspected. But several of her fingers were still black and deep purple.

"I suppose tea can be bitter without there being poison in it," the other woman said.

*Not the same tea*, Jo thought, but did not say. The first tea. Her last memory before waking up in a wretched state and being told she was ill. But Jo sank now into warmth and oblivion and could not speak. She allowed the pools of swirling warmth to envelop her. She sank further into her bed, into darkness, even as the women standing beside her watched.

# Chapter 55

"Who made this?" Eliza asked the one-eyed woman behind the apothecary counter. She held up the bundle.

"Where did you get that?" Mrs. Johnston replied.

"A boy dropped it on the street," Eliza said. "I want to know who makes this. I've been told you can get them here."

Mrs. Johnston scratched her chin. "Yes. That would be the work of Harriet."

"What can you tell us about her?" Angelica said.

Mrs. Johnston shrugged. "She works for us, cleaning the place up, running errands, making deliveries. That kind of thing."

"What else do you know about her? Why does she make such things?" Eliza asked. She was grateful for a quiet day at the establishment. But now Mrs. Johnston twitched.

"I've asked her not to sell those here. This is a respectable apothecary." Her face grew red. "But she's got a reputation, now, amongst certain women as being a spell maker."

Angelica snorted. Eliza drew back. Spell maker? She'd never heard of such a thing. But she understood exactly what it was. She needed to tread carefully. She didn't want to raise suspicions in Mrs. Johnston.

"How might I contact her?" Eliza asked. Angelica snorted again in the background. "Where is she now?"

Mrs. Johnston backed away. "I don't know. It's her day off." Her one eye squinted. "I can leave a note for her to reach out to you."

"Where does she live?" Angelica said.

"Why should I tell you? What do you want with her?"

"We want to buy the bundle of trinkets," Eliza said after a moment.

"I don't believe that. Not for a minute." Mrs. Johnston cackled. "If you have an ailment, I can help you with proper medicine." She was not a stupid woman.

"Listen," Angelica said. "A friend of ours was murdered. And one of those bundles was found amongst her things. If you don't wish us to go to the constable with that information, you need to tell us where we can find her."

Eliza's face heated as she watched the woman shift her weight, bite her lip, then lean forward. "She's at a card game."

Eliza's heart nearly tumbled out of her chest. "Card game?" Rebecca loved cards. It had been mentioned more than once.

"It's a secret gathering of women who like to play cards," Mrs. Johnston said in a hushed voice. "Secret," she repeated.

Eliza didn't need to ask why it was a secret. Unless it was a card game at home with her family, it was unseemly for a woman to play cards. Especially for money.

"I expect money is involved," Angelica said, once again voicing Eliza's opinion. Angelica's voice matched that of Mrs. Johnston's.

The woman nodded.

"Where is it held?" Angelica said. "Murphy's?"

Mrs. Johnston shook her head. "From my understanding, it's held at the Van Horn residence."

Van Horn? They had just been there and were told Mrs. Van Horn was not at home. Of course, it was not the first time someone had lied about being available to visitors. But what was Mrs. Van Horn involved in? And how were Rebecca and Jo involved?

"Why would they let Harriet attend these card games? She's not in the same social sphere as the Van Horns," Angelica said.

"That's something I've also wondered," Mrs. Johnston admitted. "Harriet is a popular figure, both at the games and with the women playing."

It didn't make sense. There was something they were missing. They didn't have a complete picture, but they had gathered more information than they initially possessed. If only it all made sense.

"Thank you very much, Mrs. Johnston. You've been most helpful," Eliza said.

"You are most welcome, Mrs. General Hamilton," she said and moved on to a customer who'd just entered the premises.

Angelica reached for Eliza's arms and pulled her out of the establishment into the biting air. A snow flurry drifted in front of them.

What had Eliza's life come to, with spell makers and card players now in her orbit? As she and Angelica walked arm in arm, she wondered what her Hamilton would think of them now. She and her favorite sister ambling down the street, huddled together against the freezing wind toward Alice's house on Pearl Street, where McNally waited with the carriage.

McNally surveyed them as they went by. "It's snowing."

"We'll not be long," Angelica said.

He nodded.

Eliza knocked on the door. This time, Alice opened it and embraced her. "Please come in."

As they got situated, Alice filled them in on seeing Jo and her condition. "I wanted to bring her home. But they are concerned about her fingers and toes. She's been frostbitten."

"There is also her mind. She seems in shock," René said.

"She remembers nothing useful. Can barely talk," Alice said.

"But she is alive. All of that will come later, surely," Eliza said.

The women sat for a few moments, basking in the truth of Jo still being alive. Even if damaged and struggling, she still had her life.

Eliza drew in air. "Did Mary tell you I learned who is pinning the vile notes to your door?"

"I've not seen her," Alice said. "She's been making deliveries."

"It's Sally Connors," Eliza said.

Alice sat straighter. "The dressmaker?"

Eliza nodded.

"Too much competition?" Angelica asked.

"Pshaw. There is enough room for all of us. She's a gifted mantua maker. Why would she concern herself with us?" Alice asked.

"She was interested in Rebecca working for her."

"Yes, but it makes no sense that she would leave such threatening notes . . ." Alice said and drifted off.

"Also, there was this strange bundle of things in Rebecca's trunk. A boy dropped that same kind of bundle in front of me today and I found out who makes them." Eliza folded her cold hands in her lap.

"We learned a lot more. We found out about a women's secret card game in town," Angelica went on.

"Yes! Rebecca said it was too rich for her," René said.

"Makes sense, but that Harriet goes to it makes little sense. She is the woman who is a spell maker and works at Johnston's Apothecary," Eliza said.

"Spell maker?" Alice sat straighter. "Is that what they call witches now?"

Eliza shrugged. "All I know is she makes these bundles to ward off evil. Rebecca had one in her trunk."

The room silenced.

"Rebecca was very superstitious," René said. "I can see her purchasing such an item. But why?"

"She must've believed herself cursed," Alice said. "And that breaks my heart."

# Chapter 56

On the way home to the Grange, Eliza and Angelica once more huddled together to keep warm. It was a quiet ride, but Eliza's head was noisy. There was a lot to take in. Jo was alive, though they may have to amputate two of her fingers. Would her mind ever snap back?

She reflected on her own dear Angel, who was traumatized by her brother Philip's death, as they all were, but she'd never recovered. Before the change, she lived a typical teenage life, attending dances, excelling in school, and showcasing her musical talent on the pianoforte. Her musical instrument was the only remaining touchstone of the old Angel.

Eliza and Hamilton had taken her to countless physicians. None of the treatments helped. Not yet. Eliza consistently sought out information on medical breakthroughs for her daughter. A sliver of hope cascaded through her. Maybe treatments existed to help both Angel and Jo. If not now, maybe next month or next year.

Eliza had drifted off to the rhythm and swaying of the carriage. She was abruptly awakened by her sister elbowing her. "Card games. Can you imagine? Cards are expensive. Most are imported from England with hefty taxes. Of course, there would be wealthy women playing them."

"I can't imagine Mrs. Van Horn doing anything so . . . so . . . out of order." Eliza straightened herself. Her neck ached from her odd sleeping position.

"And out of her sphere. I wonder what the women of the WMA would have to say about that."

Eliza chuckled. "Well, maybe as long as they are married and giving their husbands children, it would not matter to them at all."

"Now that Lucretia is gone, I wonder who will be in charge next." Angelica's face was pink with the cold but sparked with interest.

"We will have to watch the paper," Eliza said.

"I assumed they were the ones pinning those notes to Alice's door."

Eliza's brain clicked into gear. "Maybe Sally is a part of the group. Maybe her rancor is about that and not the competition between the concerns."

"It's a grand idea. Even if Alice and friends were running her out of business, why would she write such vile things, unless she espoused those beliefs?"

"She can have those beliefs and not be a member, I suppose," Eliza said.

"So true. But most people are too busy with their own lives to care about what a group of women do in their own home," Angelica said.

"Indeed." Eliza paused. "So, I figure Jo must've found out what happened to Rebecca—"

"And she witnessed too much, stumbled on something . . ."

"But why was she not killed too, if that were the case?"

"It's a good question, and it's one I've been asking myself as well."

"We've assumed the murder and disappearance were connected, but perhaps that's wrong." Eliza's statement hung in the cold air, with the carriage rumbling and squeaking in the background.

"We have one hope of justice," Angelica said. "It's locked in Jo's mind."

Eliza shivered. "You may be right, but we've other lines of inquiry. The Van Horn connection, for one. If we could get her to talk, we might find out what happened with Rebecca."

"And therefore, maybe Jo." Angelica nodded. "What are the other lines of inquiries?"

"Finding out more about the WMA. They may have nothing to do with this, but it seems unlikely they'd run an advertisement in the paper about women and marriage the same day the news about Rebecca is broken."

"What about Ramsay? He was acquainted with Lucretia. We saw him come out of her home."

"On the very day she was killed."

A few minutes passed, with each sister in her own ruminations.

"There is also the bundle of objects," Eliza said, breaking the silence.

"The spell maker's bundle?"

Eliza nodded. "There was a connection between them. If Rebecca went to the spell maker and we can find out why, it may help to sort this."

The carriage began its long ascent up the hill to the Grange, where Eliza's family was. She could not wait to lay her eyes on them. They had an unsettled few months ahead, as they would leave their home. So she planned to savor her time with them there. Was Christmas next week? She'd quite forgotten the dates. This year's Advent had a different tone from what she'd wanted, what she'd planned. But then again, how could she envision her friends at Pearl Street House would face such tragedies, one on top of the other?

There was never any question in her mind that she must do what she could to help them. She was a widow, like them, but she had standing and family, both of which could vanish at any moment. Her circumstance had changed. She was now the Widow Hamilton and would forever be. People did not need to know what dire straits he'd left her in. He was unaware he'd succumb when he did. She'd seen his diary—he'd made plans for later on the day he was shot.

If the bank took their house, then so be it. She surely could take care of her children in a smaller place, just as she'd always done before. The Hamilton family were survivors, if nothing else.

★ ★ ★

The aromatic scent of molasses greeted Eliza and Angelica as they entered the house. Removing their coats in the foyer, they proceeded to the dining room where the children were busy placing cookies into tins.

"What do we have here?" Eliza asked as she lifted Philip onto her hip.

"Baking!" James said. "We told you we'd keep the children busy, and we meant it."

"It resembles a bakery in here." Angelica pointed to little Eliza. "Was this your idea?"

Little Eliza giggled.

"Let's get this cleaned up and then off to bed," Eliza said.

"How is Jo?" Alexander asked as he closed the lid on a tin of cookies.

"She's in shock. They are trying to save her fingers, but they're quite frostbitten," Eliza replied.

Little Philip placed his head on Eliza's shoulder. She swayed with him. "Did you take a nap today?"

"He did not," James said. "But he's almost asleep right now."

"I'll take him up to bed." But by the time she placed her youngest son on his bed, he was sound asleep. She gazed at him as he slept. He would not recall his father. He was far too young to have firsthand memories. But she'd make sure he learned about him. So many children did not know their fathers. Rebecca's child, for instance, would never know his real father or mother. Eliza hoped and prayed whoever had the boy was treating him well.

Many children had wandered in and out of her and Alexander's lives. They always took in more children, if needed. Alexander and Eliza never said no to any child in need of a home. And as the city grew, even more children became parentless. Either they were born without a father, or both parents had died. Sometimes, people just gave up their children because they could not tend to them. It was unimaginable. Eliza was eager to begin work with the orphanage.

She left her son and went downstairs, where, under the supervision of Angelica, the table had been cleared off.

"Mrs. Cole has made an oyster stew that smells wonderful," Angelica said.

"She made enough for an army," James said.

Eliza smiled. "Of course she did."

"Sounds like you two have had quite a day," Alexander remarked, after listening to Angelica and Eliza's recounting.

"Yet we have no proper answers," Angelica said. "Just more questions."

"I disagree," James said. "You've learned several things you didn't know two days ago. Foremost, Jo is alive. And when she gets better, she can tell you herself what happened. Justice will be served."

"We also learned about the card game," Eliza added.

"Yes, that is rather preposterous," Alexander said. "Women playing cards for money?"

"Why shouldn't they?" Angelica teased. "Men do it. Why shouldn't women? I enjoy a good card game."

"I know you do, but you certainly aren't sneaking around and playing for money," Alexander said.

"I might. I simply have not considered it." She grinned with slyness.

"Oh no," Eliza said. "You've given your aunt an idea. London will never be the same."

Laughter erupted around the table.

"I shall start first thing on my arrival back in London," Angelica said.

Laughter lifted Eliza's heart and spirit. As she laughed, her chest filled with warmth. But her smile faded, even as she relished the lightness of the moment. She silently gave thanks, grateful that Jo, though injured, was alive and her own children were unharmed. For she was there to protect them. That much she could give them.

Women like Jo and Alice had no real protection. They only had each other, which could only go so far. Even when one of them was murdered, the law looked the other way. Eliza could only hope Jo would lead them to the killer—and justice for Rebecca.

# Chapter 57

The biting cold of dawn found Alice making her way to the hospital. Bright orange and pink streaked the sky, but the chill cut through her cloak as she walked.

The hospital stood at the corner of Broadway and Pearl Street, a squat building in the middle of a silent, slumbering city. The streets, usually crowded by carts and vendors by midmorning, were eerily still, save for the soft crunch of Alice's footsteps on the frozen ground.

She held her satchel close. Nobody was on the streets yet. But what she had inside the satchel was food for Jo. The other women were at work, their hands diligently creating scarves, hats, and embroidered handkerchiefs for the upcoming Christmas holiday. These were gifts for others to give, yes, but they were also survival—a way to make ends meet in a city where every penny mattered.

The New York Hospital's corridors reeked of sourness and despair. Narrow cots lined the walls, their occupants ranging from merchants' wives to street beggars, all equally humbled by illness. A harried nurse hurried past; her apron stained with substances Alice chose not to identify. The wooden floors, though recently scrubbed, held the ingrained memories of countless spillages.

The smell of sickness and sweat lingered as Alice walked through the hospital halls, the air thick with the breath of the ill. Gray walls stretched ahead, and the soft murmur of the few waking patients reached her ears as she passed rows of sleeping bodies. She walked past rows of sleeping people and found Jo in one of the few rooms for patients.

The hospital ward's miasma of illness made Alice's eyes water as she approached Jo's bed. The thin cotton sheet did little to disguise how much weight her friend had lost. Jo's collarbones stood out sharp as knife blades against her skin. But it was her eyes that struck Alice the hardest. Those once bright eyes stared vacantly ahead. Alice's throat tightened. Minds fractured. But not Jo. Not Jo.

Jo's small private room—a concession to her status as a person of interest to the constabulary—offered little more comfort than the common ward. The single window allowed in the weak winter light that did nothing to dispel the room's chill. A tin cup of willow bark tea sat cooling on the bedside table, the standard treatment for every ailment. A nurse probed Jo's frostbitten extremities.

Alice sank into the chair beside Jo's bed, her pulse throbbing in her neck. Jo was alive. Barely, but alive. The steady rise and fall of her chest were a fragile miracle, and Alice whispered a prayer—something she rarely did—but whatever force had kept Jo alive, she couldn't deny its power.

Jo stirred in her bed.

Alice promised herself she would find the person responsible for this. Who had sucked the life force out of Jo so badly that she couldn't speak? At least not yet.

"Mrs. Rhodes," the nurse whispered. "She spoke a full sentence last night."

Alice's heart leaped. She leaned forward. "What did she say?"

"That she wanted cake."

"Cake?" Alice echoed. Of all things. But it was pure Jo. It was a good sign. She was hungry and had expressed it. The weight on Alice's chest lifted.

"And did you give her some?"

"We did, and she went back to sleep."

So far, she only talked about tea and cake. Things a hungry person might ponder. A thread of hope spun in Alice. Maybe she would remember more details, like who held her captive and if she had discovered what happened to Rebecca.

Alice clicked her tongue. She'd only seen justice a few times in her long life. Eliza had observed it when her son was accused of murder. But no justice came for the man who killed her husband. He'd slithered into the South like the snake he was.

That thread of hope tugged at Alice. Unfortunately, they'd have to get a constable involved at some point, depending on what Jo told them. Alice balled her fists in her lap. She didn't care for the lot of them. Even Schultz always appeared smug. Yesterday, she told him about the notes and who had been leaving them at their door. Again, Schultz's eyes had narrowed with a smugness as if she were wasting his time. He hadn't believed her, not for a second. "Do you mean to say Eliza Hamilton herself witnessed the woman leave the note?" he'd asked, in a dismissive tone.

Alice grunted, "She did."

René convinced her against approaching the woman directly. "We've got enough to take care of right now. Just go to Schultz. He will see to the matter."

That she did. And then he didn't believe her.

No, they'd only involve the constable when necessary. Too much could go wrong with their involvement.

Jo rolled over onto her side and opened her eyes. She blinked.

"Good morning, Jo. I brought your favorite biscuits and jam. Are you hungry?"

Jo sat up, nodding.

Alice reached into her satchel, pulling out the biscuit.

"What are you doing here, Alice?" Her voice was so perfectly Jo. Tears of relief stung Alice's old eyes.

# Chapter 58

The next morning, Eliza was surprised to find Constable Schultz on her doorstep. "Please come in out of the cold."

"Thank you, Mrs. General Hamilton." He wiped his boots on the scraper and came inside.

Eliza led him into the sitting room, wondering what brought him here. "How can I help you?"

He sat on the chair closest to the fire. "Yesterday, your friend Alice came into the constabulary."

"Did she?" Eliza leaned forward. "Is she all right?"

"Yes, yes. Didn't mean to startle you." He paused. "She came in to report the woman who'd been leaving notes on her door."

Angelica came into the room, and the constable nodded at her.

"Yes?" Eliza asked Schultz. "Do go on."

"She said you observed the person doing so," he went on.

"I did. Angelica and I followed her to her place of residence. Sally Connors, the mantua maker. Isn't that what Alice told you?" Eliza asked.

"Yes, but she used your name as well, so I felt as if I should check with you," he replied.

"You didn't believe her." Angelica sat next to Eliza.

"It's just that she's been under so much duress. And Sally Connors's reputation is above reproach. Why would she leave those notes?" His head tilted.

"Alice's reputation is also above reproach." Angelica crossed her arms. "The notes are vile, and she'd been posting them for quite some time. We viewed her doing it."

"I'm curious," Eliza said. "I don't know Sally. But what do you know about her? You say her reputation is good. Yet why did she pin notes on Alice's door?"

The constable just shrugged.

"We assumed it was out of jealousy. She wanted Rebecca Dickens to work for her. Instead, she worked for Alice," Eliza said. "What else could it be?"

"I don't know why she'd do such a thing. Honestly. She has a thriving business, goes to church, and is a member of several charity and social organizations," Schultz replied.

Eliza and Angelica exchanged glances.

"Would the Women's Morality Alliance be one of those organizations?" Eliza asked.

"I believe so, yes," he said, cupping his meaty fingers together on his lap.

"There you have it. The group has run several newspaper advertisements preaching how unnatural it is for women to not have husbands," Eliza said. "These notes, though, point toward the same thing. It's vile and unconscionable."

He crossed his legs and leaned back in the chair. "She claims she did not do it."

"Of course she does. I am happy to come into town with you and identify her," Eliza said. "We have other errands to attend to, as well." She wanted to check in on Jo and had ordered some ribbons for her daughters' stockings.

"The children are outside with Alexander and James. I shall tell them what we're doing," Angelica said.

"Are you coming with us?" Eliza asked.

"I wouldn't miss this," Angelica said.

They journeyed into Manhattan swiftly, with McNally pushing the horses as fast as he could. Houses, woods, and establishments went by in a whirl. They lurched to a stop in front of the constabulary, Schultz right on their tail.

A large woman sat at a desk inside. A woman in the constabulary was an odd sight Eliza had never witnessed. Schultz gestured for Eliza and Angelica to sit near the woman. Eliza glanced at the woman and smiled. She was a pretty woman with startling blue eyes and perfect lips. Dressed impeccably, she sat with regal posture.

"Mr. General Hamilton, Mrs. John Church, this is Mrs. Regina Conners, otherwise known as Sally," Schultz said.

"What?" Eliza said. "This is not the woman we saw pin the note on the door."

Sally smiled. "Thank you. I told them you must be mistaken."

"But the woman walked into your shop," Angelica said. "And she had keys to allow her entrance. You must employ her."

The woman's face fell. "Oh dear."

Schultz cleared his throat. "Who might that be, Mrs. Connors?"

"That would be Marcy," she said. "But I let her go yesterday."

"Why?" Schulz asked.

"She was stealing from me," she replied.

"How much?" Schultz asked.

"It wasn't money," she said. "Oh, she didn't have access to the till. It was fabric. I found pieces of expensive fabric amongst her things. She's been taking it. I don't know what she planned to do with it. Maybe sell it?"

Eliza at once remembered Rebecca's commonplace book with scraps of fabric cut into dresses and hats.

"Where does she live?" Eliza asked.

"She and her son used to live in a room above my shop." Her face grew red. "But I couldn't have a thief living above my shop. I believe she went back to her parents' home."

"With her child?" Eliza asked.

"Yes," she said. "He was a good boy. But his mother often let him run in the streets. His father was killed a few years ago, and she came to me seeking work. She was talented with a thread and needle. Quick too."

The story was familiar. Women left alone, trying to earn their way. Eliza suspected the young woman lacked a supportive family.

"Do you know where her parents' home might be?" Schultz asked.

"Her family farms out on Long Island. I suppose she might be there." She turned to Eliza and Angelica. "I must apologize for her behavior. What was she thinking pinning notes to the doors of women?"

"They were indecent notes, accusing them of many things," Eliza said.

Sally nodded. "Sounds like her. She was very opinionated and had quite the imagination."

"The women who live there are hard workers, just trying to get by," Angelica said. "To suggest otherwise is absurd."

"I quite agree." Sally stood. "May I go?"

Schultz nodded. "Of course, and I am sorry for any inconvenience."

"Nonsense. With my name on the line, of course it was no trouble at all," she said.

"Pleased to make your acquaintance," Eliza said and stood and extended her hand.

Sally shook it. "And yours."

After Sally left, Schultz turned to the sisters and shrugged. "I suppose I'll be needing to go to the farm to find Marcy."

"You do that, but I'm afraid she won't be there," Angelica said. "Tale as old as time. I'm sure there was no husband, and that her family abandoned her."

"Let us hope you're wrong," Schultz said.

# Chapter 59

Eliza and Angelica traipsed off to pick up the ribbon, candy, and oranges for the children's stockings. Christmas was only a week away. Eliza had a lovely dinner planned, and Angel was working on learning special songs. But a pall hung over Eliza's preparations. She thanked God for sparing Jo's life but grieved for Rebecca and longed to find justice.

She and Angelica braced themselves for the cold walk to the hospital to check on Jo. Turning the corner, they nearly collided with a young woman carrying a child and a suitcase. No wonder she was not paying attention. Eliza recognized her right away. Marcy. So she had not gone to live with her parents on the edge of town.

"Excuse me," Eliza said and proceeded on her hunch. "Are you Marcy?"

Her eyes widened and jaw clenched. "Who wants to know?"

"Allow me to introduce myself and my sister," Eliza said, giving their names.

The woman backed away. The boy tugged at her. "Nice to make your acquaintance, but I have to go."

"Where are you going?" Angelica asked.

"I'm looking for a new position. I was let go from my job. There's the little one to feed." She was breathless.

"Maybe we can help. What do you do?" Angelica asked.

"I sew, make dresses and things." The boy tugged at her again. "Just a minute," she told him.

"Why were you let go?" Eliza asked. "And right before Christmas. It's doesn't seem right."

The woman shook her head. "She didn't say why. Instructed me to gather my belongings and go."

"There must be more to it than that," Angelica said.

"Well, I . . . I brought trouble to her."

"What do you mean?" Angelica leaned in.

"Someone followed me, after I'd done her dirty work."

"I'm confused," Eliza said.

Angelica crouched down to gaze at the boy. "My favorite sweet shop is right over there. Would you like some sweets?"

"Can I, Ma?" The boy's eyes sparked with hope.

"We must go," she said. But then she took in Eliza and Angelica and said to him, "Please come back quick."

Eliza led her to the side of the walk. "What dirty work were you doing?"

"Why should I tell you? Why do you want to know?" The woman still didn't trust Eliza.

"Because I am the person who followed you after I observed you pinning vile notes on my friend's house."

The woman's face fell. "Vile?"

"Didn't you read them?" Eliza tightened her scarf against a sudden wind.

"I can't read, madam. I have tried, but the letters go lopsided in my head. Thank God I can work a needle," she said. "So, you followed me."

"I did. And we accused your employer. We were at the constabulary earlier. She blamed everything on you."

"Hmph. Of course she did."

Eliza considered what she learned. This young woman could not even read. She had been doing the bidding of the woman she worked for, Sally. And Sally was a member of the WMA. Marcy was clueless about her actions.

"Do you have a place to stay?" Eliza asked.

"I found a boardinghouse for women, but I have no idea how I will pay until I can find work." Her chin quivered. "Such hard times."

Eliza dug in her satchel and pulled out money, her fingers numb from the cold, even through her gloves. "Take this." She handed it to the woman. "You've helped us a great deal by telling us what you did."

"I hate to take money from you . . ." But she did. "Thank you, Mrs. General Hamilton. I will pay you back."

"That's unnecessary. But perhaps you could tell me more about Sally."

Marcy gazed at Eliza. "I'll tell you anything you want to know."

Soon she was walking with Eliza and Angelica to the boardinghouse on Jane Street. Despite the boardinghouse being full, she secured a room thanks to her acquaintance with the proprietor. Marcy and her son now had a small space, no larger than a folded-out trunk, to call their own. Marcy then shared her story with Eliza, Angelica, and her son while they all sat together in the sitting room.

# Chapter 60

"Sometimes memories are so painful or shocking the mind blocks them," the doctor said to Alice. "But she may get them back and I warrant it won't be pleasant."

"I see," Alice said. "We'll take good care of her."

Jo wore her sturdy wool cloak, brought by Alice, and it weighed on her bones.

"We'll give her plenty of good food, and the women we live with will fuss, no doubt."

"I'd like to see her in a week. I will stop by," the doctor said. He turned to Jo. "You've been through an ordeal. Please rest."

As if she could do anything else. She nodded and managed a slight smile. "Thank you, Doctor."

She and Alice clutched one another to fight against the cold as they walked toward their home. Houses. Shops. People. All appeared sharp and real in her view, yet she had no memory of them. Did she? Her breath escaped in puffs. Her legs shivered with weakness. The walk was so long. She'd need to sit soon. Had she always been so weak?

They rounded a corner, passing through a gate into a small courtyard. Two women stood knocking at a door. Her door. This was home. She recognized it, even surrounded by mounds of snow. That door. A flash came to her, of running out of it, searching for someone. Fear pulsed through her veins and motioned her forward. Who was she searching for?

She stopped. She contemplated the house, unsure if it was a good choice. Would it be like the last place? She'd been so mistreated that she had to escape.

"Jo?" Alice said. The other women turned.

Alice's voice stirred Jo, deep and curling around inside of her. Comforting.

"Jo, these are friends, Mrs. General Hamilton, and Mrs. John Church."

The first woman stepped forward. "Please call us Eliza and Angelica."

*Eliza. Angelica.* The words rolled around in her mind. Names. Faces. She could not connect the two. She merely smiled.

"Let's get you inside," Eliza said.

Alice took out her key and unlocked the door. The sound of rattling keys set Jo on edge, but when she opened the door and Jo walked inside, only one word came to mind: home. Warmth spread through her as she eyed the old settee and chairs, the fireplace, the embroidery hoops left on the stairs.

Alice helped her off with her cloak. "None of the others are here or you'd have a gaggle of women fawning over you."

Instead, there were just three of them.

"I'll get the tea," Eliza said.

Alice nodded. "I'll stay with you," she said to Jo. Her eyes shimmered, as if she might cry at any moment.

"I'm all right. I remember this place." She'd found words. Why were words so difficult? They didn't come out as she planned. There was a strange cadence to them. So different from what was in her head. She sat next to Alice.

"I'll help," Angelica said to Eliza.

She could hear the two women in the kitchen downstairs.

"How do you feel?" Alice leaned closer.

"Strange. I recall this place. This is a good place." Her words were getting better.

Alice cracked a smile.

"There are terrible places, and I can't remember them. Just that they are bad." And left her frightened, and hopeless. Empty.

Confusion played across Alice's face.

"It's almost like a game in my mind. But it's very shadowy. Dark images, mostly." It was difficult to explain. Jo wasn't sure she was capable.

Alice squinted. "Maybe it's best you can't make sense of them. Maybe you shouldn't try."

Eliza and Angelica came into the room then with tea. Angelica poured as Eliza sat in a chair next to the fireplace.

Jo watched the steam from the tea curl around. She lifted the saucer. Plain white dishes. No flowers. The pink flowered teacup in her memory swirled. She blew on the steaming tea.

"There was someone giving me tea. It's the last clear memory I have. But I can't conjure her face. Just her plump, bejeweled hands. And the pink flowers on the cup."

Alice sat back, frowning.

"Half the women in this city must have teacups with pink flowers," Angelica said.

"But not all have plump fingers," Eliza responded.

"Might you recognize this woman's voice?" Angelica asked.

Jo closed her eyes, willing herself to remember a voice. But when she considered the sound, all she recalled was a rush in her ears. And then nothing.

# Chapter 61

Something was missing in Jo. It wasn't just because she'd lost so much weight. Her eyes had lost their spark. Also, their bright quickness. Now they appeared dull and almost lifeless. Perhaps as she healed, Jo would look more herself. Eliza chided herself. What did she expect? Who knows what she had been through?

"We will not push you to remember anything," Alice said. "We just want you to get stronger and rest. If the memories come back, fine. If not, that is fine too."

A knock erupted in the quiet room.

"I'll get it," Eliza said, rising. When she opened the door, she was half startled to see Constable Schultz.

"I understand Josephine is at home. May I see her?" he asked.

Eliza's protective hackles raised. "That's not a good idea. She is exhausted. And still recalls nothing. Can you come back tomorrow?"

He frowned. "I shall try."

She stepped out into the cold and shut the door behind her. "Her condition is troubling."

"I'm sorry to hear that."

Eliza folded her arms close to her. "But I need to tell you that we ran into Marcy."

He titled his head. "How so? Her parents have not had a word from her in years, they said."

"Quite literally on the street. We talked with her and made sure she had a place to stay."

"Where is she then?"

"She's at the women's boardinghouse on Jane Street. I imagine she'll stay there until she finds work. But listen, she can't read or write. Sally Connors wrote those notes." Eliza shivered.

He leaned forward. "Is that what she told you?"

"Sally Connors paid extra for each note she left."

"But what was the reason for the notes?" His face reddened. Eliza was unsure if it was because of the cold or his embarrassment.

"As I understand it, she considered it her duty to rid the neighborhood of 'unnatural women.'"

He frowned. "I shall talk to both of them." He paused. "That is harassment. Plain and simple. Thank you for telling me." He started to walk away.

"One more thing, Constable Schultz."

"Yes?" He turned.

"Marcy said Sally was unkind to her. She forced her to do unseemly things as well."

"Like what?"

"Entertaining her foreign gentlemen friends," Eliza stammered. "Do I have to say more?"

He shook his head. "No, madam. You need not say more. This conversation has been helpful. Thank you. Good day, Mrs. General Hamilton."

Eliza slipped back into the warmth of the house. "That was Constable Schultz. He will return tomorrow," Eliza said as she reentered the circle of women.

"Constable?" Jo said. "Whatever for?"

"We all want to find the person who did this to you," Alice said. "But if we find the person first, then we have no need of the constable."

"Besides, you are in no condition to speak with them," Angelica said. "It was good of you to send him away, Eliza."

"We certainly appreciate their help in finding you," Alice said. "But they've not done a thing to find who hurt Rebecca."

Jo's eyes widened. "Rebecca? What's happened to Rebecca?" She stood. "I must find her."

Eliza stood. "Please sit back down. You are—"

She shoved Eliza away. "No! What's happened? You must tell me."

"I'm sorry to tell you that Rebecca is dead," Eliza said.

"Dead? How?" Jo sobbed. "How?"

"She was murdered," said Eliza.

Jo gasped and fell backward onto the settee. Alice wrapped her arms around her as she crumpled.

"I don't believe it! I don't believe it."

It was a lot for the woman to take in. Her first day back at home, surrounded by people she barely remembered. Eliza worried it was too much for her fragile state.

Alice pulled Jo away, holding her shoulders, meeting her eyes. "We are going to get you strong. You'll remember who did this to you and what happened to Rebecca."

"What do you mean?" Jo asked. "Was I there?"

"You went in search of her. She'd been missing."

Jo bit her lip. Her eyes darted back and forth. "I don't recollect the details, but I think I was searching for someone. That makes sense to me." She sniffed.

Eliza occupied the seat across from her. "My daughter has had problems remembering things. Her doctors say it's important not to tax herself, force herself. The memories will bubble up in due time."

Jo paled. Her eyes slackened.

"Let's get you to bed," Alice said, standing. "Let's not mull this over right now. Rest your mind."

Alice led Jo out of the room, leaving Angelica and Eliza sitting there.

"I don't think she wants to remember," Angelica said. "And I can't blame her."

"Nor can I," Eliza said. The longer Jo's memory remained elusive, the greater the likelihood of a murderer going unpunished. Just like Burr. Of course, one could not hurry a hurt person in a matter as delicate as this. This was different. People recognized who Burr was and grasped what he had done. Yet there were still similarities. The constables had turned a blind eye, just as they had done with Rebecca's death. Because she was found dressed as a man, outside a gentleman's club. And because she was not wealthy. Eliza didn't know which was worse.

⋆ ⋆ ⋆

The next day, while eating luncheon with her family, Eliza received mail. She set aside the notice from the bank and focused instead on the letter from Williamsburg. It was from Rebecca's cousin, Lily Binns.

*Dear Mrs. General Hamilton,*

*I am saddened to learn of Rebecca's passing. She was dear to me. It is with the deepest gratitude that I write to you.*

*We had tried to get her to come and live with us, but she had declined. But she said in her last letter to me she was saving her money and would come for a visit soon. She said she had found a way to earn more money, with little effort on her part. I worried she'd been gambling, as it was a weakness of hers. She had a mind for figures and games.*

*I looked forward to that visit as we had not seen each other since I wed at 15. We have maintained a steady correspondence.*

*I can give you the name and address of her brother, but if I were you, I would not bother. He is a shameful and cruel man. He is—I hope you will forgive such crudeness—the father of the child you asked me about. Abomination.*

*The child was adopted into a wonderful family, and I suspect Rebecca found out who and was watching him from afar, as best she could. Though she would not say. She did not like to talk about him or her brother.*

*If you find out anything more about her death, I implore you to reach out to me. I will rest easier when I know justice has been done.*

*Regards,*
*Mrs. Lily Binns*

"What is it, Eliza?" Angelica took the letter from her shaking hand.

Rebecca had money somewhere. Did she get it from the secret card game? And her child was somewhere in the city. The child her own brother made with her. Eliza steadied her hands by placing them on the table. Receiving such news at unmoored her. What could she do?

"Now we know," Angelica said after reading the letter. "It's good to have such knowledge. Another piece added to the puzzle of her death." She passed the note to James. The blood had drained from her face, and she reached for Eliza's hand and squeezed it. "My God," she whispered.

Were the women of Pearl Street House aware of any of this? Did Jo know? She and Rebecca had appeared to be the best of friends. Jo had gone searching for Rebecca, without even stopping to pull on a cloak. Eliza imagined her running through the streets, calling for her friend, then happening upon her body. That would send the best of them into madness.

Eliza pushed away her half-eaten biscuit as her stomach turned. She could not stand the smell of the butter. She held her napkin to her face, with sick creeping up her throat. She stood, ran outside and threw up her midday meal.

Angelica and James trailed behind her. Angelica wrapped her arms around her sister and rubbed her shoulders. James stood on the other side of her.

"Are you quite all right, Mother? This has been an ordeal. Let's get you inside and off your feet."

They walked her back into the foyer, where the bust of Alexander stared at her. She turned her face away. *Not now, my love. I cannot feel the weight of your expectations on me. I can't.*

They brought her into the parlor and sat her on the settee. James lifted her legs. Angelica brought in a wrap to place around her shoulders. A few minutes of silence passed, and then Alexander bounded into the room with the letter in hand. "I know this man!"

"What man?" asked Eliza.

"Rebecca's brother, Jacob! He is a nasty piece of work. Please don't go off and talk with him," James said as he sat down on the edge of the settee.

"There is no need," Eliza said. "What has happened is in the past and poor Rebecca is dead."

"I agree," Angelica said. "Let's stay as far away from him as possible."

Mrs. Cole entered the room with a pot of tea. "It's mint tea. It calms the stomach. "

"Thank you, Mrs. Cole," Eliza said.

James stood and poured the tea. Eliza held the warm cup in her hands and breathed in the mint.

"There is one thing I found curious about the letter," Alexander said. "It says she has money saved. Do you think the women of Pearl—"

"No," Eliza said. "They cleaned out her things and pulled their resources together just to bury her. They don't have the money."

"Maybe she was telling a tale to her cousin," Angelica said. "So she would not worry after her."

"Maybe, but there was mention of gambling and I immediately recalled that card game," Alexander said.

"I did as well," Eliza said.

"I suppose we must visit with Mrs. Van Horn and not play nice," Angelica said after a few moments.

"Letting her know we know about the card game? I'm not sure we want to," Eliza said.

"Mother's right," James said. "If she finds out we know, she'll cover her tracks. All the players will scatter, as gambling is illegal."

"And we don't know if Rebecca was involved or not. She may have been involved elsewhere. There must be more of these card games throughout the city. It's getting bigger each day," Alexander said.

"Mrs. Van Horn did not know that Jo was a woman. She assumed she was a man. She would not have invited her to the games," Angelica said.

Eliza sipped her tea. Once again, it came back to the relationship between Mrs. Van Horn and Rebecca, which was hard to put a finger on. "Maybe this is something Jo can shed light on after she remembers more."

"*If* she remembers more," James said. "Look at our dear Angel. She's never been the same since Phil died."

"But that doesn't mean she won't be someday," Eliza said, refusing to give up on her daughter. She also refused to give up on Jo.

"The mind is not as easily healed as a broken bone," Angelica said.

# Chapter 62

The mint tea helped soothe Eliza's stomach but not her mind. Her thoughts bounced to and fro like a child's ball. She kept coming back to the fortunate fact that Jo was home. Whatever had happened to her, at least she now was with women who cared for her.

Rebecca had no such luck. The path her life took gave her ample reason for bitterness, anger, and sadness. And yet Rebecca had seemed the happiest of them all. Always smiling and laughing. Happy to help anybody with anything. But it caught up with her in the end.

She died alone on the street, with nobody to hold her hand. Nobody holding her. She certainly did nothing to deserve that. And yet, Aaron Burr and his ilk got away with murder and walked freely about the world. Eliza's chest burned with the need for justice. Burr would never get it. But maybe Rebecca would.

She shivered, even as the fire burned hot.

What had happened to Rebecca? Who poisoned her? It wasn't as if she was poisoned there on the street. She was poisoned in someone's sitting room, as she drank tea or ate cake. Alice surmised it was from street food. But street food did not have arsenic in it, or else others would've been keeling over.

Rebecca had been at Mrs. Van Horn's, who said she'd gone to the apothecary. She went to Johnston's Apothecary. So, between

Johnston's and where her body was found outside the gentlemen's club, she'd stopped somewhere to drink or eat.

*If it wasn't so bloody cold. I'd walk that path myself. There must be something, someone along the way.*

James ran into the room. "Mother, you must come immediately."

"Whatever is the matter?" Angelica glanced up from her embroidery.

"We were placing Rebecca's trunk on the back of the carriage to take to the Widow Society, and . . . well, you must see it to believe it!"

Eliza and Angelica followed him outside to where the carriage sat. McNally was gathering something with his hands. Paper? Leaves? The trunk was splayed open, its bottom having fallen out. As Eliza got closer to it, she understood it was not leaves or paper McNally was clutching, but bills of credit. Hundreds of them. Or rather the bills of credit Rebecca could've taken to the bank for gold and coins. Bills of credit were easier and lighter to hide.

"Money!" Eliza exclaimed.

"And a lot of it," Angelica said, stooping down to help McNally place it back inside what was left of the trunk.

After it was all secure, he stood and asked, "Now what?"

Angel came up beside Eliza and wrapped a blanket over her shivering shoulders. Eliza looked at Angelica, who raised an eyebrow.

"I don't know," Eliza said. "Do we take it to Alice? The police?"

"For now, Mother, let us take it back into father's office," Alexander said.

"I'm not certain. That must be evidence. There is something larger Rebecca was involved in that none of us know anything about. Where would she have gotten so much money?"

The question hung in the air, frozen.

"I suggest we take it back in. Tell Alice and the others what we found and then go to the law," Alexander Jr. said.

Eliza nodded. "Fine."

"I had hoped to stay home today," Angelica said.

"That was the plan," Eliza said.

The carriage was already prepared, so all that remained to journey into town was for Eliza and Angelica to dress.

"We'll just be a minute," Eliza said to McNally. "We need to get our winter clothing."

"I'll stay with the children," Alexander said. "We'll go searching for wood for the fireplace. They quite liked it the last time we did it."

"Father was quite right about this big house in the winter. It's using a great deal of wood to heat," James added.

Hamilton had been right. The house was cold and not meant for winter—even with its eight fireplaces. They were spending their first winter in the Grange, which was originally meant to be a summer home. The family spent the first few years of homeownership wintering in lower Manhattan, near Hamilton's office.

"Make sure you dress the children warmly." Eliza turned and trailed Angelica and Angel back to the house, where she found her wool stockings freshly dried. She slipped them on, along with as many pieces of warm clothing as she could find. *Oh, I am so tired of this cold weather.*

She wrapped several scarves around her. Angelica lifted a fur blanket. "I had quite forgotten I brought this with me. We can use it in the carriage."

"Why would you forget something like that?" Eliza asked.

"I suppose I've had a lot on my mind," Angelica said.

"I suppose you have," Eliza said.

McNally stood at the carriage waiting for them. James was already inside. He and McNally helped the two women inside.

"I've never seen so much money in my life," James said. "I estimate it was over a thousand notes."

"I believe so." Eliza imagined what she would do with that kind of money. For one thing, she'd keep her house and the two people she employed. As it stood, she'd have to let at least one of them go. She'd been dreading it. But she had no need for a carriage in the city. She'd sell the carriage and the horse and send McNally on his way. But she was not happy about it.

"She was a gambler," James said. "That is probably where she got the money."

"Must have been quite the gambler," Angelica muttered.

"They say she was. She was also good with figures." Eliza situated the fur blanket around her shoulders.

"I don't understand. If she had money, why was she living with the other women and working for Alice?" James said as the carriage moved, bobbing them around.

"Maybe they weren't her bills of credit," Angelica said after a few moments of listening to the wheels and carriage moaning and sighing with movement. "Maybe she was holding it for someone."

"Maybe," Eliza said after a few moments. "But who did she know who had that kind of money?"

"Many of the households she worked with," James stated. "Starting with the Van Horns."

# Chapter 63

"Come again?" Alice leaned in.

Did Eliza Hamilton just say that Rebecca had thousands in bills of credit in her trunk? That could not be right. None of the women in her house had piles of money. She studied Eliza. Could it be true? Why would Eliza lie to her?

"A hidden compartment in the trunk broke when James and McNally lifted it."

"I see." Yet, she did not. She had assumed Rebecca was forthright. But now, suspicions swirled in her.

"Could somebody have known she had that money and come after her?" Angelica pressed.

"I'm afraid I don't know. This is a shock to me." Alice's jaw twitched.

"We know she liked cards. Do you know if—" Angelica began.

Alice held up her hand. "I know nothing. Turns out I knew nothing of Rebecca."

"Alice, I know you are a keen observer of people," Eliza said.

"Yet I know nothing about this particular matter." Alice paused. "She was living in the Widow Society, doing chores for a place to stay. If she had hidden money, why would she do that?"

"Maybe she'd received the money during the year she lived here," Angelica said.

"What's all this?" René asked as she walked into the room.

Eliza related the story. René's jaw dropped. "Lord," she said.

"Has your friend given you any information about Mrs. Van Horn?" Eliza asked.

"Yes, I am just coming from her. You are already aware of the card games. That is mostly what she told me about. But . . ." She eyed James and her face reddened. "Mrs. Van Horn has been having an affair."

"What?" Eliza's hands went to her chest.

Eliza was such an innocent in some ways, mused Alice. It didn't matter a woman or man's station or rank. Some were controlled by their lust. Alice was less surprised by this news than by the news that Rebecca had hidden money.

Angelica's lips curled into a grin. "Who is it?"

"She's uncertain," René said. "But she thinks it's Ramsay."

"Thinks?" Angelica said.

"He's around the house a great deal. At first, she assumed it was nothing, but he turns up at odd hours," René said.

James cleared his throat. "Ramsay is up to no good, I'm sure. But where is Mr. Van Horn?"

Where was Mr. Van Horn, indeed? What was happening in the banker's house? Alice grunted. Secret card games. Now an affair. And Rebecca was in the middle of it somehow.

"Perhaps Jo could offer some insights into this." Eliza said. "She and Rebecca were close."

"If Rebecca were involved in something untoward, I doubt she'd tell Jo. Jo is straight as an arrow," Alice said. "Always has been."

"I agree," René said. "But what if Jo stumbled upon the secret?""

Alice stood. "I'll ask Jo if she knows anything about this business."

Jo had been not sleeping right. She tossed and turned most of the night. Alice only half slept for her worry about Jo, listening to her every movement. Alice considered it best to leave the poor woman alone while she healed. She rapped on the door and opened it. Jo sat on the bed and lifted her chin.

"Hello. Do we have visitors?"

Jo looked more like herself this morning, still thin and pale, but her eyes were regaining their spark.

"Yes, and they brought news." Alice sat on the bed beside her. "I know you have little memory about the details. But I wonder if you remember anything about Rebecca having money stashed in the bottom of her trunk."

Jo's expression was blank.

"We are concerned she was involved in something that may have led to her death."

"Like what?" Jo folded her hands in her lap.

Alice chortled. "Use your imagination, girl. There was a card game at Mrs. Van Horn's. Very secret-like."

"Hmph. I don't recall if Rebecca ever played there." Jo rubbed her thumbs against one another. "If she did, she kept it to herself."

Alice took her in. Was she just not remembering? Or was she lying? Jo would never lie to her. The old Jo, at least.

"Rebecca liked to play cards, but I don't think she ever played with women. When she played, she was dressed as Rob."

"Good to know," Alice said, pausing. "I've found out a lot about Rebecca since she died. It seems like you were the closest person to her."

Jo frowned. "She was very private. I knew she had a son, though."

"What of him?"

"He's in the city somewhere. She liked to keep an eye on him. Never interfered," Jo said.

Alice wondered if she should push Jo more or let her rest.

"When I was ill . . . I had this feeling I was searching for someone. It was a panicked feeling," Jo said. "Was I looking for her?"

Alice nodded. Maybe she would not have to push. Maybe it was inside of Jo, wanting to come out.

Jo stood and paced in the tiny, windowless room. "Why?"

"She'd been missing. As soon as we understood, you dashed into the cold with no winter things."

A change came over Jo's face like storm clouds gathering: first a shadow, then a darkness that seemed to swallow her previous vacancy. Her hands, still bandaged from frostbite, trembled, and her breath came in short, sharp gasps.

"Where did I go? Why was I in such a hurry?" Her eyes lit.

"You went to Mrs. Van Horn to ask after Rebecca and then you went to Johnston's Apothecary. That is all we know."

Jo squinted her eyes. "It's as if the memory is right in my head but surrounded in a mist." A tear ran down her face.

"Let's stop trying for the day," Alice said. "Why don't you lie down while I see to our guests?"

Jo sank into the small bed as Alice tucked her in. She stood for a moment and watched as Jo closed her eyes.

Alice's bones creaked as she made her way downstairs to where everybody was sitting. "She remembers nothing about money." Alice walked toward them. "But there is something her mind is working on."

"What do you mean?" Eliza asked.

"She is trying to recall why she was so panicked about Rebecca. I guarantee when she does, half of this mystery will be solved."

# Chapter 64

Eliza's brain was exploding with information. "What next?"

"We wait," Alice said and shrugged.

"I wonder if we take Jo to the places she went that day . . ." Eliza said.

James expressed concern. "It may not be good for her. It might break what's left of her mind. We've tried similar exercises with Angel."

"Perhaps we go to the constable with what we know," Angelica said. The room silenced. "I mean, they have to be interested in the money we found."

"Do you mean you think she came into it illegally?" René said.

Alice clicked her tongue. "It makes the most sense, but it's difficult to believe."

"Maybe she uncovered something she shouldn't have and used it to blackmail someone for money," Eliza suggested.

"It's possible. She was wily." Alice paused. "But maybe she won the money playing cards."

René cleared her throat. "Not with the women, remember? If she played cards, it would've been as Rob. She did say she had figured out a way to win."

Angelica's lips curled into a grin. "All gamblers think they've got it figured out. Until they don't."

Eliza shivered. While she lacked knowledge on such matters, Hamilton had recounted tales of men who lost everything to gambling. What did Rebecca know? She spoke with Mrs. Van Horn, then went to the apothecary, then her body was found outside the gentlemen's club. "Could Mr. Van Horn have been in the club?"

"Edwin Van Horn in a gentlemen's club?" James said. "I can't imagine."

"I can," Angelica said flatly. "He's so absent from his home that his wife is having card parties he does not know about."

"And don't forget—my friend says Mrs. Van Horn is having an affair," René said.

For Eliza, the story grew darker and hit deep in a hollow spot in her chest. She never liked to dwell on the affair her husband had been accused of having. Would she have paid money to keep it quiet? To not suffer the humiliation? *Yes. Yes, she believed she would.* "So, let's say both Mr. and Mrs. Van Horn had secrets, and our Rebecca learned about them. Someone was paying her to keep quiet."

"And that person ran out of money—or patience," James said. "But Rebecca was poisoned. Which means either Mrs. Van Horn poisoned her, someone at the apothecary poisoned her, or someone at Lucille's, then they dragged her outside."

Eliza shivered. The motive made sense. But they needed proof. How to get such proof?

"I say we go to Mrs. Van Horn and plainly ask what went on," Angelica said.

Eliza's humiliation was always beneath her skin, and she tried to place herself in Mrs. Van Horn's shoes. "I'm not sure it would give us much. I'm not sure she'd admit to anything yet."

"Perhaps the thing to do is to go to Lucille's club," Alice said. "She would know if Mr. Van Horn spent his time there."

"She won't tell you," James said. "The lists of visitors to those establishments are secret."

"However," Angelica mused, "If we could place him there, particularly on the day Rebecca died . . ."

"Leave that to me," Alice said. "They buy linen from us often." Alice rose and headed toward the door, where she slipped on her cloak.

"And I shall go to visit Mrs. Van Horn," Eliza said.

"I'll go with you," Angelica said.

"How can I help?" James said.

"By staying out of the way," Angelica answered.

René stood and showed them out. "Be careful," she said to all of them with grimness in her voice.

# Chapter 65

Eliza knocked on the door of the Van Horn house. Soon enough, Mrs. Van Horn's maid came and let them in.

"Mrs. General Alexander Hamilton and Mrs. John Church to see Mrs. Van Horn," Eliza said.

The maid spoke, her voice deep and Prussian. "Can I take your cloaks?"

"Of course." Eliza and Angelica slipped out of their cloaks, even though the place was cold for Eliza's taste.

"She'll be just a moment." The woman showed them into a smaller, warmer sitting room.

A lively fire danced in the fireplace. Eliza and Angelica stood in front of it with their hands splayed out.

"Ladies," Mrs. Van Horn said as she entered the room. "I'm so glad you could stop by. The tea will be here shortly. Please have a seat." She was tall, carrying herself with the grace of a gazelle, even though the years of raising nine children had added to her figure. "Whatever are you doing out on a day like today?"

"We came into town for personal business." Eliza tugged at her collar.

"We needed to deliver some items after a friend of ours passed. We went to the Widow Society," Angelica added.

"What a necessary place. I've volunteered there from time to time and met some wonderful people," Mrs. Van Horn said.

"I had the good fortune to do the same," Eliza said.

"Speaking of fortunes, well . . . the most wonderful thing has happened," Angelica said.

Eliza stiffened. *What was she doing? They hadn't discussed this at all.*

"Really? What is that?" asked Mrs. Van Horn.

"Oh, look," Eliza interrupted. "Here is the tea. I'm in such dire need of a cup of good tea." She tried to nod to Angelica, who ignored her.

Mrs. Van Horn's head tilted in curiosity, and she smiled. "Happy to oblige."

The maid poured. Eliza was glad of the warmth and the interruption. But she was loathe to drink another sip of tea.

"As you were saying?" Mrs. Van Horn prompted Angelica.

Angelica's hold on the cup and saucer was graceful, as if elegance was her birthright. "Well, as our man lifted the trunk, an exceptional amount of money fell from the bottom. Turns out our friend Rebecca had more money than anybody understood. She was stuffing it away."

"Who is Rebecca?" Mrs. Van Horn asked. Her dangling earrings sparkled against her blonde curls.

"You may have known her as Rob," Angelica said.

Mrs. Van Horn's fingers shook when she lifted her cup, and her eyes darted to the door at every sound. Money, it seemed, bought neither peace nor safety. Confusion played over her face. She set the cup down. "I don't understand. The day you told me he died, you omitted this. What shenanigans are going on here?"

"I am sorry, Mrs. Van Horn," Eliza stuttered. "Rebecca dressed as a man to be safer as she moved about the city."

Mrs. Van Horn paled.

"Ironic, isn't it?" Angelica quipped. "She did everything in her power to be safe and smart, yet someone murdered her anyway."

Quiet filled the room. Then Mrs. Van Horn erupted; a wailing noise Eliza had never heard come out of another human being—even herself. Eliza set her cup and saucer on the table and dashed to her.

Angelica was already there. "Are you all right?"

Mrs. Van Horn sucked in air. "I warned him. Her." She paused, her face full of wet tears.

Eliza handed her a handkerchief. Her heart raced so fast it might burst from her chest. *What was this about? What had she warned Rebecca about?*

"Come now," Eliza said. "You must unburden yourself. This is a safe place. You are amongst friends." Eliza meant it. As she reflected over her visits with Mrs. Van Horn, it made sense. The sense of it unfurled in her mind.

"I don't know where to begin," Mrs. Van Horn sobbed.

"Let's see if we can start at the beginning. When you first met Rob," Angelica said.

She calmed. "He was delightful. Now I know he was a woman, everything makes so much more sense. He became a friend, of sorts. I know we're taught not to get close with service people. But he—or she—was such a dear."

"So you established a relationship," Angelica said. "I must admit, I've had a few servants I've gotten too close with myself."

"Thank goodness you know what I mean. They are just people, like you and I, but born into different circumstances."

Eliza's affection for Mrs. Van Horn grew, realizing they shared similar beliefs.

"He, um, she loved to read, and we often chatted about books. I gave her a few of mine and we discussed them."

That was one mystery solved. Eliza had wondered where Rebecca had gotten all those books.

"I have saved your books," Eliza said. "They were amongst her things. Had she been delivering to you for a year?"

She nodded. "She also ran errands for me from time to time."

"Did you give her money for it?" Eliza asked.

"Yes, but not nearly as much as what you are talking about. If I am to be honest with you, we both shared several passions. One was reading, and the other was playing cards. Oh, I know ladies shouldn't do it. What poppycock! If we like to play cards, why shouldn't we?"

Eliza watched as Angelica's lips curled into a grin, for it was almost the same thing she'd said earlier.

"She learned of my secret ladies' card game, but because I supposed she was a man, I never invited her to sit with us."

Eliza burned to know who the other players were, but she held her tongue. She had much to consider. It was scandalous for a member of society to behave so blatantly against society's norms.

"He, I mean, she taught me a great deal, and I won a lot of times, using the system she showed me. I'd then give her part of my earnings, and she'd take it and make even more money."

"What? How?"

"By employing the same card methods she taught me."

"Go on, please. Where did she do this?"

"A card game at Murphy's. She couldn't go all the time, but when she went, she won." She paused. "Maybe that's where all the money came from."

Could it be? Eliza and Angelica exchanged glances. A woman was beating the male card players—and they didn't even know her gender.

"Did she owe anybody?" Angelica asked.

"I do not know."

"But you said you warned her," Eliza added.

"I did. Because one woman in my game was acquainted with someone who plays regularly at Murphy's, and they suspected her of cheating."

"Was she?" Angelica asked.

"No. She just remembered who held what cards. She devised a method of remembering. But I can see how others might think so." Mrs. Van Horn sighed.

"But the day she died . . . she had been here. Then she went to the apothecary and ended up outside a gentlemen's club. Had she been playing cards?" Angelica asked.

"I don't know. She was not running an errand for me. She said she needed to go to the apothecary for tonic. And yes, to visit a friend. She sometimes took refreshment there with the daughter of the proprietor."

"Did she have refreshment here?" Eliza willed her voice not to tremble. They were so close she could almost taste it.

"Not that day. But she did from time to time."

Alice had gone to Lucille's. And Eliza feared it was a waste of time. She now understood that the apothecarist's daughter—or someone else there—had poisoned Rebecca. But why?

"Does she play cards?" Eliza asked.

"Not that I am aware of. The Johnstons are good people. I can't see why they'd poison her. The daughter, Harriet, is a little off, but Rebecca thought fondly of her," Mrs. Van Horn said.

"How fondly?" Angelica asked.

Mrs. Van Horn shrugged. "They were friends."

"Then who poisoned her? Why would you poison a friend?" Angelica asked.

Her words hung in the air. Eliza chilled as she remembered her conversation with Mrs. Johnston. Harriet worked there. She created the charm bundles. And Mrs. Johnston had neglected to mention she was her daughter.

# Chapter 66

*She is in love with me.*

The words made no sense to Jo. But they came to her in Rebecca's voice.

*She is in love with me.*

Jo sat back against the wall in her room, cross-legged on the bed.

*She is in love with me.* The words sent ripples of terror through her.

*Rebecca! This is a problem!*

Rebecca's laugh.

Jo's fear. It was with her. Now. Lodged in her chest, about to erupt.

*What was she so afraid of? Who was in love with Rebecca?*

Someone knocked at her bedroom door and entered. It was René. "How are you?"

"Afraid." Her voice trembled.

"Come now. You are home. There is naught to fear here." Her voice soothed her—but only to a point.

"There is something I keep hearing in my mind."

"What is it?" René sat next to her.

"She is in love with me."

"You?"

"No, Rebecca. It's Rebecca's voice. In my head."

"A woman was in love with her?"

Jo nodded. Surely, René had heard of women falling in love with other women. Men with other men. But she looked as if she did not. Her face grew pink and her eyes watered.

"But who was it?" Jo asked. "It's stuck in my head. What does it mean?"

René seemed to gather herself. "Let's consider this. She was on her way to deliver goods to Mrs. Van Horn. Could it be her?"

Jo shrugged.

"She then went to Johnston's Apothecary and was found dead outside of Lucille's Gentlemen's Club."

Jo could picture those places in her mind's eye. But not the people. "We need to go to those places. Maybe it will help me remember."

"You arc not well enough to go out in the cold city today. Maybe tomorrow." René warped her arm around her shoulders. "It's very important you don't push yourself right now."

But her sense of urgency persisted. "I must go today. You may come with me, of course. But I must go today."

"But Alice said—"

"Alice isn't here."

René gazed at her, as if trying to figure out who Jo was. "Very well. But I insist we take it slowly. Where are we going?"

"Johnston's Apothecary. That's where she went, correct?"

"After Mrs. Van Horn's."

"But if she made it to the apothecary, Mrs. Van Horn would not have poisoned her."

"I suppose you're right. But some poisons act slowly."

"Not arsenic." Jo stood. "Let's go." Jo didn't know if this exercise would be folly. But she simply had to do something. This room was beginning to feel like the other room she'd been held in. She was compelled to leave and hoped it would lead her to her own mind. Her own memory. The right thread to untangle her mind.

*She is in love with me.*

Why so panicked when she heard those words in her mind?

She slipped her arm through René's. The wind bit her face when she stepped outside. She didn't care. At least she felt it. Felt the biting cold. Her senses alert and sharp. Felt the warmth of an arm through hers and each painful step. She wanted to run and dance through the streets, fly to the stars. But René anchored her.

# CHAPTER 67

Lucille herself showed Alice to a private room. They walked past several other rooms with the doors shut.

Alice had always admired the decor here—understated, tasteful decor, not gauche as some might imagine. She sat in a comfortable chair as Lucille shut the door. Lucille then turned to Alice. "I wondered how long it would take for you to come here in person."

"You know how it is. I can't do everything," Alice said. "But I'm here now. I see you're doing well."

"Business is thriving." She walked over with a slight limp, her dress swishing. "I know you don't approve, but we provide a service."

"Aye," Alice said, then clicked her tongue. "That you do."

"Shall I get us tea?"

"No, thank you. I won't be long."

"How can I help you?"

"What do you know about Rebecca?"

"Do you mean the woman dressed as a man?"

"I do. She was one of mine. You know that."

"I see." Lucille took a deep breath. "The girls quite liked him, er, her and wondered why their flirtation was never reciprocated."

"After delivering to you, did she stay around?" Alice had told the women not to. It was unseemly. You should deliver the goods, say good day, thank you, and leave.

"Somewhat. She never stayed long. She appeared uncomfortable with us." Lucille laughed a throaty, raspy laugh. "I should've known she was a woman. Most men are not uncomfortable."

Alice frowned. "Was she here that day?"

"No, we'd not seen her in quite some time," Lucille said. "But there's a curious rumor about her, come to think of it."

"What's that?"

"I heard Rob was courting Harriet Johnston."

Alice's heart raced beneath her layers of warm clothing. "Come again?"

"Yes, some of the girls were talking about it. Harriet and Rob were close, and her mother had been to a dressmaker."

"It's the first I've learned of it," Alice said.

"Well, that's the thing. There could be no wedding or marriage if Rob was a woman. Now I can assure you I've known many such partnerships, but the church or court does not sanction them." She smiled.

Alice mulled those words. She'd learned a great deal about Rebecca since her death, but Rebecca would never mislead someone into expecting they'd be married. "It's curious to me. I doubt Rebecca knew of Harriet's hopes for marriage. She didn't mention it. And I don't know about the personal lives of the women who work for me. I never pry. But Rebecca wasn't deceitful."

"Well, that's the thing," Lucille said. "The girls say Rob was completely innocent. He'd never asked the girl to marry him. Harriet just assumed."

The apothecary's daughter was in love with Rebecca and was planning their wedding. Her mother was already talking to a dressmaker. "Who was the dressmaker?"

"Sally Connors, I believe," Lucille said. Her eyebrow lifted. "She's quite talented and expensive."

What had been murky in Alice's mind became clear. Did Harriet poison Rebecca because of her heartache? She had the knowledge. But what did Sally have to do with this?

Alice dug in her bag and placed coins on the table. "Thank you, Lucille."

"Oh, please, Alice, keep your money. I am swimming in it. But I appreciate the gesture."

For a moment Alice imagined she had gone into the wrong business, moneywise. But she caught herself. What those women had to stomach! Alice could not do it, let alone ask others to.

She placed the coins back in her bag. "Thank you, Lucille. I came looking for one thing and found another."

"As is usually the case, isn't it?" Lucille laughed.

"How much longer can you do it, old friend?"

"Oh, I don't do any of it anymore. I just take care of the girls who do." She waved her off.

Alice perceived the similarities between herself and Lucille. Always had. Alice didn't craft as much as she used to, but she kept the others on track. But this business with Rebecca and Jo . . . she'd failed them.

"Ever lose one of them?"

"No, but some of them were beaten so badly they had to retire early." Lucille's cheek twitched. "And I tracked down the men who did it to them too."

Cold swept through Alice. Isn't that what she herself was doing now? She stood. "I must go. Thank you for your help."

"Where are you going?"

"I'm going to Johnston's to clear up this matter. Rebecca was poisoned, you see. Then I figure her body was moved to your back alley. She died alone, and it haunts me." Alice started walking toward the door. She turned. "Who knows more about poison than the apothecarist? Or his daughter."

Lucille's jaw firmed. "You are quite right."

# Chapter 68

Eliza and Angelica stopped outside of the apothecary. "Should we make a plan before we go in?" Eliza asked.

"We just need to get a feel for these people. I mean, we suppose someone here poisoned Rebecca, but we don't know who and we have no proof."

"No, but Mrs. Johnston is definitely hiding that Harriet is her daughter."

"I've been considering that. It seems odd, but maybe she just didn't think to mention it."

"I believe it was a deliberate omission."

"Let's go in and get an elixir for stomach problems. We don't want them to suspect we're on to them yet." Angelica slid her arm through Eliza's.

"We should go directly to the constabulary after this," Eliza said.

"Agreed."

Angelica cracked open the door, and they walked in. There were only a few other customers milling about. One was in deep conversation with Mr. Johnston. The shop's familiar herbal scents turned cloying for Eliza. Dried herbs hung from the rafters like hanged men, their shadows dancing in the weak winter light. Each creak of the floorboards under Mrs. Johnston's feet set Eliza's nerves on edge. A draft from the ill-fitted door made the candle flames waver, transforming Mrs. Johnston's face into something almost demonic for a heart-stopping moment.

Mrs. Johnston approached them. "Mrs. General Hamilton, Mrs. John Church, it's good to see you."

Each glass jar on the shelf seemed to hold a weapon now. Eliza's eyes moved from bottle to bottle as she wondered which innocent-looking powder had ended Rebecca's life. The shop's medicinal scents—clove, rosemary, mint—suddenly seemed sinister.

"Likewise," Eliza said.

"How can I help you?" Mrs. Johnston's hands moved constantly as she spoke, measuring harmless chamomile into paper twists, but Eliza couldn't help wondering what else those hands had measured out.

"We're seeking a stomach elixir," Angelica said.

"What ails you?"

"It's my daughter," Eliza said. "She's very nauseated. We just need something stronger to calm it, I fear."

"Do you have a daughter, Mrs. Johnston?" Angelica asked.

"Indeed, I do," she said. "I'll be right back." She walked over to a group of bottles and examined each one. She pulled one and handed Eliza the bottle. "This will do you."

"I doubt it, but we'll try. I think it's all in her imagination," Angelica said. "You know how young women sometimes are."

The woman cracked a smile. "Yes, I do. My own is marrying age, and she has her own ailments."

Angelica laughed. "I see. Is she looking for a husband?"

Mrs. Johnston leaned in. "Aren't they all?"

*Mine is not*, Eliza wanted to say. Her poor Angel was marrying age but would never take a husband. "I'm afraid my daughter . . . she will never marry," Eliza said as she took the elixir and paid Mrs. Johnston.

"Why is that, if you don't mind my asking?"

"She is troubled," Angelica said.

"Maybe I can help? If you allow me to examine her, maybe I can find the imbalance in her system."

Eliza had had doctors examine her daughter. But this woman? No, thanks. "Perhaps."

"And what of your own daughter? Is she well?" Angelica asked.

*Angelica was so good at baiting people.* She was a master manipulator. Eliza herself used to be baited by Angelica as a child.

"She has her own troubles. The young men these days are not what they used to be. She's heartbroken, and it's hard to see as a mother," she said.

"I agree. It's dreadful," Angelica said. "My daughter had the same. You just want to throttle the young man, don't you?"

Mrs. Johnston nodded.

The mother in Eliza understood. If anybody hurt her children, she'd want to throttle them. But kill them? Kill anybody? No. It was something Hamilton had wrestled with as a soldier. Taking another man's life was difficult for him to deal with.

A young woman emerged from the shop's back room. She was tall and broad, with a comely face and shiny red hair.

"Speaking of daughters . . . this is mine. Harriet, please meet Mrs. General Hamilton and Mrs. John Church."

The girl blushed. "Pleased to make your acquaintance."

"Harriet?" Eliza said. "Are you the woman who makes those charm bundles?"

"Aye," said her mother. "But there will be no more of that, will there?"

"No, ma'am."

"Harriet," Angelica said. "I remember where I've heard your name—"

"There are so many Harriets," Mrs. Johnston said quickly.

"No, it was this Harriet, I'm sure," Angelica said. "I have a friend who recently passed. She spoke of Harriet."

The girl shifted her weight.

"She spoke fondly of her. You might recall her as Rob, for she moved about the city as a man. For safety, of course. Her business took her to many places."

As Angelica babbled, Eliza observed the girl reaching for her mother's hand.

"I used to worry so about her," Angelica went on. "That she felt she had to hide her identity to make her way. It says so much about our culture. It's so unforgiving for women."

"Did you know Rob?" Eliza asked when there was a pause in her sister's words.

"I knew him, er, her." Harriet lifted her chin.

"We didn't know he was a woman," Mrs. Johnston said in a hushed tone. "Odd creature."

"There was nothing odd about her. She helped run a concern. And you know how difficult it can be for unmarried women," Eliza said.

"Aye, that I do." Mrs. Johnston placed her arm around Harriet.

"Mrs. Johnston, are you having a party over there?" Her husband's voice came ringing loudly. "I could use your help."

She rolled her eyes. "It's difficult for married women too." She walked away toward her husband.

"So, Harriet, your mother says you want to marry," Angelica said.

"As all young women do," Eliza said.

"I don't know . . ." Harriet gazed off into the distance.

"Maybe it's all mothers who want their daughters to marry," Angelica said with an air of flippancy.

Harriet, the spell maker, cracked a smile as bright as the sun.

A voice came from behind them. "Personally, I'd rather have my daughter do as she pleases."

Eliza turned to see Alice. What was she doing here? She was supposed to be at Lucille's. She must have also figured out that

Rebecca's poisoner worked at the apothecary. Eliza tried to imagine the sweet-faced spell maker Harriet poisoning Rebecca. They had been friends. But Harriet saw Rebecca as a man. Could there have been some misunderstanding? As Eliza eyed Alice, whose eyes were blazing, she hoped they were about to find out.

# CHAPTER 69

It was as if Alice were thirty years younger. Her face took on a whole new vitality. She stood straight and eyed Harriet. "Are you Harriet?"

"Who wants to know?" Harriet asked as Mrs. Johnston sidled back to her.

The door opened again, but Eliza didn't take her eyes from Alice. What was she going to say? Do? What did Alice know that she did not?

"My name is Alice Rhodes, the purveyor of the House of Pearl."

"How can we help you?" Mrs. Johnston asked.

"I'd like some arsenic."

Eliza held her breath. That was the substance that killed Rebecca.

Harriet's face drained of color.

"We don't sell arsenic. You'd have to go to the Manhattan for it," Mrs. Johnston said.

"Oh, I see," Alice said. "What do you have that can poison a person?"

Mrs. Johnson, befuddled, cleared her throat. "Many of the medicinals can be taken as poison if the wrong dose is given. But surely you don't mean to harm someone?"

Alice squinted. "Which one of you—"

"Alice," Angelica interrupted. "Turn around."

Both Alice and Eliza turned their heads.

Jo stepped forward with René next to her. Alice went over to her. "What are you doing here? You should be in bed. René!"

"There was nothing I could do," René said. "She wants to remember, and this is the place she wanted to come to."

"What is going on here?" Mr. Johnston came out from behind the counter. "If you're not here for medicine, move along." His face was red and projecting hatred.

Jo jumped. René and Alice flanked her.

"Sir." Angelica stepped in. "Our friend has been quite ill. Something traumatic happened to her and we're searching for medicine to help her memory return."

"How many of you have to be in my shop at once?" Mr. Johnston asked as he inspected Jo. "Are you the ill woman?"

"I am." Her voice was a quivering rasp. She blinked hard. "This place . . . The way it smells." Her voice grew stronger.

"Don't tax yourself, my dear," he said. "I have a relaxing tincture. Let me find it." He moved back behind the counter and rummaged through his things. Eliza perceived him, but her eyes were on Jo.

"What good is relaxation? Will it bring back her memory?" Alice snapped.

"It might," he said. "When the body is at rest, the mind sometimes allows memories to come through. Sometimes it works, sometimes it doesn't."

Alice sized him up as she spoke to Jo. "Do they look familiar?"

Mrs. Johnston and Harriet froze in their positions, giving the impression of mice caught in a trap.

Jo took them in. "I remember them. I've been here before." Jo stepped back with sudden force. Her face trembled. "You knew my friend Rebecca."

"Rebecca?" Mrs. Johnston said. "Rebecca who?"

"You knew her as Rob," Alice said in a flat voice. She gazed at Harriet. "You were in love with her, weren't you, my dear?"

"I'm going to ask you all to leave. We're closing," Mr. Johnston said. "I don't know what's going on here, but you all need to leave the shop. Now."

"I'm sorry, sir," Eliza said. "We mean no disrespect. But we are not leaving until we have answers."

"Mrs. General Hamilton, I have no idea what you're talking about. What is going on here?" Mr. Johnston said harshly.

"Your daughter was in love with a person she presumed was a man. Rob," Eliza said.

"Your wife was already making wedding plans, and had a dress ordered from Sally's," Alice said.

"But then," Angelica said. "She found out Rob was not a man. Rob was a woman. Our friend Rebecca."

Mr. Johnston's face grew redder and redder by the minute. "Is this true?" He glared at his wife.

"I suppose it is," she said, shrugging. "But what of it?"

"Engagements are broken all the time," Harriet said with a soft voice.

"Engagements?" Alice roared. "You were never engaged! If there's one thing I know about Rebecca, I know she was honest."

She had been honest, but she also had secrets. Eliza struggled to follow all of it. Why would this young woman imagine herself engaged to Rob or Rebecca if she wasn't? Misunderstandings happened. But it seemed like a huge one.

"Why would you say you're engaged if you were not?" Angelica asked.

The girl crumpled into herself. "I loved him. And I thought he loved me. He was always kind, and we talked about literature. And he held my hand once." She looked up at the small group of people watching. "We spoke of marriage, dreams of the future. I believed we were talking about us." Her chin quivered.

Eliza's heart went out to her. The young woman was ignorant of the ways of the world. It was the way most parents brought up their daughters. At one time Eliza herself had been as stupid and innocent as this young woman was. Parents were not doing their girls any favors in keeping them shut off from reality. Or at least not this much. It was then that Eliza realized they were all looking at Mrs. Johnston. Even Mr. Johnston.

# Chapter 70

*She's in love with me.*

The words spun in Jo's mind. She studied Harriet, surmising that she must be who Rebecca had spoken about. Her mind flashed back to her last memory of Rebecca.

"Please, Rebecca, you must not tell her like this. You must wait until someone can go with you. She might take it badly," Jo had said. "And this could affect everything we've worked for. Our livelihoods! We can't let it get out that we disguise ourselves!"

"I know. But I have to be honest," Rebecca said. "I didn't mean for any of this to happen. Her mother had a dress made! For the life of me, I can't figure out why she misunderstood our friendship."

"Rebecca! How can you be so innocent? You are dressed as a man. Men and women cannot be close friends. At least not unmarried ones. You know this."

Rebecca laughed. "It's hard to remember I'm a man when I'm dressed as one. I need to be more careful. I don't want to break anybody's heart." She patted her face. "I can't say I blame her. I'm a handsome bloke."

Jo laughed. "Promise me you'll wait to see her until I can go with you. I have a shawl to finish and deliver today. When I return, we'll go together."

But Rebecca never promised. She just nodded and went back to her embroidery.

The next day at breakfast Jo noticed Rebecca was not at the table. "Where is Rebecca?"

"I've not seen her since yesterday. She had a delivery to make to the Van Horn's," Alice said. "Is she not in your room?"

Jo's chest slammed with pending danger. "No. Where? Where did she go? What did you say?"

"The Van Horns', my dear."

Jo stood and paced. "She should be back by now."

"Whatever is the matter?" René said. "She comes and goes as she pleases, as we all do."

"This is bad," Jo said. "I'm trying to not assume the worst."

"Then don't," Alice said. "What is happening?"

*Find Rebecca,* a voice had said loudly in her head. Her legs sprang into action, and she ran out the door, leaving Alice and René in the doorway.

*Find Rebecca.*

Jo knocked on the Van Horns' door. Mrs. Van Horn reported Rebecca had been there, but then was off to the apothecary.

Dread filled Jo. She ran to Johnston's, slipping through the alleys and back streets where there were fewer crowds. Her senses were on high alert. The cold, crisp air burned her lungs, and she breathed deep. She kept running, into the alley behind the pharmacy. And then . . . what was this? A woman was standing over a heap of clothing, holding it. Jo slowed and approached.

The heap was actually a person lying on the ground. The woman was trying to lift them into a cart.

Jo gasped. "What are you doing?"

The woman dropped the body, turning her head. She lunged at Jo, who tried to fight her off. Jo slipped and fell, and all went black.

The face of the woman had been a blur until this very moment.

"You killed Rebecca," Jo said.

The apothecary hushed.

"Don't be ridiculous," Mrs. Johnston said.

"I saw you in the alley with her. You were dragging her." Jo's eyes would not leave the woman.

"Young lady, please leave the premises. You're causing a scene and you're accusing my wife of hurting someone. I won't have it," Mr. Johnston said.

Harriet's face was red and crumpled. Mrs. Johnston's mouth dropped open, as if shocked by Jo's audacity. Angelica reached for Eliza's hand and their sweaty palms clutched. Eliza was too afraid to move.

Jo raised her chin. "I'm happy to go. I'll go straight to the constable."

Mrs. Johnston leaped from behind the counter and grabbed Jo, encircling her neck, knife in her hand.

"What—" Mr. Johnston husband exclaimed.

"Everybody out or I'll slice the girl's throat," Mrs. Johnston ordered.

Eliza ignored the people pushing through the doorway. Was there someone coming in while the others rushed out? She only half perceived the commotion, as her eyes did not leave Jo.

"You won't hurt her in front of us," Alice said. "You're stupid but not that stupid. Let her go." Alice walked toward Mrs. Johnston.

Eliza tried to stop her. "Alice, no—"

Mrs. Johnston's eyes were bulging and angry. She threw Jo on the floor—hard. If Jo were healthy, she could've bounced back up with ease. Mrs. Johnston then lunged at Alice. "Come on, old woman!"

"Sarah, stop—" Her husband pleaded and went to them both as she cut Alice across the face.

Alice shrieked as blood spurted. Mr. Johnston went to his wife and held her back. Just then James and Constable Schultz and another constable walked into the scene. James rushed to Eliza and

Angelica. Eliza swooned. The room spun, and she clutched her son to keep from falling.

"Alice . . ." Eliza said. Alice was helping to lift Jo from the floor, even as blood dripped from her cheek.

A constable went to them and Schultz went to the Johnstons. "I'm afraid you'll have to come with me." He paused and took in the family. "All of you."

"For what?" Mrs. Johnston said. "I was only defending myself."

"Against Mrs. Rhodes?" Schultz said. He laughed. "You are as delusional as I assumed you were. I'm arresting you for the murder of Rebecca Dickens." He scanned the shop. "I don't need a crowd here. If you've nothing to do with this, move along."

The other constable stood next to Alice and Jo. Alice, her face bloody, gazed in Eliza's direction. She wiped blood from her face with her cloak sleeve and then nodded, letting Eliza know she was okay.

"Jones is taking Mrs. Rhodes and Ms. Ambrose to see a doctor, just to make sure they are all right," Schultz said. He turned to Eliza. "You three need to go home. We've got this."

"Wait a minute," Angelica said. "What do you mean? We know who killed Rebecca. But what about Jo? What happened to Jo? Where is her justice?"

# CHAPTER 71

Both Eliza and Angelica slept through breakfast the next morning. But Mrs. Cole knocked on the door until they were awake for luncheon.

"She's awful," Angelica groaned.

"She just wants us to eat," Eliza said.

"Yesterday was exhausting." Angelica slipped out from under the covers.

"Yes. I imagine we'll see nothing like it again."

"Let's hope not."

Soon Eliza and Angelica made their way together to the table, where the rest of the family was gathered.

"Are you staying at home today?" Angel asked.

"I am," Eliza said. "I've no reason to go into town today."

She felt good about that. The woman who killed Rebecca would spend the rest of her days in prison. She warmed. But there were still questions about what had happened to Jo.

Mrs. Cole handed Eliza the mail, as she always did at breakfast. Eliza set it aside until she finished eating. She noted an envelope from the bank, and she didn't want to spoil her hardy appetite. She heaped her plate with biscuits and gravy.

"Christmas is the day after tomorrow!" Little Eliza said.

"Are you excited?" Angelica asked.

"Yes. We'll go to church and have sweets and—"

"And stockings!" Angel said, in a tone suggesting she was much younger than her age.

This year Eliza had asked Alice and her crew to knit new Christmas stockings for the children, as their old ones were moth-eaten. The new stockings were red wool, trimmed in white lace for the girls, no trim for the boys.

As Eliza finished her breakfast, she sat back, eyeing the stack of mail. She pulled out a note from Isabella Graham, opened it and read:

*Dearest Eliza,*

*I hope this note finds you well. I wanted to let you know of our good luck. We've secured the funding for the orphanage, as we've been talking about. We just need to find a rental, which should not be a problem at all.*

*We shall have our orphanage!*

*Fondly,*
*Isabella*

Her dream was becoming a reality. Just imagine how many children they could help! Homeless, parentless children were more and more populous.

"Eliza?" Angelica said.

"It's the orphanage. Isabella Graham has secured the funds for it."

There were gasps around the table.

"To Mother," Alexander said and lifted his glass of water. They all did. And Eliza's heart overflowed.

"It's not me." Heat rose in her face. "Isabella succeeded with the funding."

"I know you had much to do with it and will have much more to do with it. It is a wonderful idea, and one sorely needed in the city," Angelica said.

"Here, here," James said.

Eliza took in the tableau at her table. Her children, some of them grown. Gratitude swept through her. The scene should have brought her more peace, but Eliza couldn't shake the hollow awareness of who was missing. Both Hamilton and Philip's chairs were empty. She'd never make her peace with it. She'd always remind people of Hamilton and his importance in founding their country. Even the house itself seemed to sense these absences, its rooms too large and too quiet despite the rambunctious children. The winter wind found each crack and crevice, as if trying to remind her that this home, like so much else, might soon be lost to her.

She bore a sharp pang of sorrow when she thought of leaving the house Hamilton had built for this family. But she needed to focus: As long as they were together, it did not matter where they lived.

Rebecca and Jo were fresh in her mind. Rebecca's child was out there, somewhere, never having known his mother. Eliza also considered Harriet, who fell in love and whose mother killed her friend. She contemplated Marcy, another woman whose son did not have a father, and whose life had been touched by Sally, a scheming wretch of a woman.

The city was unkind to women trying to make their way, women whose circumstances were not as good as her own. What right did she have to complain?

She slid the letter from the bank out of the stack and tore it open. But she needed privacy to read it so she slipped into Hamilton's study. Her hands trembled. She took in the room, exactly the way he'd left it—the same books, the same paper, even his favorite quill still waiting in the inkwell. Was her mind so grief-stricken that she was losing a sense of reality—or did his scent still linger here? Ink. Leather. That blend of tobacco he'd favored. How many nights had she found him here, working by candlelight? Now she was going to lose even these ghost-filled rooms. How could she go on? She traced the edge of his desk, the wood smooth from years of his touch. The idea of strangers here, dismantling their home, made her chest ache with fresh grief.

She gasped after she read the letter. Could it be true?

Angelica ran into the room flanked by James and Alexander, the rest of the children trailing behind.

Overcome, Eliza handed the letter to Angelica, who read it out loud.

"Dear Mrs. Hamilton, we happily inform you that a group of investors has purchased your home. And they are willing to sell it back to you for half of its value." Angelica paused before saying, "Well, that's an absurd amount!"

Eliza nodded. It was very low. It was as if God had answered her prayers. She could keep her home, and the children would grow up here in the place their father wanted them to thrive.

Alexander took the letter from his aunt. "How did this happen?"

Eliza tried to find the words. Instead, she shrugged her shoulders and basked in the moment. Their family could stay here, stay in their home. She exhaled deeper than she thought possible.

* * *

The Hamilton family bundled up to gather greenery. They wanted to fashion it into a wreath for the front door of the Grange. With no leaves on the trees, the view of the city from the top of the hill was unencumbered. They walked down the hill, at the top of which sat their home, and toward the river, where a stand of trees, some of which were pine, waited for them.

"I'm so happy to know that you'll stay here." Angelica bent over and picked up a pine branch.

Eliza drew in the pine-scented air. "Me too." She looked up toward their home. "Hamilton wanted our children to grow up here." From where she stood, the garden of Hamilton's dreams was outlined in snow, with bits of brown scrubby plants poking out.

"I think we have enough." Alexander's arms were full, as was James.

"Shall we go inside for hot chocolate?" Angelica asked Little Eliza.

"Yes!" she squealed.

As the family headed home and walked up the hill, a horse came into Eliza's view and then she saw Constable Schultz standing there. He must have news! Eliza picked up her pace, as did Angelica.

Eliza turned to Alexander. "Please take the children inside."

He nodded.

"Constable Schultz! How can I help you?" Eliza said with Angelica next to her. The others spilled into the Grange.

"Very good to see both of you. Sorry to bother your family during the holiday, but I come with news."

"Shall we go inside?" Eliza asked.

"Thank you, but that's not necessary."

"What is your news?" Angelica asked.

"We found out more about Josephine's circumstance." He shifted his weight and clasped his gloved hands together. "According to Harriet, Mrs. Johnston gave her to Sally, the mantua maker, to pay for a wedding dress she'd had made, thinking Harriet was going to marry Rebecca. Sally was attempting to sell Jo."

"Sell her?" Eliza exclaimed. *Sell.* Jo was to be *sold.* Her hackles rose. She abhorred the sale of enslaved people, and it had almost happened to Jo. Who knew what kind of life she would have had if she hadn't escaped?

He nodded. "She was to be sold to a Pennsylvania farmer."

Angelica folded her arms and harrumphed.

"Will Sally be arrested?" Eliza asked.

"Not just her. There is a ring of people who have been selling women, sometimes off the street."

Eliza's mind went to Marcy, the woman she'd met on the street who had been fired by Sally. Did she know what was going on? "Into marriage?"

"Yes." He took a deep breath. "Josephine was being held at Sally's residence. They medicated her and told her that she was ill and that they were taking care of her."

Eliza drew in the cold air, and it burned in her throat. "How is Jo?"

"Fine," he said reassuringly. But then he frowned. "She's better than could be expected."

Eliza chilled.

"Who are these people selling women?" Angelica asked.

"It may have started as a legitimate organization, wanting to match people together. But somehow it became, uh, warped. But the WMA had quite a hand. Lucretia Short and Sally are sisters."

There it was. The missing puzzle piece. Eliza and Angelica looked at one another and back to Schultz.

"It's diabolical," he said. "I realize that. And I hate to bring you such news. But I know you'd appreciate knowing what happened. We are taking care of all of it, and the streets will be safer because you have helped bring this to the attention of the authorities. Thank you."

"Do you know anything else about Lucretia's death?" Eliza asked.

"Yes. She was killed by the father of a young woman who was a victim of an arranged marriage gone wrong," he replied. "He's in jail for the time being."

"My God," Angelica said.

Eliza was speechless. The Schuyler sisters stood clutched together in front the Grange. Eliza said a silent prayer of gratitude.

As Constable Schultz took his leave, poor Harriet entered Eliza's mind. She'd gone from expecting she would be married to now being in prison, heartbroken—after her own mother had killed the person she'd loved. She said another silent prayer for Rebecca's soul, a victim of her own kindness, and for Jo, whose healing from this incident had surely just begun.

*Three Months Later*

*My dearest Angelica,*

*I miss you frightfully and pray that you and your family are well. We are all quite well. Alexander Jr. will soon be graduating, and I hope that he stays close to home. The other children are also well. The little ones are growing so fast!*

*Well, our Jo is as back to normal as can be. She has been able to continue lace making even with half a finger gone. Our friends on Pearl Street continue to thrive. Isn't it wonderful? They have used the money from Rebecca to add on to the house, and their landlord is quite happy about it.*

*With the constabularies continuing investigation, they found Ramsay and Sally, along with Lucretia, were colluding. Both are now safely tucked away in prison. Murphy's has also been shut down for illegal gambling and sundry other activities.*

*Mrs. Van Horn continues to have her card games, and I really can't see the harm in it, can you? I know not if her husband is aware.*

*The best news is that Isabella and I have found a place for the Orphan Asylum Society in the City of New York, in Greenwich Village. I will be the second directress, the first being Mrs. Sarah*

*Ogden Hoffman. Isabella continues as the directress at the Widow Society. But we will be working closely together. I look forward to it. I wish you were here, dear sister.*

*The gardens are not yet blooming. I await the blooming of the tulips, hyacinths, and lilies Hamilton chose for the front gardens. It's as if the buds want to burst into life at any moment. Hamilton loved this garden and house. I'm so pleased we've been able to stay. I can almost feel him here. I know it sounds a bit deranged. But so much of life is!*

*I will keep you informed about the orphanage. I believe our dear Hamilton would be proud.*

*Your loving sister,*
*Eliza*

# Notes

In *The Lace Widow: An Eliza Hamilton Mystery*, I first imagined Alice and her group. Since that book was published, I've often been asked if there were women living together in early America and making their own way. My answer has always been that it makes sense to me that there were, but this group is entirely fictional. But shortly after *The Lace Widow* was published, I ran into a podcast from Elfreth's Alley Museum in Philadelphia. The first episode was "The Dressmakers," and it focused on the lives of three women living together, making a living by dressmaking. It is worth noting that two of them were a couple.

Another podcast plays into the research for this book: Ben Franklin's World, where Jen Manion was interviewed. She wrote the book *Female Husbands: A Trans History*, which is a fascinating read. So, while I leave the question of my characters' sexuality up to the readers, these books and podcasts helped inform them. Another book I found helpful in understanding the norms of the time was *The Sewing Girl's Tale: A Story of Crime and Consequences in Revolutionary America* by John Wood Sweet. This book not only details the first rape trial in the United States but also gives a dark, thoughtful slice of life into a working woman's world at that time. Contrary to popular belief, issues surrounding gender and sexuality are not modern inventions.

Researching the orphans in the city proved trickier. There were no orphanages in New York until Eliza and Isabella Graham joined forces. But just looking at the orphanage Eliza helped to create, we know that the home for orphans opened on May 1, 1806, in a rented two-story frame house on Raisin Street in Greenwich Village. Twelve orphans were admitted during the first six months. By the end of its first year, two hundred children had been admitted. They were taught reading, writing, arithmetic, and sewing, as well as given religious training. On July 7, 1807, the cornerstone was laid for a new home on Bank Street on land donated by one of the trustees.

The orphanage that Eliza helped to start survives to this day as the Graham Windham organization, and it is still in New York City. Also, sometime before then, Eliza started a school in Harlem. But for purposes of this book, I focused on the orphanage.

As for the hospital where Jo spent her time, it did exist. In 1805, New York Hospital was in lower Manhattan, at Broadway and Pearl Street. The hospital occupied a large tract of land in this area, near what is now known as City Hall Park. The hospital had moved to this location after its original building was damaged by fire in 1775, just before it was set to open. After the Revolutionary War, the hospital reopened in 1791, and its main building stood at this site for much of the nineteenth century. This location was significant because it was accessible to the growing city and played a major role in providing medical care to its residents.

Later, in the 1870s, New York Hospital moved to a new location on West 15th Street and eventually it became part of what is now New York-Presbyterian Hospital.

The story of how Eliza kept the Grange is true. She did later move from the Grange after all her children, except for Angelica, were on their own. Angelica stayed with her mother for most of the rest of her life.

As to the matters of Christmas and Advent, from almost every source we have about Eliza Hamilton, it's noted that she was a deeply religious woman. I supposed she would hold Advent dear, but I have no proof of that. Also, I have no proof if the Schuylers and Hamiltons celebrated Christmas in any particular way. I supposed, with her Dutch heritage, her family would have had kept custom with the Christmas tree being part of it and, perhaps, stockings for the children. But most of America at this time did not celebrate Christmas like this—nor did they drink advocaat, unless they had a generous Dutch friend.

Once again, I hope I've done honor to Eliza's memory, as I've tried to remain true to what we know about her while also taking a flight of fancy into the realms of murder, kidnapping, secret card games, and underground wife markets.

Acknowledgements

Second books in series are always challenging for me. It's a bridge between the first book and (one hopes) the third, and it's a bit of juggling act. So I was very relieved to find Martin Biro in my corner again. He's the best editor I've had in my long career. I also happen to think he's one of the best people I've had the pleasure of knowing in this business. After so many books together, I feel as if I owe him an enormous debt of gratitude. As any writer will tell you, a good editor who actually gets you and your writing is worth their weight in gold. Thank you, Martin. I'd like to thank the agent who introduced me to him many years ago, Sharon Bowers. I'd also like to thank the agent who represented me for this book, Jill Marsal. I've been blessed to know and work with both.

I'd like to thank my beta reader Mary Rike, and my daughter Tess for talking with me about Eliza Hamilton and about this book, ad nauseum, especially when she was writing her own book. (I predict she will have a wonderful career! "Just you wait!") I'd like to thank the many, many, many bloggers and reviewers who helped make *The Lace Widow* so successful.

For me, independent bookstores are the best things on the planet, right along with libraries! I'd like to thank Stone Soup Books in Waynesboro, Virginia; Bluebird Bookstore in Crozet, Virginia: Fountain Books in Richmond, Virginia; The Book

Dragon in Staunton, Virginia; and Mechanicsburg Mystery Bookshop in Pennsylvania. Thank you all so much for your hospitality and kindness.

There are so many wonderful people at Crooked Lane. I had a chance to spend time with two at Bouchercon last year, Dulce Botello and Matt Martz. I'm thrilled to be working with them again. A special shout-out to Thaisheemarie Fantauzzi Perez and our many emails about this exquisite cover, and Rebecca Nelson, for keeping track of all the balls in the air. I imagine it's a bit like herding cats. Thank you, and I look forward to working with you all more in the future.

Both of my daughters, Emma and Tess, have been on quite a journey with me, personally, and with my writing career. In first grade, one answered a school questionnaire about what her mother does for a living by writing "she sits at the computer." Years later, they snap photos of my books in stores during their travels and tell their friends about my books. Knowing they are proud of me makes all those hours of "sitting at the computer" more than worth it.

Most of all, thank you to my loyal readers. I am honored you choose to spend your time reading my books.

Thank you all.
Mollie